PRIMAL DESIRE

Ty shook his head. "I don't get it. Why should I hide certain parts of my body?" He looked sincerely puzzled.

Kelly's gaze slid lower. "Exposing your sexual organs is an invitation to have sex."

He raised one expressive brow. "Do you *want* me to wear shorts?"

There it was, the direct challenge. Her brain shouted *yes*, but her senses rose up as one and proclaimed, "No."

His smile was hard and predatory, his lips soft and mobile. She was really conflicted about that smile. Hard or soft? She'd have to touch, taste before making a decision.

"I know what's in your eyes. Hunger." Ty stopped as he reached the side of the bed. "Recognizing things like that is one of the perks of having a primitive soul hot-wired for sex."

Eternal Pleasure

NINA BANGS

LEISURE BOOKS NEW YORK CITY

Mega thanks to Gerry Bartlett, who not only took time from her busy schedule to read Eternal Pleasure, *but also suggested changes that made it a much better book.*

A LEISURE BOOK®

July 2008

Published by

Dorchester Publishing Co., Inc.
200 Madison Avenue
New York, NY 10016

ISBN 10: 0-8439-5953-3
ISBN 13: 978-0-8439-5953-6

Visit us on the web at www.dorchesterpub.com.

Eternal Pleasure

Prologue

Oblivion.

Sudden. Unexpected. One instant alive, and then . . . Nothing.

Only the unraveling of time—months, years, centuries.

Awareness.

Sudden. Unexpected. One instant nothing, and then . . . Everything.

His essence, his *soul*, had returned, and it sought sensations. No sight, no sound, no *body*. But he knew he wasn't the same, even if he couldn't remember what that same had been.

When the memories came, they battered at him, flashing images of another time. Primitive. *Fun*. The hunt, pounding after his terrified prey. The kill, quick and bloody. The feeding, a gorging frenzy. And afterward the mating, all mindless instinct and primal satisfaction. Savage joy filled him. Anticipation. He'd do all that again.

Then the voice, the one he'd always listened to. *Obeyed*. Warning him that he was rising to a new world. No indiscriminate rending and tearing. Damn. He'd have to control the violence, the urge to destroy. Because he was no longer what he had been. He was human.

What was that? He liked the remembered version of himself better.

And because he couldn't stop it, he allowed the voice to fill him with everything he'd need to know after he rose.

Wave after wave of knowledge left his mind spinning—culture, language, history, and on and on and on.

Finally, the voice explained what he was, *who* he was. And things clicked into place. *He remembered.* Not just the images he'd seen in his mind, but all that had gone before. And the voice became a name. Fin. His earlier joy took a major hit.

Impatience tugged at him. He was the impulsive one. Something he'd have to temper. But not now. He wanted out. Pushing mental feelers through the tons of earth and rock separating him from the surface, he found the male, no, *man* waiting for him above. And with the man was his new body.

Eager, he shot upward, his essence sliding easily from the earth and into the empty body. His new home. He didn't bother thinking about what he looked like. Instead he glanced around, searching for prey, for other predators. A habit from that other time he'd never lose.

"Wow, this is so cool. It's exactly 11:11 P.M. on November eleventh, 2011. Eleven, eleven, eleven. Just like Fin said it'd be." The man looked up from the lighted face of his watch and leaned toward him out of the darkness. "And you're Ty."

Ty clenched his teeth so he wouldn't snarl. Along with a million other random details, Fin had emphasized that eating strangers wasn't good for the image of the Eleven.

"You'd better be Steve." The guy wasn't a danger to him, so Ty glanced away to scan the area again. It looked like they were in some kind of cave. "Where are we?"

The man slapped the side of his head in a gesture Ty didn't understand. "Sorry. I forgot this is all new to you. Yeah, I'm Steve. I'll be taking you to Fin. And you're inside Newgrange."

Ty could see fine in the dark, but Steve couldn't. The man pulled a flashlight from his pocket and turned it on. The predator in Ty stirred. Humans didn't have good night vision. Advantage, predator. "Newgrange?"

"Yep. We're not supposed to be here at night and definitely not without a guide. But Fin took care of it."

Ty tried out a smile on his new face. Fin was good at "taking care" of things. The smile faded though when he thought about his new name. Fin had a warped sense of humor.

"Newgrange is a prehistoric passage tomb in Ireland. One of the oldest surviving structures in the world." Steve raked his fingers through short blond hair. "Let's get outta here. Small enclosed places give me the creeps."

You have no idea. Fin did things like this. He'd given Ty a bunch of information down to the tiniest details, like what a watch and a flashlight were, but he'd forgotten to tell Ty where he was.

"How old?" Not that Ty cared. He followed Steve through the narrow passage, trying out a few of the curses Fin had poured into him when he banged his head against a low spot at the end of the tunnel.

"Five thousand years old." Steve waited for him to be impressed.

He wasn't. "Fin wouldn't have sent you if you weren't one of us. So what kind of soul do you have, Steve?" Did he sound friendly? Fin had said not to scare anyone willing to help them.

Steve shot him a nervous glance, the first hint he'd given that he might be worried about being here alone with Ty. "A horse."

Prey. Ty smiled again.

Steve swallowed hard.

Then Ty forgot about the other man as he stepped out of the tunnel and into the Irish night. Raising his head, he stared up at the few stars visible through the cloud cover.

They were the first stars he'd seen in sixty-five million years.

Chapter One

Come on, come on, come on. Kelly was *not* a patient woman. None of the Maloys was. It wasn't in their genes. She tapped out her irritation on the steering wheel. The plane was late, and she was tired of waiting.

Fin is paying you crazy money to wait. He's also paying for your apartment with the nice soft bed. Yeah, there was that. Besides, the job was pretty straightforward. Nothing complicated. Pick up the guy Steve was bringing in from Ireland. Then drive him around wherever he wanted to go until he left Houston. A few weeks, tops. The best part? Once he was gone, she'd have enough money to finally get her degree without eating peanut butter and crackers for dinner every night. It was worth taking off a semester to play chauffeur.

She stopped tapping as she thought about Fin. She'd never actually met him. His assistant, Shen, who ducked and dodged all meaningful questions about his boss, handled the face-to-face stuff. But Fin's money was very green, so she was very satisfied. And if she had a few unanswered questions about what her boss was doing in his big penthouse condo, well, she wasn't being paid to ask questions.

A few minutes later Steve walked out of the building, and she sighed with relief. But she had to suck her breath right back in again when she saw the man behind him.

Whoa! He rang the bell on her personal demigod meter. Tall, muscular, dark hair, great face, and . . .

She didn't get any further. Unusual, because she was

a detail person, and she hadn't gotten anywhere close to an inch-by-inch appraisal.

Something was coming. Something big. Kelly sensed it on a level that didn't answer to logic. It was the moment between the lightning strike and the thunder. You knew the boom was coming, but you didn't know how loud it'd be.

It struck. An emotion so raw she wanted to clutch her stomach and scream, a darkly erotic punch in the gut that was more about pain than pleasure. What the . . . She tried to crawl free, but the images and impressions followed her—heat, hunger, violence, *sex.*

Kelly gripped the steering wheel until her knuckles turned white, but it didn't help. Her common sense was trying to drag her battered psyche to its feet when the second emotion flattened her.

Terror. The black crow of panic was perched on her shoulder. She'd never felt this scared in her whole life.

Don't open the door. She pried one hand free of the steering wheel and reached for the door to lock it. Wait. That's stupid. Run like hell. In the fight-or-flight mode, flight was a winner. She was getting out of Dodge.

Steve knocked on the closed passenger window, and whatever weirdness had a stranglehold on her loosened its grip. *Thank you.* She shook her head, trying to clear away the residual terror. What was that about?

"Unlock the damn door." He didn't sound like the goofy Steve she knew and avoided.

She blinked. When had she locked the doors? "Sure." Keeping her eyes carefully averted from the man still standing a short distance behind Steve, she released the locks.

Steve yanked the door open, but he didn't bother saying anything about the locks as he leaned into the car. "Look, I'm not riding back with you. I'll get home some other way." He hooked a thumb at the man behind him. "He's all yours."

Hers? Until she untangled her emotions, she'd like a buffer in the backseat. As Steve started to turn away, she leaned across the seat to shout at him. "Wait. You can't just go off. Why aren't you riding back with us?"

He stared at her, his face pale, with eyes that showed a lot of white. "I flew across the ocean with him. Felt like I was sitting next to death the whole way. By the time we landed, everyone around us had moved." He held up a hand to ward off questions. "Don't ask. I don't know why. The dude just scares the crap out of me. Scared everyone else too." His smile was grim. "And don't tell me you don't feel it."

Shocked, she watched Steve drag his bag to the taxi line. They didn't make white knights like they used to. Warily, she cast her soon-to-be passenger a glance before waving him over. What she felt was primal, instinctive, and didn't make one bit of sense. She'd either overcome it or lose her job. She'd take steak over peanut butter and crackers every time.

Still, she had to renew her grip on the steering wheel when the man slid in beside her and slammed the door closed. His presence filled the car, and she fought the return of her panic, her *need*. She pressed her lips together as she tried to wall off her feelings until she could figure them out.

"No bags?" She forced herself to turn her head and meet his gaze.

"I travel light." His voice was a soft, sensual rasp. He could use that same tone to say, "I want to have sex with you," or "I'm going to eat you, little girl," and Kelly would've believed either statement.

She didn't think she had any breath left in her lungs, so

she just nodded as she drove away from the airport. Once on the freeway, darkness wrapped itself around them. And if someone didn't say something soon, she was going to pull the car over and do a great impression of a gazelle across someone's field.

"Fin said your name is Ty. Ty what?" A last name would make him seem more real, more solid, *less dangerous*. Maybe.

"Endeka." He clenched and unclenched his hands as he watched traffic whiz by.

Maybe he wasn't used to busy highways. That tiny glimpse of vulnerability helped dispel some of her fear, but it didn't do much for her other problem. *It* waited, dark and threatening, in a shadowed corner of her mind. It didn't have a reason for being; it just was. *Sex.* Not just ordinary sex, but a craving so powerful she knew taking him inside her would never be enough. Only absorbing every single cell of his body would quiet the need.

She almost snorted. Great. Kelly, the human amoeba. She beat that stupidity back and tried to bury it under who she was—a woman who chose her men based on a whole bunch of *sensible* criteria. I-want-your-body wasn't one of them.

"That's Fin's last name. You guys related?" She smiled. Okay, so it was a little shaky around the edges.

He didn't smile back. "Cousins."

Kelly took her attention from the highway long enough to sneak another glance. Less dangerous? Maybe not. For the first time, she really took stock of what he looked like.

About six-four, broad shoulders, with a muscular build that came from real work and not a weight room. Dark hair that was a little too long, and a hard face with gray eyes she didn't think she wanted to study closely right now. He had a sensual mouth, his only softening feature. Jeans, a dark gray pullover, and a short leather jacket completed the picture.

She looked back at the road. Nothing about him should cause the suffocating fear she'd felt, *still* felt. But logic wasn't a passenger tonight.

"*Your* name? Fin forgot to pass that info on." He stared out the side window at the darkness rushing by.

Kelly frowned. Tension rolled off him in waves. She didn't have to be particularly sensitive to feel it. "Kelly Maloy. I'll be your driver until you leave Houston." When in doubt, ask. "Is something bothering you?"

He paused, and for a moment she thought he'd tell her. He didn't. What he did do was fumble for the button to lower the window and then stare into the woods they were passing. "Stop."

Startled, she put her foot on the brake and eased the car to the side of the highway. "What? Do you feel sick?"

Mr. Scary didn't answer. He shoved the car door open and leaped out. While she watched open-mouthed, he raced into the woods.

"Well, hell." No matter how terrifying this guy was, she couldn't go back to Fin and say she'd lost him. She needed this job. Besides, she knew how miserable carsickness could make you feel. He'd probably run into the woods to throw up. She should make sure he was okay.

Grabbing the pepper spray and her cell phone from her purse, along with the flashlight she kept under the seat, she locked her car and followed Ty into the trees.

Kelly heard the screams first, followed by what sounded like the roar of some animal. A *big* animal. And not one she recognized.

Common sense said that bad things were happening when people screamed like that, and whatever animal was out there would probably snicker at her pepper spray, right before it swallowed her whole.

Common sense also suggested she go back to her car and lock herself inside until Ty came back. But what if he didn't come back? What if he was in trouble? With a muttered apology to her common sense, she kept going.

A wild thrashing in the underbrush was her only warning as four men burst from the trees. Kelly planted herself and readied the pepper spray. Wasted effort. They ignored her, racing past and disappearing into the darkness.

She exhaled the breath she'd been holding. That had gone well. But where was her missing paycheck? She found him a few seconds later.

Kelly stepped onto the old dirt road that ran through the woods and froze. Her mind checked off the obvious— white Honda, windows up, two terrified faces pressed against the back side window, Ty standing a few feet from the car, and . . .

Her mind refused to put a check beside the last item. It looked like there was some huge ghostly shape dissolving around Ty. Whatever it was, it disappeared even as she stared. She shook her head. No, she hadn't seen that. It was just her stress, fear, and the night playing games with her senses.

Before she had a chance to ask what was going on, the faces disappeared from the window. Kelly could see the two teens, a girl and boy, scrambling into the front seats. A minute later, the boy started the car, and they raced away, leaving a cloud of Texas dust in their wake.

She took a deep breath and forced herself to walk over to Ty. "Explain."

He shrugged. And then he smiled.

Kelly felt her fear ease into that other emotion, the one she wouldn't give a name because it didn't need any encouragement. He had a great smile, if you liked smiles laced with promises of danger and secrets. Evidently she did.

"The men who probably passed you on their way out were trying to rob the people in the car." His smile widened. "They changed their minds."

The logical question was *why*? Kelly didn't ask. She was too busy fighting the fear-and-sex thing. Besides, she'd had about all the strangeness she could take for one night. And she had a suspicion his explanation might involve the ghostly image she definitely had *not* seen. Hey, denial was her friend.

"We need to get moving. Fin will be calling to find out what's happened to us." She turned and headed back to the car. Even though she couldn't hear him following her, she sensed Ty with every primitive instinct remaining in her modern human body. She controlled the urge to run. *Never run from a predator.* Where'd that thought come from? Kelly pushed it away.

They spent the rest of the long drive from Bush International in silence. Questions stood shoulder to shoulder in Kelly's mind. How had he known something was happening in the woods? What was the animal she'd heard? Why were those men so terrified? Why hadn't the two in the car at least rolled down their windows to thank Ty for saving them? And what was . . . No, she wouldn't think about that again.

She didn't ask any of those questions because, well, he might answer them. Maybe tomorrow she'd be ready for answers.

There was one comment she felt safe making. "Rushing in to save those people in the car took guts."

Ty threw her a puzzled look. "I wasn't trying to save anyone."

Uh-oh. Maybe she didn't want to hear this. But she couldn't drive with her hands over her ears.

"I was there for the hunt. Too bad you interrupted." He smiled again. "I could like Texas. A lot."

His smile sent icy worms slithering and wiggling down her spine. Okay, small talk done for the night. They didn't exchange any more conversation for the rest of the trip. He seemed fascinated with Houston, and she didn't try to distract him.

By the time she turned off Memorial Drive and stopped at the front entrance to Fin's high-rise condo, her muscles ached from tension. She nodded toward the door, where someone was already headed their way. "That man will make sure you get up to Fin's condo." She watched Ty climb from the car, then turn to stare back at her. "I'll wait for you."

Tonight as she lay in bed, she'd have to come to terms with her feelings. She couldn't let phantom fears derail her plans to get her degree. And the sexual thing that was totally not her? That was a curiosity she needed to lay to rest.

She worked up a real smile for him. "I'll see you in a few hours." She'd end this on a light note. He wouldn't want someone around him who radiated fear every time he looked at her. "And I'll be ready to drive you to hell and back if you need me."

His expression gave nothing away. "Remember that promise." And then he strode away.

When would this freaky night be over? She'd park the car in the underground garage, take the elevator up to the condo's lounge, where she could get some caffeine in her system, and wait until he needed her.

A short time later, she settled onto a leather couch with her cup of coffee and one of the books strewn around the lounge. A serial-killer mystery. Good. She needed something simple and ordinary to calm her down.

Chapter Two

Ty closed his eyes as he leaned against the elevator wall. He'd spent too much time in confined spaces during the last few million years. Fin had done his mental show-and-tell act to explain planes, cars, and elevators, but knowing something was a long way from *living* it.

On top of that, he could feel his aggression level punching through the roof. He wanted to kill something. Fin had warned him about this. Ty would never be able to stay close to Fin for any length of time without snapping that slender thread holding him to the human world. Something about Fin fed the animal in him. Good in a fight. Bad when he was trying to fit into this time, this place.

Could he make it work? Ramp up the need to hunt, the need for mindless savagery, the need for sex, and what you had was a walking disaster ready to blow.

The sex thing could be an immediate problem. Maybe Fin should get a male driver for him. If he hadn't jumped from the car in search of prey, Kelly Maloy might've had a first night on the job she'd never forget. He allowed himself a smile born of all his deprived hungers rolled into one baring of the teeth. No, forget the male driver. He'd keep the small blonde with the big brown eyes and hot body.

The elevator doors slid open, stopping all conjecture about sexy drivers. He scanned the open area for danger before stepping out. Empty. No place for another predator to hide.

The pale walls, absence of windows, and white tile floor made him uneasy. It was alien, enclosed, and as the elevator doors slid shut, felt like a trap. The building's strangeness made him want to roar and tear holes in things. He tightened his control, but still his need to strike out strangled him, made his breaths come in hard gasps.

There was only one door in the opposite wall. He took the seven strides necessary to reach it, then waited. Fin knew he was there.

The door opened.

There were three of them. A few inches shorter than he with lean, muscled bodies created for speed. They all looked the same—short spiky blond hair, bright blue eyes, and hard faces.

Nothing like him except for one thing. They all watched him from predators' eyes that gleamed with challenge. They smiled.

Ty returned the smile, making sure they understood he was the biggest badass in this particular cave. "Three of you to take me down? Not impressed." *Go ahead, push me so I can kill you.*

Two of them stopped smiling. The third laughed and stepped forward. "Nah. One to take you down and two to watch." Behind his grin and cold eyes, the man assessed Ty. Any weakness would be noted and stored away to be exploited later.

This guy was fighting the same battle as Ty. His need to destroy lived in his eyes. He controlled it, though. Barely. Too bad.

As for weaknesses, he wouldn't find any. But Ty would make sure he kept all three of them in front of him anyway. A hunting pack could do plenty of damage. "Want to move aside so I can come in." It wasn't a question.

Tension thrummed between them. Ty let it hum and build, enjoying the feel of it singing through his blood. He wanted a fight, *needed* it. And when the other man finally nodded and stepped aside, Ty felt bone-deep disappointment.

"I'm Utah." The guy didn't offer his hand. "These are my brothers." He didn't introduce them. "You're the last one."

Ty said nothing. He waited for the three brothers to go into the room ahead of him. Let another predator get behind you often enough and you ended up missing body parts.

Respect touched Utah's eyes for the first time. Glancing at his brothers, he did some silent communicating. They led Ty inside.

Ty ignored the marble staircase along with everything else meant to distract as he scanned his surroundings for danger or prey. Only when Utah and his silent brothers led him into a large room did he stop his search. He'd found the danger.

All the info Fin had crammed into his brain had given him a serious case of mental indigestion. But now his thinker burped out an immediate ID—dining room, entire wall of floor-to-ceiling windows, barrel ceiling covered with some kind of shiny metal, dim lighting coming from somewhere he couldn't see, and stained-glass double doors probably leading to the kitchen. The walls were one giant mural—lots of trees, grassy fields, and glimpses of prey in the shadows. Color. *Home.*

He forced his gaze away from the mural and thoughts of home. Houston was his home now. The men sitting around a long table near the windows claimed his unblinking attention. Utah and his brothers took their places, and then everyone returned his stare.

Ten plus him. The Eleven. Together. In one room. It had never happened. *Ever.* In the past, Fin had kept them far apart from one another, from him. Fin's psychic link had been their only connection. Ty didn't know the faces or the men behind them. He took the last seat, between a guy in a suit and one wearing a black duster with his hair in a long braid that almost slapped his ass. Beneath the table, Ty curled his hands into claws. *Control.*

Then Ty watched everyone watch one another.

Silent aggression filled the room. Ty gathered himself in response to the unspoken threats bouncing back and forth. As the violence potential ratcheted up another notch with each passing second, he made his plans. He'd take out the guy with the duster first. After he grabbed that braid, he'd yank the man's head back and slit his throat.

He hesitated. Problem. No sharp knife, just a dull-edged, useless piece of crap lying next to his spoon. Hell.

"No."

The voice was soft, compelling, *familiar.* Not a voice he'd ever ignore. Everyone jerked his attention to the man at the head of the table.

Fin.

"I did *not* almost kill myself putting your sorry asses in the ground sixty-five million years ago for this. I did *not* monitor your safety for sixty-five million years for this. I did *not* drain myself yanking your aforementioned sorry asses out of the ground after sixty-five million years for this. You *will* respect one another."

Fin's voice was a weapon, each "not" a psychic punch to the side of Ty's head. The final "will" was a kick in the gut that almost doubled him over. Good thing Fin wasn't seriously angry. Ty leaned back in his chair and gasped for air.

He cut his gaze to his neighbors to find they were doing

the same thing. Ty closed his eyes and shoveled earth on his need for violence. Okay, fire banked for the time being. He opened his eyes.

"Where'd you get our bodies?" The guy asking the question was bigger than Ty, with a need-to-kill gleam in his eyes.

Ty smiled. He'd always hunted alone, but if Fin ordered them to team up, he wouldn't mind partnering with this dude.

Fin scanned the table before answering. Probably checking to make sure lots of respecting was going on. "I rose last year. Then I searched for big male bodies." His pause left the suggestion out there that maybe he should've looked for small female bodies.

Everyone sucked in a breath.

"I claimed the bodies right after their human souls turned out the lights, locked the doors, and went on permanent vacation." Fin's smile made even Ty shudder. "I'm good at breaking and entering." He shrugged. "After that it was just a case of some minor tweaking. I gave you faces women would lust after so none of you could bitch about not getting laid. Every body's in prime condition. Keep it that way."

Fin stopped smiling. "Because here are the hard facts. If someone destroys your bright and shiny new human body, you're down for the duration. Sure, your body can heal from most injuries, but you can't grow a new head. So don't lose it. Yes, I can yank your soul out of your body if it dies, but my power's pretty much tied up right now. I'd have to tuck your soul away for safekeeping somewhere. Not the way you want to end up."

Ty intended to hang on to his body. No way was he taking any more extended naps.

He looked around again. Yeah, Fin had gotten it right. He'd seen a lot of human males on his trip from Ireland, and the men around him were definite upgrades. Ty glanced back at Fin. "Man, you're going to stand out in a crowd. Why'd you make yourself look like that?"

For just a moment, Fin lost his supreme-leader expression. He grinned. "Because I could."

It wasn't a case of *could* but *should*. All the others except Fin had hard faces, dangerous in a way that would make people think twice about fucking with them.

Fin's look said, *Come to me. Stay with me. Be awed and amazed by me.*

His long silver hair fell over his shoulders and down his back. Not gray, but *silver*. Each strand sparkled in the dim light. His eyes were metallic silver rimmed in black with a hint of purple when you looked at them just right. Their cold brilliance was freaking weird if you asked Ty. Women would think his face was beautiful. Fin's image promised that he was a benign god who never grew angry, never harmed. What a crock.

"You just hurt my feelings, Ty." Fin's eyes gleamed with wicked amusement.

"Yeah, well the guys we're hunting won't have any trouble finding *you*. They can just follow the glow in the sky." Ty had stopped worrying about Fin rooting around in his thoughts a long time ago.

Fin smiled, a smile that turned all that beauty into something really terrifying. "Think of me as a big, shiny spider sitting in the middle of my superglue web. You guys are out there at the end of the web waving your arms and giving out invites to visit me." His smile widened. "I eat visitors."

Okay, that made Ty feel better. Fin was . . . Fin. He'd

always drawn people to him, made them forget what he really was. But he took care of his own. Ty didn't know how he knew this. He couldn't remember ever seeing Fin's physical body before, but somewhere he knew he had. When . . . ?

"Don't think about it, Ty. Keep focused on the enemy." Fin wasn't smiling anymore.

"How about filling us in on this enemy? We need details." The guy with black hair across from Ty sounded like he thought all this talk was a bunch of crap. His expression said, *Let's get on with the good stuff*.

Ty added his personal vote to that thought. He liked the man's attitude. Ty took a moment to wonder what he'd been before. Not that it mattered. *Now* was what mattered.

"And why didn't you warn us before you did your disconnect thing with our souls? I was in the middle of—"

Fin turned his gaze on the guy, and he shut up. "Dinner's ready. I'll answer questions while we eat."

On cue, the double doors opened and a small man rolling a cart filled with food came through. Ty, along with all the others at the table, eyed the covered dishes and then the man, trying to decide which was dinner.

The man met their gazes and growled. Predator. Ty lost interest.

Fin narrowed his eyes. "This is getting old fast. You're human. Act it. Get over the predator-prey thing. Here it's all about friends or enemies. Greer is my chef. He's otherkin. His soul's *other*. Like us." His mental message was, *Not exactly*.

Greer nodded, but his expression said he'd never turn his back to any of them. Smart man.

Ty watched as Greer put the uncovered dishes on the

table. He forced himself to remember the how-to-eat-like-a-human lessons Fin had poured into his head along with everything else. He wanted to pounce on the steaks, drag them all onto his plate, and devour them before any of the others could try to take them away. He only took two. Ty ignored the potatoes and vegetables. Maybe he'd try them at another meal, but for now he wanted meat.

While Ty resisted the urge to abandon his knife and fork in favor of his fingers, he eyed the chef. "Great food. What are you, Greer?"

The chef almost smiled. "My soul is tiger." His eyes said the men at the table might scare him witless, but a tiger didn't cringe.

Ty nodded his approval.

Fin watched the chef return to the kitchen. "Ty's experience tonight is worth mentioning."

What experience? Ty paused in his eating.

"Houston isn't a hotbed of otherkin, but from now on I'll make sure any of them that come in contact with you guys have predator souls." Fin glanced at Ty. "Steve won't be coming back to work. By now he's probably in Dallas. You were broadcasting your need to kill and get laid so loud, I almost reached for my earplugs. Oh, and right now Kelly is trying to figure out why you sent her into a panic and what her sudden craving for sex was all about."

The other men at the table grinned. Fin didn't. His stare wiped the smiles from their faces. "Here's where everyone pays really close attention. Ty went hunting tonight."

Everyone except Fin looked envious.

"When he found his prey, he got excited. His soul form bled through and scared the shit out of his intended prey. Luckily for everyone, Ty's driver showed up and distracted him." The glance he sent Ty wasn't condemning. It just said, *Don't do this again.*

"I don't care how hard it is—start blending. You're human. You'll never be anything else again. I've done the last nifty body exchange I'll do for a long time. So learn to fit in." He left the *or else* unsaid.

Ty looked down the length of the table, met every man's eyes. "Hell, all of you would've done the same thing." Satisfied, he watched their gazes slide away from him.

"So would I." Fin's murmur silenced the table. No one moved; no one *breathed.*

Ty's imagination couldn't begin to wrap itself around what it would mean if Fin ever lost control. Death and destruction like the earth had never known. *He'd seen it happen once.* The thought took root and refused to budge. His memory was wrong, though. He'd never *seen* Fin before tonight. Then what . . . ?

Fin fixed him with an unblinking stare. "Forget it." Fin never raised his voice. He didn't have to.

Ty frowned as the thought faded. It hadn't made any sense anyway.

"We need to know what we're facing." The guy in the suit sitting next to Ty spoke up for the first time.

"Once I woke you, I had to decide what to tell you first. I chose to fill you in on the nitty-gritty day-to-day stuff." Fin studied all of them. "I thought I'd have time to explain everything else to you tonight. But it's not going to happen. You'd tear each other apart long before I finished. I underestimated what being close to me would do to you." He pushed his chair away from the table, rose, and strode to the wall of windows. Standing, he was about six eight.

Ty and the others joined him. Far below, the lights of Houston looked like some giant connect-the-dots picture.

From Fin's expression, Ty figured he wouldn't like what the finished shape revealed. Fin's smile didn't reach his eyes. "That's your jungle down there, all the dark alleys and deserted streets. The hunting will be good."

"And who'll be hunting *us?*" Someone behind Ty voiced the question they all wanted to ask.

"The same beings that wiped us out sixty-five million years ago. Nine powerful immortals plus their leader, the granddaddy of them all." Fin's expression didn't change, but his eyes gleamed cold and hard.

"Why?" the voice behind Ty asked for all of them.

"Because no one has ever said no to them. Until now. They've worked the absolute-power-corrupts-absolutely truth since the beginning of time. They foment destruction and chaos. It puts them in their happy place." He curled his lips back from his teeth. "I'd like to put them in their dead place."

"How do they make it happen?" Ty figured what had worked millions of years ago might not work now.

"They only target the dominant life form of the planet. They encourage evil, and if Earth isn't harboring any intelligent evil at the time, they work up a few cataclysms. Sixty-five million years ago, it was an asteroid strike."

"Why wait millions of years if they get such a kick out of it?" Ty raked his fingers through his hair. If he didn't get action soon, he'd explode.

"They don't have a choice. Earth's life is measured in time periods. At the end of each period, a cosmic door opens and the bastards can return for a short time until the new period begins. They're here now. And this time they plan to take out the whole human race."

No one spoke, but rage and the need to kill was a living, breathing presence in the room.

"We weren't strong enough to fight them last time. But now?" Fin smiled. Not a nice smile. "Now is different."

"How soon?" Utah's blue eyes blazed with his desire to hunt.

Fin's gaze grew distant. "The present time period ends on December twenty-first, 2012, at exactly eleven eleven. Winter solstice. Then the cosmic clock resets to zero, and time begins again. What we do between now and that moment will decide whether humanity still walks the earth when the new period begins." His expression turned savage. "And I don't know about you, but I have a vested interest in the human race. There won't be another Great Dying."

Ty didn't question how Fin knew stuff like this; he just did. "Why will this time be different?"

"We're the Eleven. Numbers have power, and eleven is a master number. It defines who we are. When the clock hits eleven eleven on that December twenty-first, we'll be at our strongest. Humans with all their high-tech toys won't have a clue how to fight this war. It'll take primal violence to win, and we're the only force on Earth with a shot at kicking cosmic asses."

"What about the humans? Don't any of them understand the danger?" The guy with the long braid sounded disgusted with humanity. "Why aren't they doing anything about it?"

Fin shrugged. "Probably a few sense what's coming. They ask questions like why the ancient Mayans ended their long count calendar on that date, and why more and more people are seeing the number eleven wherever they look. But for the most part, they're clueless. The universe tries to send messages, but most humans don't listen."

Ty glanced at his watch. 11:11. Damn.

Fin turned to face the men behind him. "We'll hunt the

enemy down one city at a time." His smile was a thing of nightmares. "And when we find them, we'll make sure they aren't around to party in 2012."

Ty glanced out the window and froze. A roiling black cloud outlined in glowing red was racing toward the window. "Shit!"

All the others except Fin followed his gaze. Fin didn't even turn around to look.

As the cloud blanketed the windows, the glass shook. Ty felt the waves of energy bouncing off the building. "What the hell is that?"

They all backed away from the windows. Fin stayed. "That's death and despair and all kinds of fun stuff. It's a welcome-to-Houston message from our enemies."

"Don't they have names?" Ty watched the glass vibrate, waited for it to crash inward.

"The windows won't break." Fin reached behind him and placed his palm flat against the glass. The shuddering stopped. "And *they* would be many things. They've been called the Galactic Masters, Lords of Time, Gods of Death, and probably names I've never heard."

He paused. "Personally, the names all sound a little too *Dr. Who* for me." He turned to look at the cloud, and it slid away into the night. "They're just numbers to me. That was Nine tapping on our windows."

"What would've happened if you weren't here and we weren't connected to you?" The questioner wore black pants and a black shirt. But he wouldn't blend into the night with that long blond hair.

"The wall of glass would've exploded. Then all of you would've taken headers out the windows. Compulsions are a bitch. You'd survive, but you'd scare the shit out of anyone walking their dogs down below." Fin speared them with a hard gaze. "You've all learned something tonight. Keep the mental airwaves open between us. Always. As long as we're connected, I can protect you from the psychic stuff. You can handle physical attacks on your own."

Ty watched Fin walk back to the table. He didn't sit down. "Looks like we'll have to skip dessert. Greer will be disappointed. But hey, I'm tough. I'll force myself to eat your share."

Some of the men remained frozen, that dangerous still-ness of a predator just before it attacked. The others paced restlessly. Ty chose stillness.

"I've rented apartments in five different parts of town. Four apartments in each building. Your drivers will use two of them. The other two are for you. I'm pairing you up, but you'd kill each other if I made you share an apartment."

Drivers. Ty had a question about that. "Are all the driv-ers human? Why can't we just learn to drive ourselves? And what excuse did you give for us running around at night?"

"I expect you to learn how to drive. But we need human drivers right now. Nine and the others can sense us." Fin nodded toward the windows. "You saw what just happened. We have a raw, primitive energy they can track. So I searched out drivers with the strongest possible human life force. They help mask our presence as long as we stay close to them. Besides, the enemy can't kill humans di-rectly. They don't have that problem with nonhumans. Make the most of your time with your drivers. You need practice interacting one on one with humans."

Fin grinned. "And I told them you're missionaries try-ing to save the poor lost souls that wander the mean streets after dark."

Someone snorted his opinion.

Ty scowled. Every answer Fin gave just led to more questions. He'd have to do some damage control with Kelly. After his little run through the woods, she might not believe he was hunting for lost souls.

"You staying here, Fin?" The guy with the braid was a pacer.

"Absolutely. This is my building. I bought it. Everyone who lives here is with us. I've built protections around it from top to bottom. Don't worry, your apartments are safe too." Fin looked at his watch. "It's time for you to go. A few of you are having a tough time holding it together. If it's any comfort, the longer you're human, the easier it'll be to control your aggression. Try to sleep during the day. You'll hunt at night."

"Hunt *what?*" Ty could feel his temper slipping away even as he grasped frantically for it. "I need more freaking info. What do the Lords of Time look like? Where do we find these guys, and how do we kill them?"

He heard mumbled agreement all around him.

"I'll fill you in while you're sleeping. Hope none of you are screamers." Fin's smile said the dreams would be that bad. "There's a pile of CDs on the table. You'll each find a laptop in your apartment. Watch the CD. All of you are on it. Memorize names and faces, and then destroy the disc."

"Speaking of names, the ones you gave us suck." This from the black-haired guy again.

Fin looked insulted. "I thought the names were sort of clever. I looked all of you up and gave each of you a shortened version of your scientific name." He shrugged. "Some turned out better than others."

"One more thing. What about women?" The black-haired guy got everyone's attention with the word *women*. "Humans fall in love and get married. Sometimes forever." His expression said the whole forever thing puzzled him. "What if that happens to one of us? How will that affect the Eleven?"

Fin exhaled deeply, his expression one of long-suffering patience. "I wouldn't worry about it. Women won't be falling over each other to marry you."

"Why not?" Black-haired Guy didn't sound as if he believed that.

"You'd have to find the one woman on Earth who was strong enough, who loved you enough to walk into the heart of your beast and claim a piece of your soul. That has always been our way. What're the chances?"

That had always been their way? What way? Ty didn't remember anything like that. He'd always gone for the "see her, mate with her, and leave her" way. But as inevitably happened when he tried to think deep thoughts about some of the things Fin said, they drifted away and were gone.

Before anyone could ask another question, Fin picked up his cell phone from the table. "Shen gave all the drivers a choice of going home until he called them back or staying here. Kelly was the only one who stayed. I'll have Shen call the rest of them now." He glanced at Ty. "You can leave. She's down in the lounge on the ground floor."

Ty scowled. That was a dismissal if he'd ever heard one. He headed toward the door.

"Oh, and, Ty, you scared Kelly. Make it up to her. We need her. She has a special skill that'd be tough to replace." Fin was in cryptic mode. "You might want to ease up on the sex-every-second thoughts, too. You can wait a little longer."

"You try waiting sixty-five million years," Ty muttered, not caring if Fin heard him.

"I have." Fin sounded hungry.

Kelly had tried getting into the serial-killer book. She really had. No luck. All she could think about was Ty. Did she believe he was a man of God trying to save souls? Uh, no. She'd seen his expression back in those woods. He'd mentioned hunting, but she didn't think souls were involved.

She refused to obsess over the fear and lust she felt whenever he was near. Kelly had her feet firmly planted on the ground; there was no way she could blame those feelings on him unless her feet achieved liftoff. And she wasn't ready yet to label herself a wacko.

"I'm ready to leave." His voice sounded right behind her.

She choked back a startled squeak. "Jeez, don't sneak up on me like that."

Ty walked around to stand in front of her. For just a moment, his grin looked almost boyish. He'd gotten a kick out of catching her by surprise. Then the smile changed, becoming more personal. "Where's the car?"

The words didn't match the smile. But she wouldn't let the smile make her uneasy. She was too relieved his return hadn't triggered another massive dose of terror and sexual craziness. The tension and awareness she felt now were normal. He was chest-thumping alpha male, and she was female. No biggie. "In the underground garage. I'll bring it around to the door."

But when she stood and started toward the elevator, he walked beside her. "It's late. You shouldn't go anywhere by yourself at this time of night. Lots of dangerous people are out there."

You're so much safer? She didn't think so. But still . . . It was nice that he thought about her safety. Fine, so *nice* was too bland a word for Ty Endeka. And she could pretty much take care of herself.

Once in the elevator, he looked nervous during the short drop. She remembered noticing the same look on the car ride back from the airport. Huh, maybe he was claustrophobic. When in doubt, ask. "The elevator bothers you?"

"Yeah. I don't deal well with small, enclosed spaces." His frown said he didn't like admitting any weakness.

But the admission relaxed her. He was just a normal guy. Uh-huh, and she really believed that. The elevator door slid open, and they walked to the car in silence. As she drove from the parking garage, she searched for a casual way to get the answers to some questions she had. He beat her to it.

"Fin said you have some kind of special skill. What's he talking about?" Ty didn't even try to sound casual. Her answer was important to him for some reason.

Special skill? "Haven't a clue. I don't do anything special."

"Wrong."

She didn't have to see his face to interpret that one word. It was a sensual male purr that said she was a woman so she had a *very* special skill. For a moment the remembered need flared and then just as suddenly died. Huh?

Kelly took a deep breath before shutting off all interpretations of the word *wrong.* "No, really. I was born and raised in Houston. And when I'm not driving missionaries around in the dark, I'm getting my masters in music from Rice University's Shepherd School of Music."

When she chanced a glance at him, he was staring

unblinkingly at her from those gray eyes. "So what're you learning at your school of music?" He looked like he actually cared.

She shrugged. "Performance—I play a few instruments—composition, and music theory. Stuff like that." The traffic was light this time of night, and she drove a little faster than she should. Did he make her nervous? You bet.

He nodded as he turned his attention to the passenger side window. "Where's this apartment?"

"Westheimer. We're almost there. Then you can . . ." Then you can what? "Umm, you don't have any luggage. Where're your clothes?"

"Stop."

She didn't think as she stomped on the brake. He braced himself against the dashboard. What? Where? A quick scan revealed no red lights, no other car barreling toward her, no late-night drunk staggering into her path. Then why . . . ?

"Something's wrong. Stay here." He flung open the door, leaped out, and sprinted across an empty parking lot, disappearing behind the back of a furniture store.

Déjà vu. Kelly was left sitting in her car in the middle of the street with her mouth hanging open. *Stay* here? Beg, lie down, roll over? Uh-uh. Angry, she whipped the steering wheel around and pulled into the parking lot. Once again, she loaded herself down with pepper spray, flashlight, and cell phone.

Mumbling complaints about strange and unusual on-the-job idiocies, she climbed from the car, locked it, clicked her flashlight on, and headed toward the back of the building.

This time she didn't hear screams or animal sounds. She didn't hear anything. In a way, that was even scarier. Since she hadn't taken her stupid pills this morning, she moved slowly, skirting the shadows thrown by the building. Silence.

"Ty? Finished hunting souls in there?" Okay, that was dumb. God, it was so quiet she could hear her courage tiptoeing away. She swallowed hard. Fine, so she was scared. If he didn't answer right now, she'd—

"Too late. Soul's gone." His voice was hard with a sharp edge of threat in it.

Without thinking, she aimed the beam of her flashlight at the narrow alley behind the store.

At first all she saw was him standing there. She couldn't read the expression on his face. Then she glanced past him and saw the body on the ground. She sucked in her breath. *Oh, no. No, no, no.*

Ty answered the question she couldn't force past frozen lips. "Yeah, he's dead." He turned back to the body. "Come take a look and tell me what you think did this."

He was kidding, right? She'd never seen a dead body. When she was a kid, she'd refused to go to any and all funerals. Her parents hadn't forced her.

She must've made some kind of strangled sound because he glanced back at her. Narrowing his eyes, he studied her for a moment, then nodded. "Two holes in the throat. Blood drained. Must be a neat freak. No blood splatters anywhere." His voice was cold, dispassionate. "What kills this way?"

Holes in throat? Blood drained? Hysterical laughter bubbled just below the surface. This could not be happening. But she'd better find her voice soon or he might decide to bring the body to her so she could give him her expert opinion on cause of death.

"Vampires." Good. She'd managed one word; maybe

she could force out a few more. "Mythical monsters." Why was she explaining vampires to him? Everyone knew the legends.

"Mythical. So they don't really exist?"

"No." Everyone knew that except Ty Endeka. None of this made sense. She shouldn't be standing here in the dark explaining vampires to someone while a man's body . . . Kelly willed herself to stop shaking.

"Got it." He didn't look horrified at the murder, just thoughtful.

Well, he could be as detached and analytical as he wanted. She'd fall apart for both of them. "Omigod . . . the poor man."

"Police." She pulled her cell phone from her pocket with shaking fingers. "We have to report this." Kelly faced away from the body as she punched in 911. If she didn't see the man's face, he wouldn't be a person to her.

She was just about to press send when Ty reached over her shoulder and lifted the phone out of her hand. "No police."

"What?" Outrage fueled false courage and got her coherent again. "Look, I play by the rules. You find a body, you report it to the police. That's the law." She narrowed her eyes to angry slits. "You don't want to obey the law, then I don't want to work for you."

He raked his fingers through his hair. "So what do we tell them? That I told you to stop the car and then ran back here only to find a dead body drained of all its blood? Yeah, that won't make them suspicious. If we walk away now, someone will discover the body in the morning when the store opens. *They* can call the police."

Kelly could feel a line forming between her eyes as she thought it out. He was right. They had no logical reason for rooting around behind this building after midnight. And Ty had just entered the country. The police might try to make something of that.

"I don't like your idea. Someone has to report the murder now, not in the morning. The sooner the cops get here, the better chance they have of catching the killer." She wasn't sure she really believed that, but she didn't want to leave the man lying there in the dark for the rest of the night. Not that it'd matter to the corpse, but it mattered to her.

Ty put his arm across her shoulders and guided her back to the car. "I'll call Fin. He'll take care of reporting it. No one will associate the murder with us."

Even with a dead man lying a few feet away, she couldn't ignore the pressure of Ty's arm. It was . . . disturbing. Actually, it felt dangerous and strangely intimate at the same time. She forced her thoughts away from his arm. "What if someone drove by and noticed our car parked here? Maybe they could give the police a description or plate number." She pressed two fingers against her forehead to hold the burgeoning headache at bay. "Tell me I'm not thinking of agreeing to this."

"You're making a rational decision. We didn't kill him. And we're doing the right thing. We're seeing that his murder is reported." He opened the car door so she could slip in. "And exactly one taxi has passed here since we stopped. He had a fare, and neither one glanced at the parking lot. Even if they had, your car is registered to Fin. Let Fin deal with it."

When did you have time to notice all that? She wanted to say it, but she didn't have the guts. He was freaky. Everything he'd done since she'd picked him up from the airport had been freaky. But he was also fascinating, exciting, and sexy. And even though the freaky part might make her want to quit, the fascinating, exciting, and sexy tags would keep her at the wheel. He definitely wasn't boring. She hated boring.

Since he didn't look as if he was about to pull out his own cell phone, she handed him hers as soon as he climbed into the passenger seat.

He did exactly what he'd said he would. She waited until he finished talking to Fin before asking the question.

"Want to tell me how you knew that guy was behind the building?"

Chapter Three

Ty yanked at the tattered edges of his self-control, trying to close the gaping holes. He wasn't ready to deal with explanations right now. Not when he could barely think.

As he'd stood over the body, the scent of an unknown predator in *his* territory had triggered his hunting instincts. Ty's aggression had roared back to life. Whatever had killed the man wasn't human, but human or not, he'd find it and destroy it.

Unfortunately, he was also busy dealing with that other equally demanding need, the one that couldn't understand why he wasn't already running his fingers over Kelly's bare body, tasting every inch of her smooth, soft skin, and burying himself deep inside her. So far he'd controlled the "broadcasting" Fin had complained about, but only because he was concentrating like hell.

"Well?"

She threw him a glance, intense and so tempting he had to dig his nails into his palms to keep from touching her. Kelly's scent teased and tortured, almost making him forget where and what he was. Almost.

Taking a deep breath, he stared straight ahead. "I can sense when something's wrong. Don't ask me how. I just know."

Kelly nodded as though his explanation made perfect sense. "So it's like a *bam* moment? Interesting. I've never met anyone who could do stuff like that. I didn't think it could be done, but you made me a believer tonight. And what about earlier? You said you went into the woods to hunt, not to help those people."

Crap. Didn't she forget *anything*? "Guess I didn't make myself clear. I *was* hunting. For those lost souls who thought they could gain material goods by taking from others."

Hallelujah and pass the bullshit. Damn Fin and his stupid excuses for what the Eleven did at night. Why couldn't they be undercover cops working to lower crime in Houston? *That* made sense. Ty thought about it. Okay, so maybe Fin was right. Undercover cops didn't hire clueless, sexy drivers.

"Uh-huh. Got it."

She didn't say anything for the rest of the drive. Probably analyzing everything that had happened tonight and deciding whether she still wanted to be a part of Team Weird. He hoped she did. And not because of the sexual attraction he felt or what Fin had said about her having a "special skill." He grinned. Who was he kidding? It was *all* about the sex. *Wasn't it?* He stopped smiling.

The apartment was in a three-story block of ordinary brick buildings. Parking in the rear. He guessed this was one way Fin hoped they'd blend in. Fin, on the other hand, didn't give a shit about blending in as he lived the good life in his penthouse condo. Jealous? You bet.

As they climbed the stairs to the third floor, Kelly looked worried. "What about clothes? Do you want me to drop you off at the Galleria tomorrow?" She frowned. "You never said why you didn't have any luggage."

"I was doing some missionary work in Africa, and the airline lost my bags on the flight back to Dublin. Didn't have time to buy new stuff before I had to catch the Houston flight." He paused to glance down the hallway. Only four doors. Two on each side. He hoped Fin had rented the whole top floor. "No problem, though. Fin said everything I'll need is in the apartment."

"Tough luck about your luggage. I'm in the apartment across from yours. Let me know if you need coffee or anything." She pulled a key from her pocket and handed it to him. "This is for your place."

She had no idea what he needed. If she did, she'd be burning rubber out of the parking lot right now.

"I'll be fine. Go and get some sleep. You'll hear from me tomorrow night." He watched as she unlocked her door and disappeared inside.

Only after she'd closed her door did he let himself into his own apartment. Even though he knew Fin would've whipped up his own brand of security for this place, and even though all he wanted to do was strip and fall into bed, he couldn't abandon the habits of a lifetime. He checked out the four small rooms—white walls, beige carpet, and windows overlooking the parking lot. Basic and generic. Nope, he wouldn't be doing any bonding with this place.

Ty glanced around his bedroom. Okay, no Nine hiding under the bed. Kicking off his shoes, he pulled the CD Fin had given him from his pocket, then padded over to the desk where the promised laptop waited. For the next twenty minutes he matched faces with names. He had a good laugh at the end. It was the only time he'd felt like laughing all night.

No, wait. Kelly had given him a few cheerful moments. She'd be exciting in or out of bed. It'd be tough keeping her safe, though. Ty already knew she didn't follow orders.

So what would happen if she found out about the Eleven? Had Fin thought all this stuff through? Probably.

Ty didn't even try to figure out the twisted maze that was Fin's mind.

He yawned. Maybe everything would be clearer after he got some rest. Fin had promised to feed them info while they slept. He dragged off his clothes, then pulled back the covers and was asleep as soon as he hit the mattress.

But when the dreams came, he wished they hadn't.

Ty tossed and turned all night as Fin downloaded explanations along with battle plans. And when he finally woke, Ty thought nostalgically about his little plot of earth under Newgrange.

Kelly lay across her bed as she got ready to make the last of her calls before the sun set and Mr. Hot and Oh-So-Scary put in an appearance. She'd saved Jenna till last because her sister was way too nosy and always managed to hook an "extra" onto "ordinary" without even trying. Jenna could make vanilla into a sinister flavor. God knows what she'd do with Ty's dark chocolate.

"Why didn't you call sooner, sis? So what happened last night? Tell all." Jenna didn't waste time on ritual greetings like "Hello" and "How are you?"

"Nothing much." Ha. Let Jenna find something interesting in that. "I picked my client up at Bush and drove him to the apartment." No use leaving even the hint of an information trail for Jenna to pick up with her ultra-sensitive nose for news.

"Uh-huh." Jenna's tone said, *More info because I know you're holding out on me.*

Kelly sifted through last night's events to find a few that would appease Jenna while telling her nothing important. "I'm just getting around to calling you because I got a late start. I stayed in bed as long as I could this morning because the boss's secretary, or whatever Shen is, said that Ty would do most of his prowling at night." *Prowling.* The word fit the man. It took Kelly only an instant to realize it was also the wrong word to say out loud to Jenna.

"Oooh, sounds sexy and dangerous. You always liked large predators."

"In the zoo, Jenna. With lots of walls and wire between us."

"What's he look like?"

"Umm, tall, dark hair." Megalicious with a dash of deadly.

"How did he make you feel?" Jenna was into vibrations, auras, and emotional connections.

As God was her witness, Kelly hadn't meant to tell her sister anything, but it just came rushing out. Her need to confide in someone overwhelmed her. "Scared. When I first saw him, he terrified me. No reason. The fear was just there. And then, wham, I took this major erotic hit. It wasn't a smooth sensual feeling. It was all jagged glass and burning coals." The words were barely out of her mouth when she realized what she'd said.

"Oh, wow, sis." Jenna's voice was filled with excited awe.

Damn, major blunder. "Yeah, it freaked me out too. But after a good night's sleep I realized it must've been one of my crazy PMS moments. It's the right time of the month. You know I'm the poster girl for mood swings. Sure it was bizarre, but I'll deal."

"Hmm." Jenna didn't sound convinced.

"Look, Ty is incredible looking, but he's still just a guy. He didn't say or do one thing to trigger what I felt." How did she feel about his . . . gift, which she definitely was *not* mentioning to Jenna? Kelly frowned. She had no clue.

"Sure." The wheels in Jenna's head were making a whirring noise as they spun.

Panicked, Kelly tried to distract her sister. "Anyway, I had time to waste after I got up, so I tried to make this place a little homey. Couldn't. These rooms are Bland and Boring Central. Then I played the flute for a while."

"Good." Jenna wasn't listening. She was thinking. From long experience, Kelly knew things always ended badly when Jenna thought too much.

Maybe if she babbled on long enough, Jenna would lose her train of thought. "I called Mom. More of the usual. She warned me about home invasions, kidnappings, global warming, and the coming apocalypse." Kelly didn't think she'd introduce Ty to Mom.

"He's a vampire, Kelly. It all fits. Dark, dangerous, only comes out at night, can project emotions. Did you check out his teeth?"

Kelly blinked. *What?* "You need some serious downtime, Jenna. That tabloid you're writing for is warping you." The sound of the doorbell almost lifted her off the couch. Talk about nerves. "Someone's at the door. I'll call you tomorrow." Relieved, she hung up before Jenna could expand on her vampire theory.

Her visitor pressed the bell again, hurrying Kelly along. Probably Ty, but why visit her when all he had to do was call and ask her to have the car ready? A lifetime of Mom's warnings and the memory of the dead man made her glance through the peephole before opening the door. She frowned. What the . . .

She pulled open the door. The woman waiting on the other side grinned at her.

"Hi, I'm Neva." She was tall with long legs, big boobs,

and short red hair. Tight leather pants along with a leopard-print jacket and heels completed the picture. "I'm Q's driver. He's in number 304." She nodded down the hallway.

That was news to Kelly. No one had told her Fin was putting another man in this building. Why? Maybe she should've asked a few more questions. But all the money she stood to earn sort of clouded her judgment. She shrugged the thought away. Nothing illegal was going on. *You walked away from a crime scene last night.* Not really. Fin had reported it. *Hadn't he?* She'd check on that later. And even if they'd stayed, they wouldn't have had any information the cops could use. There, guilt banished.

"I'm Kelly. Can I help you?" Shen hadn't said anything about how they should dress. She'd opted for jeans and a pullover sweater. They seemed more missionary appropriate than Neva's getup.

Neva's smile was friendly. "Yeah. My man wants to visit your man in about half an hour. He says for you to pass it on."

Kelly lifted one brow.

Neva laughed. "Hey, I'm just the messenger. Q said Ty is sort of jumpy. Doesn't like to be startled by someone strange showing up at his door. Do I buy that?" She shrugged. "As long as they pay my salary, I dance to their tune." She offered Kelly a finger wave before heading back to her room.

It seemed weird had just morphed into crazy. Shaking her head, Kelly walked across the hallway and rang Ty's bell. Was she a little nervous about seeing him again? She thought about Jenna's vampire and smiled. Yeah, she had a few quivers low in her stomach, but not because she expected an undead bloodsucker to answer the door.

As his door swung open, Kelly braced herself just in

case yesterday's emotions replayed themselves. Nothing. *Thank you, God.* Wait, there *was* a low sensual hum, but she figured that was just part of Ty's sexual force field. He was that kind of guy.

He leaned against the doorjamb, thumbs hooked over the top of his jeans. They tugged at the waist just enough to make the jeans ride low on his hips. No shirt—muscular chest with a fine dusting of hair and a flat, ridged stomach. Yum, yum. Was that a professional reaction? Probably not. Sighing, she continued her inventory. No shoes. No webbed feet. She could cross devil off her list.

She took a deep, fortifying breath. His scary index was still sky high, but it wasn't the same as last night. This was a good scary. Dark and dangerous all wrapped up in a big, muscular body with a hard, male face.

"One of Fin's men sent his driver to tell me to tell you that he'll be knocking on your door in a half hour. Evidently he doesn't think you can handle a stranger visiting you." She waited for his laughter.

He didn't laugh. "Yeah, that was probably the smart thing to do."

Kelly waited for an explanation. Ty didn't offer one.

"Since he won't be here for a while, come on in so I can give you a rundown of where we'll be going tonight." He stepped aside so she could pass him.

Obviously it didn't occur to him that she'd say no. Well, he was the boss. Still, her gaze skipped around the room when she walked in. What was she expecting: a body propped up in the corner, a whiskey decanter filled with blood? She tried to block the sound of Jenna's mocking laughter from her mind.

"Coffee?" He pulled a T-shirt over his head.

Kelly didn't quite manage to squelch her stab of disappointment. "Sure. Lots of milk and sugar. I guess you were right. Fin did take care of you." She settled onto the couch.

"Yeah. He's good with those kinds of details." Ty disappeared into the kitchen and came out a minute later with two cups.

She got the impression Fin wasn't great with other details. "Where will you be saving souls tonight?" Kelly took a sip of coffee, hoping he wouldn't see her amusement. She couldn't imagine anyone looking at that hard face backed up by all that hard muscle and refusing to be saved.

He drew in a deep breath. "First off, I don't belong to any church, and I'm not saving souls for any god." Holding her gaze, he took a gulp of his coffee.

"No church? No god? I don't get it. I mean, Fin said you were missionaries." She was totally confused. But why should she be surprised? Ty had taken her out of the state of Texas the moment he slid into her car last night. She'd crossed the border into a state of permanent befuddlement.

Setting his cup on the coffee table, he rose to pace in front of the couch. "Fin gave you the wrong impression. We find people who're down and out, try to give them a second chance."

"Oh." Wasn't much she could say to that. "You came a long way to give people a second chance. Weren't there any people in Ireland who needed help?" She did some mental wincing. This was none of her business.

He paused before answering. "I'm not from Ireland. I was just staying there for a while. I was born in Colorado. Fin and all of us worked together a few years back. We decided to join up again." Ty stood to the side of the window, looking out. "I understand you had another job before Fin offered you this one."

That was a neat change of subject. "I worked part-time at the zoo to help with college expenses. Mom is a veterinarian and Dad is the Director of Animal Programs, so I grew up around exotic animals. The job didn't pay much, though."

"Didn't your parents make enough to help you?"

Her pride rose up and hissed at him. "I pay my own way. Always."

He just nodded.

Her turn to ask a question. "Where're we going tonight?"

"First we'll eat at a Mexican restaurant near here."

She nodded. "I'll drop you off and then—"

"You'll eat with us."

"That's not the usual—"

"*I'm* not the usual. You'll go to dinner with us."

"Fine." Whoa, dominant male sighting.

"Then we'll visit a few clubs." He was good at not being specific. "You'll stay in the car when we go into the clubs."

"Sure." Kelly had learned her lesson last night. Every time she got out of the car to follow him, bad things happened. Tonight she'd sit back and let him do his thing alone. She glanced at her watch. "Guess I'd better clear out before this guy shows up. Thanks for the coffee." She'd never thought of herself as a coward, but Kelly had a feeling she didn't want to be a part of their meeting.

She could feel Ty watching her every move with unblinking intensity as she put her coffee cup in the kitchen. His gaze made her feel like . . . prey. Confusion followed that thought. Prickles of fear hurried her out of his apartment even as a surge of excitement trailed her into her own. The excitement made no more sense than the fear had.

Closing her door, she leaned back against it. Time to get her act together. She'd drive him wherever he wanted tonight while remaining cool and emotionally detached from everything having to do with Ty Endeka.

Just before she moved toward her bedroom, she heard someone pounding on Ty's door. The mysterious Q had arrived.

Ty couldn't answer the door with a snarl on his face. He had to put his predator instincts aside. This was his partner, not someone competing with him for supremacy. Now that they were both away from Fin, things should be easier. But that didn't mean they wouldn't want to tear out each other's heart at the beginning.

He didn't know which of the Eleven Fin had chosen to work with him. Ty hated suspense. He needed to get this over with. Taking a deep breath to calm himself, he opened the door.

"Why'd you take so long to answer the freaking knock?" Glaring back at him was the black-haired guy who'd had so many questions the night before.

"Why didn't you ring the damn bell like everyone else?" He motioned the man into his living room because he couldn't make his lips form an invite without growling. Reluctantly, he stood aside to let the guy pass him. What he'd been before, still *was*, thought that letting another predator into his home was dumb.

"You first." The man's expression said he didn't trust Ty either.

They stood staring at each other. Ty curled his lips away from his teeth at the exact moment the other man did the same thing.

A moment rife with the threat of violence passed before the other guy suddenly relaxed and grinned. "You're protecting your place, so you get a pass this time. And yeah, you had bigger teeth than me back then, but now it's a level killing field."

Had was the operative word. This confrontation only proved he had a long way to go before beast and brain worked together. Good thing Kelly wasn't here to see him acting like a primitive jerk. He turned and walked over to the window, making sure he stood to the side of it. In his nightmares, Fin had assured him that Nine didn't think he and the others were too much of a threat right now, so he wouldn't be putting a lot of effort into hunting them down. But Ty remembered the black cloud from last night. Jumping out of a third-story window might not kill him, but he'd be doing some major hurting afterward.

The other man dropped onto the nearest armchair. "Don't worry. If you jump, I'll save you from going splat. You're lucky Fin teamed you up with me, because I'm the only one who could."

Ty threw him a sharp glance.

He laughed. "No, I can't read your mind, but your expression said you were thinking about Nine's little visit."

Ty rolled his shoulders to ease some of the tension. "Good guess . . . Quetz, isn't it?"

The other man's smile disappeared. "Call me that again and I'll tear your face off." His voice was a low, rumbled warning. "It's Q. I don't know why Fin thought his dumb-ass names would stick. He should've let us pick our own."

Finally Ty smiled. Well, well. A weapon. When an enemy lost his temper, he stopped thinking. And once he stopped thinking, his next step was dead.

He's not your enemy. Ty exhaled deeply. He really needed an attitude adjustment. But this whole working-as-a-team thing would take getting used to.

"Q it is." Ty wandered over to the couch and sat. "I guess Fin played games in your head last night too."

"Yeah." Q yawned. "Not too restful."

"Lots of complicated stuff." Ty's head had been whirling with Fin's tale of godlike immortals, the end of time, and mass extinctions. It would take a while to get it straight in his mind. "Fin seems to know a lot about these guys. Wonder how he got his info?"

Q shrugged. "I don't think we can worry too much about the big picture right now without our heads exploding. We have to take it one night at a time."

"Right." Ty nodded. "So these immortals are on a tight schedule to wipe out all humans by December twenty-first, 2012. They're hitting major cities first, gathering an army of nonhumans who'll exterminate the human race." Just like that vampire had killed the man they'd found last night. Fin had taken a look at the body before calling the police. He'd stuck that tidbit into Ty's dreams along with everything else. Too bad Ty couldn't tell Kelly her mythical monster lived. Or not.

Q frowned. "Why bother with an army? If they're so freaking powerful, why not just whack everyone themselves?"

"Who knows. Fin said they can't kill humans directly. It would probably violate some weird cosmic code." And why only kill humans? If you were going to go to all that trouble, why not get rid of everyone? Another question for Fin.

"So our job is to find out how this Nine is recruiting and stop him." Q looked worried. "I see a few problems here. One, we can't kill him. Two, we have to trap him and then send his ass back out into the cosmos. Once there, he can't return until the end of the next time period. Did Fin tell you how we wrap him up and ship him out? I don't think FedEx delivers in that neighborhood."

"With Fin, information is given on a need-to-know basis." Ty saw his own frustration mirrored in Q's eyes. "Give me a minute to change." Once in his bedroom, he quickly stripped.

There was only one positive to this whole picture. These guys were so arrogant they thought one of them could take care of a whole city. Nine was in charge of raising an army and visiting random acts of violence on humans in Houston. So take out Nine quickly, and that would leave eight remaining immortals, plus their boss Zero. Ty didn't have to worry about Zero. He belonged to Fin.

When Ty returned to the living room, Q was pacing. "We start at this Mexican restaurant. Fin said the owner is otherkin. She'll help us if she can. Then we hit some clubs to see if we can pick up anything." He raked his fingers through his short black hair. "It'd be great if we had a clue what we were searching for."

Ty grabbed his jacket and headed for the door. "Nine will need to offer an incentive or else no army. That could be drugs or something else. From what Fin said, most non-humans aren't naturally joiners."

"I don't know. The thought of world domination might interest a few demons." Q pulled the door open and walked out into the hallway. He waited while Ty locked his door.

"We only need one driver tonight." Ty stuffed the keys in his pocket.

"Yeah. I figured that. I gave Neva the night off. Told her not to leave the apartment." He frowned. "She was dressed for her own kind of hunt, so I don't know if she'll stay in."

Ty refused to acknowledge the surge of pleasure he felt at the thought of being around Kelly for the night. He'd have to make sure he didn't let himself get out of control or . . .

Wait. Q hadn't been with a female for a long time either. Just the thought of Q sniffing around Kelly triggered a killing rage. He took deep breaths, tried to hold himself together. Tearing his partner apart on the first night would sort of sour the team spirit.

"You. Will. Not. Touch. Kelly." Ty forced the words through clenched teeth.

Q smiled, not a nice smile. "Feeling possessive, huh?" But he didn't make any promises.

Ty beat back the need to rend and tear. Q wasn't stupid. Fin would lay a mega hurting on them if they didn't play nice together. Ty was so full of aggression, he hoped they'd run into Nine himself tonight. He'd get rid of lots of negative energy by launching Nine's immortal ass into space himself.

With anger driving him, Ty didn't even think about using Kelly's doorbell. He pounded on her door so hard it shook.

Q grinned. It was the kind of grin Ty knew he'd had when Q went ballistic over his name.

Growling low in his throat, he raised his fist to rain down more punishment on Kelly's door.

Kelly decided she would listen to her mom from now on, because there was a home invasion attempt going on right outside her door. She squinted through the peephole. Ty?

She opened the door and blinked. Ty had his hand raised to knock again. Kelly backed up a step as a wave of testosterone-driven rage smacked her in the face. "I heard you the first time. People ten blocks away heard you."

Kelly held her breath as he lowered his arm. Good grief, he was actually shaking as he worked on his control. What had brought *that* on? "We're ready to leave. This is Q." Ty didn't even look at the other man.

Kelly did. Tall, only about an inch shorter than Ty. Hair so black it had a blue sheen. Lots of lean muscle. The same hard, savage kind of face as Ty, but with deep blue eyes. Both men had faces and bodies that sent out a primal call to all women. A call that promised to put adrenaline-pumping excitement into their lives and bring heart-stopping sex into their beds.

She chose Ty. Not that she was in the market for all that was scary and wicked, but a little fantasizing wasn't a bad thing. And his pheromones or whatever sang to her.

"Hi, Q. I'm Kelly."

Ty glowered. She'd never seen an expression that qualified for that word, but his did.

"Glad to meet you." Q grinned as he shook her hand, holding on to it a few seconds longer than necessary.

She sensed Q was enjoying Ty's temper a lot.

"Time to move it." Ty turned away and strode down the hallway to the stairs.

Q waited while she got her purse and locked the door. "Don't mind Ty," he said. "He's a throwback to when males pounced from behind trees and then had wild sex in the grass with the female of their choice."

"Caveman?"

"A little further back."

She smiled. "And you?"

He returned her smile. "The same, but I hide it better."

By the time she reached the car, Ty was standing beside the front passenger-side door. Kelly didn't say anything as she unlocked the doors and the men climbed in. Ty gave her the address of the restaurant, and then both men lapsed into silence. But the tension between them twanged like an out-of-tune guitar string.

Sometime during dinner, the guys relaxed a little. Kelly paused halfway through her chiles rellenos. She was enjoying her meal, but not half as much as the two men were. "If you like Mexican food, you've hit the mother lode in Houston." Maybe it was just her imagination, but they ate as if they'd never tasted Mexican food before. Was that possible? Kelly mourned for their deprived taste buds.

Ty started to answer, but he never got the chance.

"Welcome to my restaurant. Fin told me to expect you." Kelly glanced up.

The woman standing behind Ty appeared to be in her seventies, with fluffy gray hair forming a halo around her face. Her body had a comfortable, grandmotherly roundness. Kelly's gaze returned to her face. Definitely not grandmotherly. No laugh lines around *her* eyes or mouth. The rest of her might say senior citizen, but her eyes said something else. Something that reminded Kelly of the terror she'd felt when she first saw Ty. And if she wasn't having a paranoid event, Kelly didn't know what the hell it was.

The woman's mouth formed a tight smile when Ty looked at her, but her eyes remained cold and assessing.

"Right. You must be Celia Gustavo." Ty's smile held no more warmth than hers.

Kelly frowned, unable to make sense of their body language.

Celia nodded. Her gaze shifted to Kelly. "Introductions." It was an order.

No matter how great her food was, Kelly hoped Celia

stayed out of the dining room. She shivered. The woman sucked every bit of warmth from the room.

Q spoke up. "This is Kelly, our driver. I'm Q, and that's Ty." He nodded across the table.

All Q's playfulness from a short time ago had disappeared. There was an edge to his voice that Kelly didn't understand. She put down her fork carefully. Appetite gone.

Celia continued to study her for a moment before shifting her attention to the men. "I see." She seemed to be trying to decide something. Finally, she nodded and turned back to Kelly. "Do you mind if I borrow your men for a few minutes?" Her expression said she didn't give a damn whether Kelly minded or not.

Kelly jumped up before the guys could push their chairs back. "No, everyone stay here. I have to visit the restroom. I'll be a while." Translation: *I'll be gone as long as you need to talk to Celia the Creepy.*

For the first time, Celia's smile seemed genuine. "Thank you. I'm so glad you understand." And for just a moment, her eyes glowed red.

Kelly almost ran to the restroom. Nope, she hadn't seen any glowing red eyes. She pushed into an empty stall, locked the door, and stood shaking. *Enough.* She had to get her imagination under control.

So she'd had an over-the-top reaction when she first met Ty. PMS. Explained.

So she'd seen her first dead body last night. Traumatic, but not unusual. Homicides happened in big cities.

So she'd seen a woman's eyes glow red. Hadn't happened. A trick of the lighting and her willingness to believe in the weird and unexplained when Ty was around.

So she'd seen . . . the woods, the terrified men, the car,

Ty, the huge ... Once again, her mind stalled at that point. She'd seen nothing in the woods. *Nothing.*

Pressing her forehead against the metal door, she absorbed its coolness and tried to chill out her emotions. Kelly Feet-on-the-Ground Maloy had better make an emergency landing or else say good-bye to Fin's cushy job.

Chapter Four

Ty frowned as he watched Kelly head for the restroom. She was upset. It was evident in her quick, determined steps and the stiffness of her body. Why now? He'd understand if it had happened last night in the woods or when they'd found the body. At least she hadn't seen the one thing guaranteed to blow her mind.

Maybe it was just a delayed reaction to everything going on around her. Made sense, but he'd still worry until he found out for sure. The big question? Why did he *care* that his driver was upset?

"How sweet. She's giving us time to talk." Celia's chuckle was all warm and grandmotherly as she took Kelly's seat. "Quickly. Tell me how I can help you."

"You're otherkin." Q pushed his plate away.

"That won't get in the way of our little adventure, will it?" She made a moue of disappointment, but her hard gaze skewered Q and came out the other side.

"We like to know who we're working with." Ty hoped he sounded relaxed and patient. Tough when all he wanted to do was shake any info she had out of her, find out what was wrong with Kelly, and then be on his way to bigger and more violent things.

Celia hesitated before admitting, "My soul is demon."

Ty narrowed his gaze. "I'm not sure that qualifies as otherkin. Demons don't get trapped in human bodies. They sort of wander in, kick out the owner, and set up shop. I think it's called possession."

She made an impatient sound, and her eyes glowed red.

Ty nodded. "Okay, explain."

"I angered an arch demon. He cast me into this body at the moment of conception. I've lived for seventy-three years as Celia Gustavo." Her eyes were red slits of frustration.

Q leaned forward. "From the info Fin stuffed into our brains about demons, I'd figure you could just find another body."

Her laugh was light, fluttery, humorless. "I'm a lesser demon. My enemy is too powerful. I have to stay in this body until it dies. And if I try to hurry along the dying process, he punishes me again."

"You don't sound or act like a demon. Where's the cursing and evil deeds?" Ty was working up a little sympathy for Celia. He understood how it felt when you couldn't express your true nature. He thought of Kelly lying naked beneath him, of him sliding his hands over her breasts, her stomach, and the lightning-bolt thrill when she closed her fingers around his cock . . . Yeah, suppressing your true nature was a bitch.

"Humans give words too much value." She sighed. "My parents didn't allow cursing, and it was easier for me to adapt than fight it. So I never formed the habit. Yes, I suppose I could've done away with them, along with their rules, but they loved me, and even a demon is susceptible to that kind of human frailty."

Ty frowned. Love? What was that? Not something he'd ever experienced. He'd never be like Celia and let human love weaken what he was. Sex was sex. You enjoyed it, then walked away. He thought about Kelly again. Not right away, though. Sometimes you stayed for a while.

Celia leaned forward. "Look around you. By acting the way everyone expects, I've built up a nice business that lets me live in comfort. This body is getting old. When it dies, I'll find one that's closer to the real me."

She shot him a sly glance. "And I've gotten in a few evil deeds in my day. Ask some of the people who've crossed me, sweetie. Oops, you can't." Another grandmotherly chuckle. "They're dead." She glanced at Ty's plate. "I torture people in my own way. La Casita de Fuego has the hottest Mexican food in Houston. Jalapeño peppers are a demon's tool. But the humans keep coming back." Celia shook her head at the wonder of it all. "Who pays to have their stomach lining burned away?"

"What *is* the real you?" Ty figured he already knew.

"Male. Big, mean, smart, and powerful." Anticipation gleamed in the demon's eyes. "I'll make up for all these years."

"Where do *we* come in?" Q's expression said he wasn't sure he trusted her.

"Fin told me what's happening in Houston. As long as I have to stay in this body, I need to protect my restaurant. If nonhumans take over and bring chaos with them, my business is finished. Vampires don't appreciate good salsa, and werewolves prefer steakhouses." Her expression turned thoughtful. "Besides, if there's a battle, someone might kill me. Then I'd be free."

"Always self-serving." Q looked satisfied. He understood Celia's reasoning.

"Always, dearie." Her kind old lady cover slipped a little. "Here's what I know. Nonhumans are killing more humans lately and not bothering to hide it. Word is there's a new gambling ring in the city that caters just to nonhumans. No one knows who's in charge, but it's getting lots of action. I hear the surge in killings and the ring are connected." She took a breath and slid back into character. "Oh, my, it's all so upsetting." Celia reached into the pocket of her dress and pulled out a card. "Try these clubs, sweetie. Maybe you'll pick up something."

Ty took the card and put it in his pocket along with his money and keys. No wallet, no ID, no way to trace him back to Fin. "Thanks. Let Fin know if you hear anything else."

Without answering, Celia rose and left the table just as Kelly returned.

"Hey, great timing." Kelly was taking forced cheerfulness to a whole new level. "Did Celia clue you in to lots of places where people need saving?"

Ty figured someone should tell her that wide eyes didn't translate into *I don't suspect a thing*.

"Yeah, she did." While Q called for the check, Ty studied Kelly. "Are you okay?"

"Yes." She glanced away. "No. But it's nothing I can't handle." Her words sounded final.

Ty wouldn't get any more out of her. He didn't waste his time pushing. When the waitress came with the bill, he paid it, and they headed for the first club.

Hours later, Ty was ready to write the night off. He'd watched humans drink themselves into stupidity and breathed in the powerful scents of arousal and sex. All he could think about was getting Kelly into one of the many darkened corners where anything could happen and probably did. The only good part was that he and Q had stayed apart most of the night. The need to kill his partner had faded.

This would be the last club. Q had already gotten out of the car and was waiting for him as Ty turned to Kelly.

"You know the routine. Windows up, doors locked, anyone bothers you, lay on the horn and get me on my cell."
He'd sense if anything were wrong, so she'd be pretty safe
in the parking lot.

"Got it." She'd set her cell phone, pepper spray, and
flashlight out on the dashboard. Pulling a book from her
purse, she prepared to spend her waiting time reading.

No novel for her. *The Hidden Life of Wolves* said a lot
about her interests. She'd be surprised at exactly what some
wolves *were* hiding.

Ty frowned. Each time they'd stopped, he'd expected
her to ask if she could go into the club with them. He'd
had all his reasons lined up why she couldn't. Wasted effort, because she seemed happy sitting in the car.

He trailed Q into the club. Music and voices washed
over them in the semidarkness. Meeting Q's gaze, he nodded. They separated and began to hunt. Ty tried not to let
the scents overwhelm him as he searched for any that
weren't human.

A path opened up wherever he went. He accepted it. In
his world, the biggest and baddest survived. He was bigger
than most of the men, and even in this time of diminished
instincts, they sensed he was dangerous. Smart. Ty wasn't
in the mood to put up with crap from anyone.

The women were a different matter. He felt their gazes
trailing him, touching him with hot and greedy looks. His
hunger fed on their desire. But when he thought of pulling
one of them beneath him and driving into her, she always
had Kelly's face. Not good.

Just when he was about to find Q and call it a night, he
caught the scent. Not human. He growled low in his
throat as he sought the source. There. Pushing through
the packed masses on the dance floor, he headed for a door

at the back of the club. Closed. He turned the knob. Locked. He shoved it hard, and it popped open. Unlocked. Looked like an invite to him. Pushing it open, he stepped into a small dark room.

Death lived in this place. It was there in the coppery scent of blood that only a predator would recognize. He scanned the area.

The nonhuman crouched in the blackness, thinking Ty wouldn't be able to see him. Ty smiled. Nothing hid from him in the dark. Beside the creature lay a woman. She had the loose sprawl peculiar to death.

"You're a hunter, so right now you're weighing your chances and feeling pretty good about them. You figure you can take me out before I make any noise. And even if I do scream, the music's too loud for anyone to hear me." Ty's personal dance of death began in his mind, a dance the humans in the other room wouldn't recognize. He didn't need music to keep the beat, just the memory of a thousand other hunts that ended with him alive and something else dead. "But sometimes the hunter becomes the hunted. Welcome to my jungle."

The man hissed at Ty, baring long fangs stained with the woman's blood. Vampire. Good thing Kelly had supplied info on them because Fin hadn't. Ty smiled. Knowing Mr. Infallible could make a mistake now and then kept things interesting.

Finally, something to fight. Excitement made his heart hammer and his breathing speed up. He couldn't kill the vampire right away, though. First Ty had to find out what he knew about the gambling ring. But afterward he'd pay for killing the woman . . .

Wait, there was a familiar scent here. Ty tested the air again. *Yes.* He'd also pay for killing the man last night.

Just as Ty was about to take that last step before leaping at the vampire, Fin spoke to him. Ty didn't let the voice in his mind distract him. He'd gotten used to Fin interrupting him at bad times. His gaze never left the vampire.

"Good. You've found someone. Al is in your territory. I'm sending him to help you and Q."

"No." His rejection of Fin's offer was an angry snarl. This one was his.

Fin didn't bother answering.

Ty would have to get the job done before help arrived. And then he'd find out why Al was in his territory. He took a calming breath. He thought about Q. Okay, *their* territory. Ty hated sharing.

For a moment, the vampire looked puzzled. Probably used to everyone being scared shitless of him. Then he got a good look at Ty's eyes. With a curse, he made for a door Ty hadn't seen because he was so focused on his prey. With a speed that surprised Ty, the vampire disappeared through the door. He slammed it shut, and Ty heard the sound of a bar dropping. Who the hell tried to lock people *in?*

Ty reached the door and hit it with his shoulder. It held. This one was stronger than the first. Metal. He backed up, then leaped into the air and kicked the door full force with both feet. It crashed open. He was in the parking lot. Scanning the darkness, he hunted for the vampire. Nothing.

Kelly. For a moment he forgot about his prey as he searched the lot for their car. Ty had to make sure she was safe from the bloodsucking predator hiding among the shadows.

He felt the wrongness at the same time the sound of breaking glass jerked his attention to the back of the lot. He found the vampire just as he saw Kelly.

No! The thin veneer of civilization Fin had tried to paint over Ty's primitive soul didn't do the job this time. With a roar of fury, Ty's soul bled through.

The last thing he heard was Q's shout behind him.

Kelly was deep into her book when she sensed movement outside her window. She glanced up, expecting to see someone getting into the car next to her . . . and saw death staring back at her.

Terror was a boulder clogging her throat. She opened her mouth to scream, but all she got out was a strangled squeak.

Her brain barked orders at her. Grab the pepper spray. Call Ty. Start the car and get your butt out of here. Or none of the above, because her butt along with every other body part was frozen in place. She couldn't even look away from him.

Eyes. All black. Where was the white? Everyone's eyes had white. She'd bet lots of white was showing in *her* eyes. His lips were drawn back to expose bloody fangs. *Fangs!*

"Get outta the car, bitch." Even with the closed window between them, he got his message of hate and violence through. He grabbed the handle and yanked. It came off in his hand.

Never. Her power to move returned with a rush. She leaned on the horn with one hand while she fumbled around for her car keys with the other. From the corner of her eye, she saw his fist coming. *Omigod! This can't be happening.* She flung herself to the other side of the car.

Kelly stared in disbelief as he punched in the driver's-side window, shattering the tempered glass. Then he reached in and unlocked the doors.

Not daring to take her eyes off him, she felt around for the door handle. Suddenly, someone jerked the door open, grabbed her arm, and yanked her out.

Kelly turned on this new source of danger.

"Name's Al. Work for Fin. Don't fight me. I'm trying to help you." He fed her the info between hard gasps, as if he'd run long and hard.

The man holding her was as tall as Ty, with a face just as hard. He wore a leather duster and his hair was pulled back in a long braid.

"Tell me that's not a vampire. Fake fangs, right?" She'd found her voice. Good. Now for a scream that would wake the dead. She glanced at fang-guy, who looked ticked off that he hadn't gotten the girl and the car. And if the dead were already awake? All the noise would bring help. Kelly had just sucked in her breath for the mother of all screams when she felt Al freeze.

"Shit. I don't believe him."

She turned to follow Al's gaze.

Kelly slapped her hand over her mouth. Cancel the scream. It was way past the time when a scream would do any good. In fact, it might call the wrong sort of attention to her.

Al backed away, dragging her with him. Backing away was fine with her. In fact, running like hell made even more sense.

Because pounding toward them was everyone's nightmare from *Jurassic Park*. She'd had fun studying stuff like that in elementary school. Even remembered a few facts from a science report—forty feet long, six-inch-long teeth. But seeing a picture in a book or even on a movie screen wasn't anywhere close to having a Tyrannosaurus rex bearing down on you in a Houston parking lot, every thud of its feet shaking the ground.

"Stay calm. You'll be okay." The man holding her didn't sound scared, just mad.

Easy for him to say. The only good thing was that the vampire—no, she hadn't really said that—wasn't focusing on her anymore. Now he seemed to be the one frozen in place as an animal extinct for sixty-five million years came charging toward him. How could something that big move so fast?

In the few seconds before the unbelievable met the unspeakable, Kelly noticed something. The T. rex had shape and color, but it seemed a little lacking in mass. She could faintly see the back of the club and parked cars through its body.

She gasped as she saw something else. At the heart of the creature was the shape of a man.

After that, images spun in her head. People pouring out of the club to see what was happening, Q jumping in front of the T. rex in a doomed attempt to stop it, and three figures gliding out of the darkness that hadn't been there a moment before. They moved toward the vampire.

They wouldn't reach him in time.

This was bad, really bad. Kelly didn't want to see what would happen next, didn't want to be here when it happened. But she didn't have a choice. Al still had a firm grip on her.

And then the T. rex was there. It towered over the vampire cringing on the other side of the car. All teeth, it was a killing machine, and the vampire had run out of options.

At the last moment, Kelly jerked her head away from the imminent carnage. But she couldn't block out the sounds of death. The screams abruptly cut off. The sounds of bones snapping and flesh tearing.

She clapped her hands over her ears and chanted a litany of, "No, no, no, no," while the scent of blood gagged her.

At last, Kelly sensed the silence. The vampire was dead. She knew it. She forced her hands from her ears and turned her head to look.

Kelly couldn't see what lay on the other side of the car. Thank God. But she forgot the vampire as she looked up and up and up. The twenty-foot-tall T. rex roared its triumph, mouth open to expose huge, bloody teeth and eyes still filled with a killing frenzy.

Once again, Q put himself in front of the monster. Kelly caught pieces of what he was yelling.

"Control it. Everything's over, Ty. You'll hate yourself in the morning if you don't. Fin's in your head. Listen to what he's telling you."

The dinosaur paused, almost as though someone *was* talking in its mind. Then it swung its massive head to stare at Kelly and the man holding her.

"Crap." Al's comment expressed her feelings exactly.

Eternity passed while the predator made its decision.

Then the T. rex simply faded away, leaving only Ty. That was what Kelly had seen in the woods, the last of the huge shape disappearing.

She didn't have even a moment to digest the fact before a wave of dread, followed closely by panic, hit her. Familiar. *Uncontrollable.* This time, though, she was sure of its source. Because Ty's fury—jagged and sharp—was so solid she could just about reach out and cut her finger on it. Terror was a logical reaction to that kind of aggression. And all that anger was aimed at the man still holding her.

Al must have recognized it too. Quickly he released her and stepped away. Ty ratcheted down his anger.

The three who'd failed to reach the vampire before death found him moved, redirecting Ty's attention. Al exhaled deeply. She understood his relief.

Kelly was emotionally maxed out. She didn't try to think. She just watched the bizarre drama unfurl.

Two of the figures—Men? She wasn't sure—leaned over the vampire's remains. One took off a coat he was wearing and laid it over the body. Then they rose, the dead vampire between them, and just seemed to fade into the darkness.

The third man walked slowly toward Ty. Dressed in a tux, with long dark hair flowing down his back, he should have looked out of place. He didn't. This was a dangerous meeting, and he was a dangerous man. Her instinct was right on this one.

Carefully, as though any sudden movement might release the beast again, he approached and then stopped. "Very impressive. But because of you, I have a bunch of memories to erase. Besides that, you dragged me away from a party with lots of entertainment potential." With no further explanation, he walked past Ty to the people milling around the back door of the club.

Once there, he simply looked at them while they stared back. "You heard a noise back here. When you came out, you saw two men scuffling over a woman. No one was hurt. You'll go back inside now and continue what you were doing."

Obediently, everyone trailed back into the club. The man turned around and returned to Ty. "The police will be here in a few minutes. We all should be gone by then."

"You're in our territory." Q's voice was tight.

"I'm Jude, and you're in *my* territory. It's been my territory for a long time."

His smile was beautiful and the scariest thing Kelly had seen in, oh, say, five minutes.

"Your guys just took a kill away from me. I want him

back." Ty's voice was a softly rumbled warning that might was right in his world, and if Jude wanted another demonstration of T. rex might, he could oblige.

Jude narrowed his eyes. "I don't know what you are, but don't threaten me."

Q held up his hand to stop Ty's response. "Fin says he wants a meeting with Jude tomorrow night."

Jude scanned the parking lot. "Where's this Fin?"

"In my head. He said he'll be in touch." Q moved to stand beside Kelly and Al.

As if this kind of communication were normal, Jude nodded and glided back into the shadows. No matter how hard Kelly stared, she couldn't see where he'd gone.

Ty's glance took in everyone. "Get into the car. All of you." He brushed the broken glass off the seat before stepping aside. "Nothing I can do about the window tonight. It's going to be a cold drive home."

Kelly slid into the driver's seat just as sirens sounded in the distance. Ty took his place beside her, and the other two men climbed into the backseat.

"Are you okay to drive?" Ty's eyes were still flat, dangerous, but the deadly anger was gone.

She nodded. No way would she say anything right now. If she started, she wouldn't stop. And she needed the steering wheel to hang on to. Without it, she couldn't control her shaking. For whatever reason, she didn't want Ty to know how upset she was. Something her mother had told her over and over as a kid popped into her mind. *Don't let an animal sense your fear.* Would that work with dinosaurs?

"I can smell your fear, Kelly." Ty's voice had lost its harshness. "I'm sorry you had to see that."

Yeah, right. Something else occurred to her for the first time. What were the two in the backseat?

"You're in our territory, Al. Why?" Q didn't sound friendly.

Their territory? What was all this territory stuff about? She concentrated on driving and kept quiet.

"The vampire was in *my* territory first. When he crossed over into yours, I followed him. He's my prey." Al's voice had a warning edge to it.

Carnivore. Definitely. Kelly gripped the wheel tighter.

The silence in the car thrummed with unspoken challenges.

Ty exhaled deeply. "Okay, everyone relax. I've done enough damage for one night." He glanced over his shoulder at Al. "Where'd you leave your driver?"

"An accident tied up traffic, so when Fin told me what was going down, I got out of the car and ran the rest of the way to the club. I told my driver to go back to the apartment."

Ty nodded. "Tell Kelly the address, and we'll drop you off there."

Once Al gave her the street number, everyone got quiet for a while.

Finally Q asked Ty the question she figured everyone wanted to know. "What was that all about, man? If the vampire hadn't been there to erase minds, we'd be in a world of shit right now."

Vampire? Jude was a vampire too? Of course he was a vampire. Stupid of her to be surprised.

Kelly noticed that Q made sure his voice didn't sound confrontational.

The silence dragged on for so long, she thought Ty wouldn't answer.

"He was going to hurt Kelly."

Silence again.

Through the horror and disbelief making mush of her brain, Ty's explanation touched something fiercely primitive in her. He'd been protecting *her*. That shouldn't matter, but it did.

She could see Al staring at her when she glanced in the rearview mirror. He looked worried. Why not? She was the eight-hundred-pound gorilla in the car. Jude *hadn't* wiped her memory. And so far they didn't have a clue what she was thinking. They'd be gratified to know that no rational thinking was going on inside her head at all.

When she pulled up in front of Al's apartment, he offered her a grin before getting out. "Great meeting you, Kelly."

"Same here, Al. Thanks for saving my behind from . . ." From what? The whole scene back at the club seemed surreal, something she could've dreamed. Except the air blowing in the broken window was real, her clenching stomach was real, and there wouldn't be any waking up from this.

Kelly watched until he went inside and then pulled away. Q and Ty didn't say anything on the drive back to their apartment building. Good. She wasn't in the mood for small talk. A million questions jockeyed for position in her mind, but she needed to get her head straight before asking them.

The silence lasted all the way to her door. Q murmured a good night, then went into his apartment. No explanations, no apologies, no "this was all an elaborate hoax—ha ha."

Ty waited while she unlocked her door. Then he put his hand over hers. "We need to talk."

Shimmers of that first erotic burst she'd felt from him shivered over her. She tried to push them away. "So talk."

He glanced past her.

"No, I'm not inviting you in. Just answer a few questions."

His gaze grew wary. "Ask."

"I'm the only human witness. Will you have to kill me?" She didn't believe he would, but the question had to be checked off her list.

The corners of his luscious mouth tipped up. "Not necessary. No one would believe your story."

"Were those guys really vampires?"

Ty shrugged. "I guess so. They weren't human. And I recognized the scent of the one who broke the car window. He killed the man we found last night."

She fought to keep her face expressionless. But her Chicken Little mind was running in circles screaming, "The sky is falling! The sky is falling!"

"Next question. What're *you*?"

"I'm otherkin."

"Explain."

"Otherkin are nonhuman souls trapped in human bodies."

"I'd say you have one assertive soul."

His scowl said he didn't think that was funny. "Fin and the rest of us are a little different from the normal otherkin."

"Normal?"

His sudden smile softened the hard lines of his face. "Right. Normal wasn't a good word. Most otherkin have no choice. Steve's soul is a horse. He was born that way. I bet if I knew him better, I'd find out he runs in marathons. Most otherkin learn to adapt or go crazy."

"How're you different?" She thought about the T. rex. "Other than the obvious."

Ty stared at the ceiling for a moment before answering. "Maybe we need to let it go for now. I've told you too much already. But after what you saw, you deserved some explanation." He met her gaze. "You're quitting, aren't you?"

"Yes." Surprised, she realized the thought of walking away from him forever didn't bring the relief she'd thought it would. "I study music and used to work at the zoo part-time. Neither of which qualifies me to be a part of whatever's going down on the dark side."

He nodded. "I don't blame you." He moved closer. "Then I guess I'd better do this now."

Before she could react, he wrapped his arms around her and lowered his head.

His mouth on hers was a hot branding. No tentative first touching of lips. It was sexual hunger in its most primal form. If there was a woman alive who could resist the burn of his need, she must be packed in ice.

Kelly wasn't a hypocrite. She'd been wondering what he'd feel like, taste like, so now she gave herself over to the experience—the tip of his tongue tracing her lower lip before demanding a deeper commitment, the heated male scent of him, the tactile sensation of firm lips and a tongue talented in so many ways.

And when he finally lifted his head, she wasn't ready for it to end.

"I'd like to see you tomorrow before you leave." He pushed a strand of her hair away from her face.

All she could do was nod. Then she went into her apartment and closed the door behind her. After making sure it was locked, she shed her clothes, leaving a trail all the way to her bed. Neatness wasn't a priority tonight. She climbed beneath the covers and stared into the darkness.

A vampire had threatened her, and she'd kissed a man tonight who had the soul of a T. rex. A T. rex who'd killed for her. Where was the hysteria? True, hysteria wouldn't change anything that had happened. Then why wasn't she beating down her parents' door so she could tell them her story? Because her story was so weird not even they would believe it. Besides, knowing what walked the darkness could be dangerous for them. Could be dangerous for *her*.

No, she'd keep what she knew to herself. She suspected Ty was counting on that. And as she drifted off to sleep, she tried to go out on a positive thought.

Maybe Ty would offer his body for her silence. She'd make that deal.

Chapter Five

Kelly played the flute while she sat on her suitcase waiting for Ty to show up at her door. Sitting on her bag was symbolic. She'd packed all her things right after she'd woken up, showered, and had a shot of caffeine to get her through the day.

Then she'd spent some time walking around the neighborhood. Thinking. Dangerous thing, thinking. When she'd returned to the apartment, she'd Googled Otherkin on her laptop and begun reading. Wow.

Now she had her behind firmly planted on her common sense and determination. As long as she didn't move, the suitcase would *stay* closed. No acting on second thoughts about the job.

And there *were* second thoughts. A dreamless night's sleep had left her rested and a lot calmer. Eight hours of oblivion had put some emotional distance between the horror of last night and today. She'd witnessed the unbelievable; therefore, it was now believable. Her motto? Accept and move on.

The second thoughts were oddly seductive.

First, she had this fascination with the dangerous unknown. At the zoo, the large carnivores had always drawn her. Not enough to climb into the cage with them, but enough to make her wonder what it would be like meeting one in the jungle. Well, she'd met the granddaddy of them all last night. And yes, the fascination lived and grew, along with a raging case of the hots for Ty Endeka.

Second, the cat with the death-by-curiosity syndrome had nothing on her. Once she walked away from this job, she'd never find out what was going on. Oh, and had she mentioned never getting a chance to find out if dinosaurs did it better?

She explored some haunting Celtic melodies on the flute, allowing the music to wrap itself around her, shield her from all those second thoughts. This time she'd made the right decision, even if it depressed the hell out of her.

The doorbell startled her out of her music. Ty. Kelly drew in a deep, calming breath. She'd handle this coolly, professionally, and make her exit from his very strange life with tons of dignity.

Kelly put down her flute, pasted a smile on her face as she opened the door, and got hit with an erotic blast that should've lifted her off her feet and bounced her off the far wall.

Backing away from him, she held her hands out to ward off a sensual sizzle that threatened to turn her common sense to hot ash. "Stop it. Just stop it." The back of her legs hit the armchair and she sat down hard.

"I can't." He spoke through gritted teeth. "God knows I've tried." Shoving the door shut behind him, he trapped all that superheated testosterone in the small room with them.

Waves of desire so strong she had to clench her fists made mush of her nice neat logic. "How do you *do* that?" She tried to contain the emotion, tried not to react.

Sweat beaded on his forehead and a slice of muscular chest exposed by his open shirt. "I heard the music. I thought of you. It happened."

He glided his fingers over her flute, and she felt it as a slide of flesh against flesh along her inner thigh. She pressed her legs together so hard they trembled. "Music does *this* to you?"

"*Your* music. It's sex with a melody." His gaze was a dark lick of erotic heat. "Like you."

Everything about him was an orgasmic trigger for her—that sensual mouth and all those sensual words coming out of it.

"It would've been a lot simpler in the old days." His lips curved up, indicating the "old days" held fond memories.

Old days? She didn't understand.

"We would've met, acknowledged the attraction, and had sex."

"Blunt, aren't we? I don't know where *you* were living, but making love had a little more ritual attached to it in the 'old days' around here." Sure, he was just being honest, but his honesty ticked her off. Did she want him to play out the ritual—tell her he admired her mind, tell her she was special to him, say "make love" instead of "have sex"? Probably. Did how he said it change what she felt? Nope.

He reached her and leaned down, bracing himself with a hand on each arm of the chair. "I've wanted you since the first moment I saw you at the airport. I controlled it then. Barely. But that music you were playing . . . It was like you were touching my bare body with your mouth. All over. You expect me to resist that?"

"Um, no?" She was still trying to get past the mental image of his bare body. Gorgeous pecs? Tight abs? Awe-inspiring sexual package? All of the above? Jeez, things were sort of spiraling out of control. She'd never been in the let-your-lust-run-free camp. She thought too much.

Releasing his grip on the chair's arms, he cupped her chin and took her mouth with his.

Thinking less and less. This time she was the one who slid her tongue across his full lower lip. And when his lips parted, she took full advantage. Her tongue knew no shame, exploring the taste and texture of his mouth. His scent of distant, untamed places pushed at her control while her tongue wondered if the rest of him tasted like rich, dark chocolate. No sugar added.

She wasn't sure who pulled whom onto the floor. She didn't know exactly when she'd worked her fingers beneath the waistband of his jeans so she could cup his perfect butt cheeks. And she definitely had no clear memory of his pushing her top and bra up to expose her breasts.

But all *who*, *when*, and *how* thoughts vanished the moment he circled her nipple with the tip of his tongue. Sensation flowed in to fill all the holes left by her escaping common sense. The heat of his mouth on her nipple became a heaviness low in her belly.

And when he scraped his teeth lightly over the sensitive nub and teased it with his tongue, she actually felt tears flooding her eyes. Between gasps for air to capture all the fast-disappearing oxygen she could, Kelly tried to think.

Useless, useless, useless. Right now she was a slave to sensation, and Ty Endeka was holding her chains.

She had to abandon his delicious ass as he worked his magical mouth across her stomach, then moved lower. His hand touched the button on her jeans and, and . . . nothing. He stopped and simply rested his forehead against her stomach.

"What?" If that one word came out a little angry, then so be it.

"I don't want you to think this is your severance pay." His words were muffled and sounded desperate.

Not half as desperate as she felt. "You really know how to stomp all over a mood." With shaking fingers, she pulled her bra and top down before he could do it.

Ty flung himself to his feet and strode to the window, giving her his broad back. "A few more seconds and I would've raced past the point of no return. You aren't ready for what would happen if I turned everything loose. It's been too long, and I want you too much."

How long? How much? She needed to know. Uh-uh, she just *needed*. But as the silence dragged on between them and she reengaged her brain, common sense fought its way past all that lovely lust. He was right. If they made love right now, she'd always wonder if he was getting what he could before she walked. Not a memory to cherish.

When the quiet became almost painful, Kelly filled it with words carefully chosen to have no sexual connotation. "While I was out today, I picked up something for you to remember me by."

At first she thought he wouldn't respond, but finally he left the window to drop onto the couch. "A gift?" His smile seemed forced. "Never got one before."

Now *that* she didn't believe. Women would bury him in offerings if they thought they had a shot at his bed. "It reminded me of you." She got to her feet and was surprised when she didn't collapse in a sexually deprived heap. She walked to the dining table and rooted around in a small shopping bag. She pulled out her gift, then handed it to him.

"A Tyrannosaurus rex?" He seemed ridiculously pleased with the small toy. "Thanks."

She shrugged, but at the same time she could feel the beginnings of a big, silly smile. The grin totally canceled her attempt at a glad-you-like-it-but-it-doesn't-mean-a-thing expression. His pleasure in her gift made her happy.

When he finally lifted his gaze from the toy, his smile had faded. "Any chance you can stay one more night?"

No, she absolutely did *not* feel a tiny spurt of joy. "I don't—"

"Q said Neva didn't come home last night."

"Maybe she found out how . . . unique you guys are."

"She didn't."

"No messages from her?" Worry niggled at Kelly. Even if Neva had hooked up with someone last night, she'd had plenty of time to call with an excuse.

"Nothing." Ty frowned. "Q told her to stay in last night. She didn't listen."

"That's because he probably didn't give her a reason for staying in. You know, Fin needs to stop hiring people under false pretences. He has a moral obligation to tell the drivers what they're letting themselves in for." Somehow, she didn't think Fin would give a damn about her take on his moral obligations.

"Right. Wanted: driver for otherkin who spends nights kicking paranormal butts. Yeah, people would be fighting to sign up for that job." He shook his head. "You weren't supposed to see any of what you saw last night. But it won't happen again. Humans will be safe from now on."

Humans. There it was. Out in the open. He didn't think of himself as human. She wanted to argue the point. "No matter what you think your soul is, the rest of you *is* human. So don't set yourself up as a UFD—that would be an unidentified freaking dinosaur—who can disconnect from his humanity whenever it's convenient."

His expression said she didn't know enough to make that call. He was right. If she was smart, she'd run away as fast as she could before Ty dragged her any deeper into his world. And maybe someday in the distant future she could deny what she'd seen last night and actually believe her denial.

"So, will you drive us around for just one more night?"

That was a definite no. "Yes." Or maybe a yes. She sighed. Her common sense was shaking its head in disbelief. Curiosity and lust made dangerous bedfellows.

"Good." He looked like he meant it. "First we'll get something to eat and—"

The doorbell interrupted him.

Kelly stood and went to answer it. Q waited on the other side. She took one look at his expression and almost closed the door in his face. Something told her he wasn't the bearer of good tidings. Sighing, she waved him in.

He stopped just inside the door. "I got a call a few minutes ago. Some guy using Neva's cell phone said we'd find her on the Ho Chi Minh Trail. Where the hell is that?"

"It's a mountain biking trail in Memorial Park." In between working part-time at the zoo and studying music she'd done a little mountain biking.

"In the middle of Houston?" Q looked unconvinced.

"Memorial's one of the biggest urban parks in the country. Almost fifteen hundred acres. Anyway, the mountain biking trails wind through some dense forest. Pretty rough terrain too. Why not call Fin for help? He's closer to the park than we are."

Ty met Q's gaze. Q shook his head. In this they were one. Neva was *their* driver. They took care of their own. "We won't need help. Let's go. We're wasting time," Ty said.

Once in the parking lot, Kelly looked around. "Car?"

Ty pointed toward a black SUV. "Ours is in getting a new window. Fin sent that over." During the few seconds it took to reach the vehicle, he thought about how much he'd hated calling Fin last night. He could've opened their mental link, but the phone put some distance between them. Yeah, Fin had been pissed, but his interest in Jude cut short the fun he was having beating Ty over the head with his own stupidity. So Ty owed the bloodsucker.

Q didn't get a choice of seats. Ty grabbed the one next to Kelly.

They'd barely cleared the parking lot before she started with her questions.

"Why the human drivers? A vampire driver wouldn't even have blinked at last night. Okay, maybe she might've blinked at you, but she could've accepted it easier. Why have drivers at all? Get yourself a GPS and you're in business."

"The things we're fighting can't touch humans directly. Fin thought that would be an advantage, but it doesn't mean they can't get their hired help to take out our drivers." Q looked frustrated. "And we need you. None of us know how to drive yet. Even if we could drive, a GPS wouldn't be able to give us the insights into the city that someone who's lived here could."

Kelly looked like she was compiling a shitload of questions about the "things" and the "None of us know how to drive yet" comment. Personally, Ty thought Q was saying way too much. Everything he'd said would just lead to more questions. At least Q hadn't told her the most important reason they needed human drivers.

"You think someone's done something to Neva, don't you?"

"Done something" translated into "killed." Ty understood why she didn't want to say it. "Yeah." No use in giving her false hope.

"Why?"

Her question encompassed all her "whys" rolled into

one. Why would someone want to hurt Neva when they really wanted Q and Ty? Why be so cryptic? If someone had killed Neva, then why not come right out and say it? And why lure them down to a densely wooded area in a local park? Ty could answer the last one easily.

"A trap. They know we'll come looking for Neva. Night plus lots of trees equals no witnesses." Ty bared his teeth in a savage smile. "I hope there're lots of them."

Q stared into the darkness and said nothing. Ty chose to watch Kelly. She'd drawn her sexy lips into a thin line of disapproval. He hadn't answered her most important question.

"It's Nine's way of saying, 'Hey, I might not be able to get to *you*, but I can eliminate the weakest members of your team.' Fin made a mistake." Ty shook his head. Didn't get to say that often. "He thought if the drivers didn't go out at night unless they were with us, they'd be safe. It didn't occur to him that one of them might not obey an order to stay safe in her apartment."

"Okay, back up. Who's this Nine and why do you call him by a number?"

How much to tell without getting in too deep? "Fin's obsessed with numbers. He doesn't know the name of the guy we're fighting, just that he's part of a gang. So Fin calls him Nine."

"You're kidding." She slanted him a disbelieving glance. "I've just learned two things. First, your Fin's really strange. Second, you lied to me about why you're in Houston. I think . . . Wait, why would Neva be safe in her apartment?"

"Fin has powers. If he protects a building, nothing gets in." Fin would be pissed all over again if he knew how much Ty was telling Kelly. So much for Ty worrying about Q flapping his lips.

"Powers? Like woo-woo stuff?"

"Yeah." Ty didn't elaborate.

Q leaned forward. "I see lots of trees. Is this it?"

Kelly nodded. "Now all we do is park and then search miles of trails in the dark." She muttered a curse. "And my flashlight's in the other car."

As she pulled into the parking lot, they saw only one other car. She stopped beside it. "Is this your car, Q?"

He nodded.

Ty watched the emotions play across Kelly's face—frustration, anger, and worry. He'd never worried about anyone or anything. He'd had no one, and no one had given a shit about him. Worry was an alien emotion. But he suspected that's what he was feeling now. All of this newfound concern should be for Neva, but a big chunk of it was for Kelly. Lesson learned from last night: cars weren't safe places.

Grabbing her pepper spray and cell phone from her purse, she climbed out of the car and waited for them to join her. "I guess it's no use suggesting you call the police and let them take care of this."

Q made a rude noise. "No cops."

Ty understood where Q was coming from, but she didn't. He'd try to explain. He owed her that much. "We're used to handling our own problems. We don't bring in outsiders."

Her expression said that was a dumb attitude. "I'll carve that on your tombstones. There's always someone bigger and badder than you are." She cast Ty a quick glance, then amended her comment. "Okay, maybe not, but the police are your tax dollars at work. Let them do the dangerous stuff."

"No." She didn't *get* them. Not her fault, Ty admitted.

"You enjoy the dangerous stuff, don't you? Q is practically glowing with excitement."

Ty smiled. *Now* she got them.

She peered into the darkness. "We could stumble around all night without finding Neva."

No one suggested that she stay in the car tonight.

"Ty?" Q glanced expectantly at him before pulling his gun from his jacket pocket.

"A gun? I thought you guys could tear them apart with your bare claws or whatever." Kelly looked uneasy as she glanced around. "What're you expecting? I want to live through my last night on the job."

Q's grin was a flash of white in the darkness. "The gun is insurance, babe."

"Nothing will happen to you." Ty reached behind her to massage the tight muscles at the back of her neck. "I won't let it. That's a promise."

Kelly relaxed a little. "Sure. After what I saw last night, I believe you." She glanced at Q. "Do I need to know what you are, or should I let it be a surprise?"

Q returned her grin. "A little birdie."

Ty felt a stirring of the primal rage he'd managed to control since last night. He didn't need to go all prehistoric just because Q was talking to Kelly. She wasn't Ty's. Would never be his. Did that reasoning help? Hell, no. They'd better get started before he tried to rip his partner into easily digested pieces.

"So do you feel anything?" Q returned his attention to Ty.

"Yeah, over there." He pointed toward the woods.

"Let me guess, it feels wrong." Kelly sounded resigned.

"Got it."

She nodded. "We'll start at the beginning of the trails and you can search out the wrongness."

Sounded like a plan to him. "Whoever took her probably

didn't go too far. Wouldn't want us to get discouraged and go home. Stay near us, Kelly."

She didn't argue with him.

Ty's night vision was good, so he forged ahead. Walking the trails would distract him from his jealousy. And, yeah, he recognized the new emotion. Worry and jealousy, human emotions he didn't need.

Fifteen minutes later, Ty admitted that as far as distractions went, this was a good one. The encroaching trees made the path a black tunnel. He felt at home stalking prey through the darkness. Kelly wasn't one with the night, though. After the first few times he and Q had to catch her when she tripped over tree roots, he pulled her close to him and simply lifted her over obstacles in the trail. "We're close."

"Uh huh." She sounded nervous.

The feel of her body tucked close to his tested his predatory nature. When he hunted, nothing broke his concentration. She came close.

"Do we have to stay quiet?" She was too busy peering at the ground in front of her to look up at Ty.

"No. They know we're here. I can smell one of them. He picked us up right after we entered the woods."

"Smell him?" She slid a glance to where the dark silhouettes of trees marched beside them. "I noticed you're not tripping over any tree roots. Must see pretty well in the dark. Do all otherkin have heightened senses?"

"No."

"So you guys are special."

"Yes."

Kelly nodded. He thought she'd ask another question. She didn't. Probably organizing what Q and he had told her into neat little columns and formulating more questions for the future. *There won't be any future with her.* The thought depressed him. Depression, another new emotion to add to worry and jealousy.

"Damn. I hate this hiking stuff." Her muttered complaint came after they'd slogged through a small stream. "I forgot how rough these trails are on foot."

Ty had just opened his mouth to answer when the howls began. They undulated up and down the scale, a chorus of hunters celebrating the night, sounding completely out of place in a Houston park.

"Wolves." Kelly didn't sound as shocked as she probably would have before last night.

Q moved up to stand beside them. "You're sure of that?"

"I worked in the zoo. Those are wolves." She glanced at Ty. "I guess this is it."

Ty was already moving in the direction of the howls. "What's the chance other people will hear them?"

"Park security maybe. The park doesn't close until eleven, but I think anyone else who hears them will run like hell in the opposite direction. I would." She was almost trotting to keep up with him. "But it's November, it's chilly, and it's pretty late. So maybe we'll get lucky."

Ty slowed down while Q strode ahead of them. "We don't want witnesses. There's no vampire around to wipe memories tonight." He hoisted her over a fallen tree.

She moved closer, and something that almost felt like protectiveness stirred in him. No. He couldn't fall prey to a bunch of human emotions just when he needed to focus on the enemies ahead. But the worry and protective feelings wouldn't be denied. Damn.

"Wolf packs don't run in Memorial Park. So what are they?"

He didn't miss her shudder.

She wanted him to say the word, so he did. "Were-wolves." Fin had filled them in on most paranormal entities. Except vampires. He'd missed the vampires.

Q came back to them. "They're right ahead." He pulled out his gun and offered it to Kelly. "I'm not sure how to use this anyway. Can you shoot?"

"Yes." She took the gun without hesitation. "You live in a big city, you learn how to protect yourself. Too bad I didn't bring the one I kept in my old apartment." The glare she leveled at Ty was lethal. "Didn't know I'd be hunting were-wolves in the park. Oh, and I think I remember reading that ordinary bullets won't kill a werewolf."

"Don't know about the killing part, but ordinary bullets *will* hurt them. When I hear the ouch, I'll come running." Ty felt the rush of adrenaline that came at the beginning of every hunt. This was what he missed—the excitement of knowing the next few minutes would tip the scales for or against his survival. It'd always been about survival. He'd never known anything else. *Yes, you did. Back when . . .* The rest of the thought eluded him. He shook it off. No time now.

His bloodlust rose as he flung open the cage door holding back the snarling savagery of his past life. Free at last, it looked for something to kill. "Stay between Q and me. Don't get out of our sight."

Her expression was incredulous. "You think I'm crazy?"

Without warning, the trees gave way to an open meadow on their left. At the fringe of the tree line, pairs of glowing yellow eyes formed a semicircle. Ty counted four of them. Neva lay in the middle of the meadow. It looked as if there was some kind of note pinned to her jacket. He couldn't tell if she was dead.

"I've been waiting for this. God, don't let the bastards decide to run." Q licked his lips in anticipation.

Kelly stared at Q. "I don't want to rain on your testosterone parade, but this is about Neva. Get me to her so I can see if she's alive."

Ty nodded and started across the open space. The wolves waited until they reached Neva before leaping out of the shadows.

"Holy hell, they're as big as ponies." Kelly's eyes were wide with shock.

"They'll all die," was Ty's promise.

She must've believed him, because from the corner of his eye he saw her crouch beside Neva.

Taking a deep breath, Ty gave his soul its freedom.

Chapter Six

A torn throat. Blood. So *much* blood. More than she'd ever seen. Kelly fought back nausea. The coppery scent of Neva's life flowing away coated the night with new urgency. Panic nibbled at the edges of Kelly's resolve, threatening to swallow her whole.

"Damn, damn, damn." But all the damns in the world wouldn't make her personal horror movie go away.

The creatures bounding toward Ty and Q weren't wolves. They were something from a mad special-effects creator's nightmare—all glowing eyes and lips peeled back to expose the scariest teeth she'd ever seen. Well, maybe not. Ty had the scary-teeth market cornered.

There came a time when the brain reached its terror limit and refused to recognize any more mindless, gibbering fear. She'd passed that a minute ago. It was only a smudge in her rearview mirror. She'd either die or she wouldn't.

Kelly watched with a weird kind of detachment as Ty's T. rex formed around him. Had a predator that huge really stalked the earth? And once again, she could see Ty's shadow at the heart of the beast. How did he do that? She'd never know, because she'd either be dead or gone by tomorrow. Right now she was leaning toward dead.

The werewolves skidded to a halt, momentarily stunned. Kelly didn't blame them. She figured if they were smart, they'd turn tail and run.

They weren't smart. After that brief pause, they flung themselves back into attack mode.

Kelly didn't watch the battle. Bending over Neva, she tried to apply pressure to her ruined throat. Useless. Her hands were stained with the other woman's blood, and Kelly doubted Neva was still alive. Only stubbornness kept Kelly at it.

The noise and fury of the fight surrounded her now. A headless werewolf fell beside her, its blood splattering her jacket, her pants.

Please, please, God. Maybe God was busy somewhere else, with someone who went to church every Sunday and didn't curse. But if He had a spare moment, she really needed Him here.

A quick glance revealed a surreal world of primal savagery. The T. rex was a prehistoric killing machine, tearing through werewolves and flinging mangled bodies left and right.

Wait, something wasn't right. There'd only been four wolves initially, but now more and more streamed from the forest. The four must've just been a tease, bait to lure Ty and Q into thinking they could win the fight.

A strange cry from above her head startled Kelly. She looked up. Omigod. Something else to add to her fright night. Q. She could see his form within the body of the huge creature sailing over her. How could something that big fly? Its wingspan had to be close to forty feet, and its neck looked at least ten feet long. Other impressions came in flashes: long head, long thin beak, incredibly long legs. *Long* was the operative word for Q's soul form.

The battle intensified as Q made his entrance. But Kelly could only think of one thing. She had to get Neva out of the path of all those leaping, snarling bodies. Ty and Q could keep her safe from four werewolves, but now there were too many of them. It would only take one wolf to sneak up behind her. She had to get something solid at her back so she could concentrate on defending her front.

Grabbing Neva by her jacket, she dragged her to the edge of the clearing, where two trees grew close enough together to protect her back. Pulling Q's gun from her pocket, she held it in one hand while she returned to putting pressure on Neva's neck. The blood flow was sluggish now. Was that good or bad? If Neva was dead, would there be any flow at all? She should've paid more attention during those high school first-aid classes.

No matter how hard she tried, Kelly couldn't keep her gaze from returning to Ty. She knew that Q's massive wings and sharp beak were inflicting tons of damage on the pack, but Ty's ferocity and savage violence clenched her stomach and brought back the fear she'd felt last night behind the club. How could he control and contain what lived in his soul?

Finally, she couldn't watch it anymore. She had her cell phone, but 911 probably wouldn't respond to a reported dinosaur and werewolf battle. Her family? Never. And she wouldn't chance a shot. She might hit Ty or Q by mistake.

She concentrated on Neva. Frowning, she looked more closely at the woman's throat. It looked as if the wound were closing. Impossible.

Without warning, an animal screamed from the forest on the far side of the meadow. Startled, she searched the tree line for the source of the cry. Not a wolf. It sounded like a big cat. But big cats didn't roam the park. Right, and those weren't werewolves leaping all over the meadow in search of a throat.

Kelly didn't have a chance to think that through because suddenly a body hit her gun arm with enough force to knock the weapon from her hand.

Instinctively, she grabbed for the gun. Before she could reach it, though, teeth clamped onto her right arm and started dragging her. Looking up, she stared into the amber eyes of a huge gray werewolf.

Oh, shit. Ow, ow, ow! Kelly fought the wolf's grip and the pain while she tried to figure out how she could reach her pepper spray. She'd put it into the right pocket of her jeans so she could get to it fast with her right hand. Now it was almost impossible to reach while the wolf dragged her.

Surrendering to mindless fear, she twisted, kicked, and screamed. *Not hard enough, not loud enough.* Her voice couldn't rise above the roar of battle. And all her panicked struggling hadn't made the wolf unclamp his jaws. Somewhere in the part of her mind not consumed by terror, she realized the animal had incredible strength. He'd already dragged her into the woods.

Think. The good: The wolf hadn't killed her yet. It could've. The bad: It was dragging her away from Ty.

Think. She stopped fighting. It wasn't helping, and by going limp she might fool the werewolf into thinking she'd given up.

Once out of sight of everyone, the werewolf dropped her arm. Kelly didn't wait to see what would happen next. Jamming her hand into her pocket, she grabbed her pepper spray and let the wolf have it.

With a yelp of pain, it leaped back. But before she could jump to her feet and run, the wolf returned to human form. Male. Naked. And pissed. Couldn't forget the pissed.

"Shit!" He bent over and coughed uncontrollably. "Why the hell did you do that?" He gasped for breath as he rubbed his streaming eyes. Crouching, he felt around on the ground.

His very real shock made her pause. "Uh, maybe because you dragged me into the woods? Hey, I read 'Little Red Riding Hood' too. I'm not playing dumb grandma to your big bad wolf." She rubbed her arm. "You bit me."

"Didn't break the skin." He paused to drag in more air. "Just a bruise."

"And that makes everything okay? Uh, no."

"Where're my freaking clothes?" He was still coughing as he searched the ground. "I was trying to save your butt." He sniffed, but his nose kept running.

"Yeah, right." Kelly pulled a tissue from her pocket and handed it to him. While he noisily blew his nose and coughed some more, she spotted his missing clothes by the trunk of a nearby tree. She retrieved jeans, T-shirt, and shoes, and handed them to him.

She should run. Now. He couldn't see well enough to chase her. She was curious, though. A dangerous state of mind at the moment. But from the way he was coughing and wheezing, it should be safe to stick around for a few more minutes.

Now that he wasn't dragging her around like a favorite stuffed toy, she could take a good look at him. *Average* was the word that came to mind. About five ten, brown eyes, brown hair, and a lean build. Passing him on the street, she'd never connect him with a huge slavering werewolf. Fine, so he didn't slaver, but it went with the werewolf image.

"Why would you try to save me?"

"My alpha sent me over to check up on the red wolves. When I saw what was happening, I knew I had to get you and the other woman outta there. Once you were safe, I was planning to go back for her." He quickly pulled on his clothes.

"I don't know if she's still alive." Oh, God, she'd forgotten about Neva. "Look, I've got to go back."

With tears still streaming, he tried to peer at her. "Why? You have a death wish?"

"I have to help fight the red wolves, and my gun is back there." Kelly started to move away, then stopped. "I want to know more about your pack." Feeling around in her pocket, she came up with a pen. "Give me your hand."

Suspicious, he stuck it out. His expression said he wouldn't be surprised if she tried to gnaw it off.

She quickly wrote her cell phone number on the back of his hand. "Contact me and we'll talk."

He looked as if he thought she was crazy for going back, but he nodded before stumbling away, still rubbing his eyes and coughing. She hoped he'd call. He might have information Ty could pass on to Fin.

Before he'd even disappeared, she was rushing back toward the clearing. Stumbling over roots and rocks in the dark, she hoped she hadn't gotten turned around.

She'd only gone a short distance before she heard the sound of running footsteps. Who . . . She slipped behind a tree to wait. Now that her brain wasn't shriveled up in terror, she realized the sounds of battle had stopped. The silence was almost as frightening.

Whoever had won was back in human form and coming toward her fast. She didn't even want to consider that it wouldn't be Ty. On a level she didn't have time to examine right now, she knew if Ty went down she'd . . . She'd what? *Slippery slope ahead.* She clamped down on her imagination. Two days did not an attachment make. She'd go home and live the rest of her life as a normal person. *You'll never be a normal person again.*

Kelly had misjudged his speed. Before she had time to bring up her pepper spray, he was on her.

"Where the hell did you go? I looked around and saw Neva on the ground, but you'd disappeared. What part of stay-near-me got past you?"

Stupid, stupid tears filled her eyes. Ty loomed over her. Big, angry, and—thank you, God—alive. "A werewolf dragged me off."

"I can't believe you decided to take a walk in the . . ." He blinked. "*What?* What did you say?"

"A werewolf—Oomph!"

Ty didn't let her get any further. He yanked her to him, surrounding her with heat and the scent of battle. "I thought I'd lost you. I was . . . worried." Then he lowered his head and took her mouth in a kiss that spoke of all the fears he was trying to cover up with angry bluster.

The tension in his body slowly eased, and his kiss softened into something else. Kelly closed her eyes and let the texture and taste of him fill her. Once back in the meadow, she'd have to deal with reality, but just for a moment, she wrapped herself in the pleasure of what he offered.

"Yo, Ty." Q's voice. Reality had come looking for them.

Kelly pulled away and stared up at him. "Neva. I left her lying on the ground. Is she alive?"

Ty watched her from troubled eyes. "Yeah."

Something about the one word raised warning flags in triplicate. "That's good, right?"

He didn't get a chance to answer as Q emerged from the darkness.

"Glad to see you're okay, Kelly." Q slapped Ty on the

back. "Thought the big guy was going to tear the forest apart when he discovered you'd skipped out on us."

"I didn't . . . Look, I can tell you what happened later. Let's get back so we can take Neva to a hospital."

"I don't think so." Ty avoided her gaze as he started toward the clearing.

"Why not?" Uh-oh, sensing incoming unpleasant revelation at twelve o'clock.

"Did you read the note pinned to Neva's jacket?" Q sounded grim.

"No." She'd been too busy trying not to throw up.

"Seems the wolves had a sense of humor. Nine ordered them to kill Neva, but they thought it'd be a giant hoot to make her one of them." Q's smile was all teeth. "They died laughing."

"Omigod." Neva was a werewolf? "Is she conscious yet?"

Q shook his head. "If we're lucky, she'll stay out of it until Fin decides what to do with her."

Fin would probably kick Neva into the nearest gutter if she no longer had a place in his master plan. "We have to take care of her. This happened because she was your driver, Q."

Ty had remained quiet through the conversation. Now he stopped and turned to meet her gaze. "We?"

Okay, maybe not exactly *we*. "You and Q are responsible for her."

Ty's smile looked as dangerous as his soul. "It's survival of the strongest. Always has been. She's a wolf because she disobeyed Q's orders. Too bad there's no pack left to take her in."

Kelly felt his rejection of Neva as an emotional slap in the face. Why did she care that he was a cold son of a bitch? She was outta here in a few hours. She'd never see him again.

But it *did* matter. A lot. "You know, I thought you were more than a prehistoric jerk. I was wrong."

Ty shrugged. "Of course, you could always stick around to make sure nothing bad happens to her. You've had experience with wolves, you said."

Trapped. He thought so too. She saw it in the triumphant gleam in his eyes. At that moment, she hated Ty Endeka along with Fin and his whole prehistoric crew. She couldn't walk away from Neva, and he was counting on her humanity to keep her with them.

Wait. There was a way out. "I didn't get a chance to tell you about the wolf that dragged me into the forest."

Ty narrowed his eyes. "I'll find him and kill him."

Good thing her would-be rescuer had gone. "He wasn't a member of the pack you were fighting. His alpha sent him to keep an eye on them. The guy thought he was saving me. The wolves that attacked us were red wolves. He was a timber wolf." She offered him her best fake confident smile. "I bet he'd help find a pack for Neva." Kelly hoped Mr. Gray Wolf wouldn't wash her number off his hand at the same time he washed the pepper spray out of his eyes.

"Hmmph." With that comment, Ty turned away and continued walking.

Kelly wasn't prepared for the carnage as she came upon the meadow. She almost tripped over a dead wolf. His coat slick with blood, he was a true red wolf now. Beyond him lay another wolf, his dying eyes still glazed with hate. *Oh God, oh God.* She swallowed hard, trying to hold the nausea at bay.

Dead wolves lay everywhere, some whole, some not so whole. None of them had changed back to human form. The pale moonlight gave the whole scene a macabre effect. Holding her hand over her mouth, she teetered on the edge of a fit of screaming hysterics. The meadow stank of death and violence.

She turned toward the trees, trying to get control, trying to make sense of all the blood. It smeared her hands, her clothes, her *soul*. And unlike Ty's soul, hers wasn't handling it too well.

Ty moved to her side, but he didn't touch her. Looking up at him, she studied his face for any sign that he shared her horror. He looked back at her from cold, emotionless eyes.

"What are you, Ty Endeka?"

"I'm what you saw tonight, Kelly. Never doubt it." A bitter twist of his lips said he knew exactly how she viewed him—as a merciless killer and someone she needed to stay far, far away from.

Looking anywhere but at him, she stumbled over to Neva. The woman's wound was completely closed. Dully, Kelly skimmed her fingers over the spot where the flesh had been torn. "When will she know?"

"I'm not sure. Someone will have to prepare her." Ty exhaled deeply. "Let's get out of here."

Q joined them. "I opened my link to Fin. Nothing. He's shut me out." He sounded worried.

Ty frowned. "Did you try your cell phone?"

"Yeah. All I got was his voice mail." Crouching, Q lifted Neva into his arms.

Numbly, Kelly followed Ty back to the trail. Q brought up the rear with Neva. Kelly wasn't up to a conversation, but the quiet gave her memory too much time to replay every terrifying moment of the last hour.

"What's your soul form, Q? It's been a long time since I studied dinosaurs."

"Hey, I'm not insulted. All of us can't be stars like Ty. My soul's a Quetzalcoatlus. Who the hell came up with that name? Fin tried to call me Quetz. I won't answer to something that weird. So I shortened it to Q. Anyway, a Quetzal-whatever was a giant pterosaur."

A little bird indeed. "Neither of you have a scratch on you. How'd that happen?"

Ty glanced over his shoulder. "As long as we're surrounded by our soul's form, we're pretty much invulnerable."

"So you're in a kind of bulletproof bubble?"

"I guess so. Don't ask me how it works, because I don't know. Fin might be able to explain it." Ty shrugged. "You can kill me by taking my head while my soul's napping and I'm in human form. Other than that, it'd be tough to do much permanent damage."

Okay, this wasn't a fun conversation. Kelly lapsed into silence for the rest of the walk out.

Once she caught sight of the SUV, she stopped dead in her tracks. A man was leaning against the hood. Wow, and wow again. Definitely a two-wow man. Taller than Ty, his long silver hair flowed down his back. Even in the pale moonlight, each strand sparkled. He wore jeans tucked into biker boots and a brown suede jacket that showcased his broad shoulders.

"Fin." Q made a disgusted sound.

She walked with the men to where Fin waited. Up close, he towered over her. Kelly remembered once hearing someone describe an object as so beautiful it hurt to look at it. Well, that described Fin's face. The angles of jaw and cheekbones played with light and shadow, forming a whole that took her breath away. And his *eyes*. Silver irises with a hint of purple in them were outlined in black. They were framed by dark, thick lashes that didn't seem to care that his hair was silver.

Fin was spectacular and totally unforgettable. But she'd take Ty with his hard face and dangerous aura any day of the week. Because there was something off about Fin. He was like a diamond that had been brought to life. The complete awesomeness of the gem left her gasping, but she'd never mistake it for anything other than a cold, glittering stone.

Everything about Fin's smile was calculated to say, *I'm incredible, but don't let that get in the way of liking me, trusting me.* Then why did she feel that the gorgeous surface wasn't Fin at all? She shook her head to clear her thoughts.

Ty watched the expressions chase each other across Kelly's face. Shock, awe, then suspicion. The suspicion made him feel a lot better. Human jealousy wasn't a worthy emotion for one of the Eleven, but he was finding that it clung to him with sharp little teeth and refused to let go.

"If you knew we were here, why didn't you drop in to help?" Ty doubted he could put Fin on the defensive, but he'd take a shot at it.

Fin's smile widened. "You didn't invite me to your little party, and I don't go where I'm not wanted." His gaze skimmed Kelly's bloodied clothes and Neva's limp body. "Fill me in."

Bullshit. Fin might be smiling, but Ty figured their fearless leader was furious that they'd kept tonight's mission from him. That was why he'd shut down their mental link and his cell phone. Ty didn't bother asking how Fin had known something was going down. Fin didn't give out trade secrets.

Q opened the door of the SUV and carefully settled Neva on the backseat. "We got a message that Neva was on the Ho Chi Minh Trail. When Kelly told us where it was, we came to get her. There were a bunch of werewolves waiting for us. We killed them. But Neva's in trouble. One of the bastards made her a wolf."

Fin nodded. "We'll take care of her."

Kelly looked surprised. She probably thought Fin would fire Neva's unconscious behind once she'd outlived her usefulness. Ty smiled at the thought. No one ever outlived their usefulness to Fin. He was really creative that way.

Fin turned his attention to Kelly. "I bet this whole thing was pretty traumatic for you."

His sympathetic expression would've fooled Ty if he didn't know Fin better. Ty bit his lower lip as he tried to concentrate. *How* did he know Fin better? Fin had been nothing more than a disembodied voice sixty-five million years ago. These strange random thoughts about Fin were starting to bother him.

"Ty?"

Fin's voice was sharp, pulling him back to the present. "What?"

"Where're the bodies?" Fin's voice had once again returned to the calm, slightly amused tone Ty was used to.

"About fifteen minutes down that trail." Ty nodded in the direction of the path. Why had Fin asked? If Fin was here, he knew exactly where the bodies were. He'd never just show up in the parking lot and hang around waiting for them to return. He would've sniffed out the action and decided whether he needed to interfere.

Nodding, Fin pulled out his cell phone and made a few calls. "I have a cleanup crew on the way."

"Cleanup crew?" Kelly asked.

Fin's smile returned. "I don't think any of us want to open our *Houston Chronicle* tomorrow and see headlines about twenty-four dead wolves found in Memorial Park.

My crew will get rid of the bodies and clean up all the blood." He glanced over at Q's car. "That has to be moved too."

Hah. Ty had known it. Fin had not only been there, but he'd stuck around long enough to get a body count.

"That's cold." Kelly met Fin's gaze.

Ty winced even as he shifted his position so he could leap in front of Kelly if Fin decided to take offense.

"I understand why you have to do it, but it still seems wrong. I mean, they were werewolves, enemies, but they were living creatures, not garbage." She looked troubled.

Fin's expression gave nothing away. Then he nodded. "I like you, Kelly. You humanize things." His gaze turned calculating. "We can use you. You can teach us the emotional responses we lack."

Now Kelly looked confused. "I don't understand. I can't *teach* you how to feel emotions. You didn't just pop in from another planet. You've lived with emotions all your life. Oh, and I told Ty I'm quitting. I'll stick around until I find a pack for Neva, but then I'm gone. The last two nights have been way too bizarre."

Ty held his breath, waiting for Fin's reaction. And deep down in his heretofore one-dimensional soul, he hoped Fin would convince her to stay. Since Ty was a big part of her "bizarre" nights, he didn't think she'd let anything he said sway her.

Fin shook his head and looked sad. Ty figured Fin didn't have any more emotional depth than he did. But Ty gave him points for putting on a good show.

"I can't let you quit, Kelly."

"You can't stop me."

"I think we both know that's not true." It was when Fin sounded the most gentle that he was at his most dangerous.

"Let's look at the facts. Nine knows you work for us, and he also knows you were here tonight."

"How? All the wolves are dead."

"Balan was here."

Ty spoke up. "Who the hell is Balan?"

"Balan is the messenger for Nine and all the others. He watched the battle and then went back to report every detail." Fin shot Kelly a meaningful glance. "That's *every* detail. You'll be in his report."

"So?" Kelly's question came out more cautious than defiant.

"Nine will have someone watching for a chance to kill you. Remember the man you and Ty found? That'll be you." Fin glanced at the SUV where Neva lay. "Or worse."

Kelly turned pale.

Fin pounded his point home. "What about your family? Nine doesn't care about collateral damage. Are you ready to put them in danger?" Mission accomplished, he smoothly shifted into his Mr. Sympathetic role. "Stay with Ty. You'll be safe as long as you're with him. Once we get rid of Nine, you'll be free to go. I'll even add a bonus to make up for mental anguish."

"You don't have enough money to do that." Her glance said she really hated him. "If I stay, can you guarantee my family will be safe?"

"Yes."

Kelly nodded, turned her back on Fin, and climbed into the SUV. Slamming her door shut, she stared straight ahead, waiting for Ty and Q to join her.

Q narrowed his gaze on Fin. "How'd you know about this Balan and what he was doing tonight?"

Fin's smile was his first sincere one of the night. "While I waited for Ty and you to finish your fun for the night, I amused myself by surfing a few wolfy minds. I was getting lots of interesting info until the cable cut out."

"What should we do with Neva?" Ty wanted to get out of here. "And I think we're finished for the night. Kelly has had enough." He lowered his voice so she wouldn't hear.

"Don't get too attached, Ty. You can't afford the distraction."

"Is that a threat?"

Fin narrowed his eyes and bared his teeth. Pointed canines. "*This* is a threat. What I gave you was a friendly suggestion."

Tension hummed between them for a few seconds before Ty backed off. This wasn't important enough to defy Fin over. Sure, Ty wanted Kelly in his bed, but when the time came to leave her, he'd walk away without a backward glance. Besides, obeying Fin was a habit, one he wasn't ready to break yet. "When did you get the vampire teeth?"

"After you told me about Jude. He's coming over in about an hour. I like to meet possible allies on an equal footing." Fin's soft laughter said he didn't need pointy teeth to do that. "Besides, they look cool. I'm feeding my inner child."

Fin's sudden mood shifts always surprised him. Ty shook his head as he started around the SUV to the passenger side. Q had already climbed into the backseat beside Neva.

"Oh, and I want you and Q there when he arrives. Along with Kelly."

"Why Kelly?"

Fin exhaled impatiently. "Do you have to question everything?"

Seeing Fin's annoyance brightened Ty's mood a lot. "When it comes to Kelly, yes. She's not one of the Eleven."

Suddenly, Fin was in his head. *"Why do you think I spent*

so much energy scaring Kelly into staying with you when I could've just hired a new driver? She has something I need, something that'll help us toss Nine's ass back out into the cosmos. I don't have it all worked out yet, but I'm getting there. So until I do, she stays. And the best way to bind her to us is if she knows what will happen to her world if Nine and the others are in control in 2012. That's why I want her there when I explain things to Jude."

Ty didn't like the way his stomach clenched as he thought about Fin manipulating Kelly. Only the fact that Fin was right kept him from ordering her to drive back to the apartment. If Fin needed her to win the war, then she had to know everything.

Fin smiled, reminding Ty that he wasn't always a hard-ass. *"Hey, I get it. You like her. You want to have sex with her. But she won't blame you for anything. I'm the bad guy. And I don't care if she likes me."* His gaze hardened again. *"I've never cared if anyone liked me."*

Ty simply nodded and climbed in beside Kelly.

As they left the parking lot, Kelly cast a glance in the rearview mirror. "He's just standing there. How'll he get back to his condo? He can't drive Q's car."

Ty didn't have a clue whether Fin could drive or not. Picturing Fin walking back to his condo gave Ty lots of satisfaction, but he knew that wasn't likely. "Fin gets where he's going in his own way. And he wants you to drive us to the condo in an hour. He's got a meeting set up with Jude."

She didn't bother looking at him. "The fun just keeps on coming."

Chapter Seven

Kelly had gone to the zoo with her parents a lot when she was a kid. She'd had these great fantasies about swinging through a jungle as Super-Tarzana and dropping onto the back of a tiger. Riding a tiger sounded like the coolest thing a kid could do. Getting on the tiger was easy. Too bad no one had mentioned that it was the getting-off part that could kill you.

She was having that same getting-off-the-tiger feeling now. So hanging on a little longer, until she could think things through, made sense. "What's on our to-do list for the rest of the night? Bust a coven of witches? Herd a bunch of ghosts into the light? Kick a few demons back into hell? One thing, if there're any animals on that list, cross them off."

Q chuckled. "Yeah, I hear you."

"And I need a shower. Bad." She couldn't do much about the blood on her clothes, but she wanted to scrub it from her skin along with the memory of how it got there. Unfortunately, the memory wouldn't go away. It was like a bad tattoo. All you could do was cover it up and hope no one ever saw you naked.

Ty leaned toward her. "Pull over, Kelly."

Groaning, she stopped the car and rested her forehead against the steering wheel. "Been here, done this." This time she absolutely would *not* follow him. She'd sit in the SUV with the gun Q had returned to her in one hand and her pepper spray in the other.

He laughed. "No, I'm not running off this time. I just have something I need to tell you." Leaning his head back against the headrest, he closed his eyes. "Fin wants you there when he meets and greets the local vampire lord."

"Why? Will all the other drivers be there?" She had a bad feeling about this. "I can't be there. Someone has to stay with Neva. Remember Neva? Q's driver? Kidnapped by were-wolves? Has a good chance of waking up furry? While Fin's having his meeting, I could—"

"No."

Kelly didn't like the sound of that no.

"No, the other drivers won't be there. And, no, you can't stay with Neva. Someone else will watch her."

Ty raked his fingers through his hair. She had a fleeting thought that running her own fingers through his hair would be . . . would be inappropriate right now, and why the hell was she thinking of his hair when she'd fallen into some weird alternate universe where werewolves and dinosaurs battled each other in Memorial Park?

"I wanted to give you a heads-up on what Fin will say."

"And we had to stop while you told me?"

"Yeah."

That wasn't good. Kelly straightened. "Shoot."

Q spoke from the backseat. "I don't know about this, Ty."

Ty ignored him. "I'll let Fin fill in the details, but the bottom line is our souls are dinosaurs because that's what we were. Before."

Before? Before what? She blinked at him. "Umm, the T. rex has been extinct for sixty-five million years."

"I know."

"Okay, just to clarify. You were the real deal sixty-five million years ago, and now you're here?"

"Right."

"What happened when ye old mortal shell went extinct?" She heard her own voice. It sounded flip, detached. Maybe her psyche had realized that to survive it would have to jettison her emotions like extra weight from a doomed jet.

"Fin put our souls in safe places until it was time for us to walk the earth again."

"You're saying that Fin is sort of a god?"

Ty shrugged. "Never thought of him that way. He's just . . . Fin."

A few nights ago, Kelly would've offered to point Ty toward the nearest mental-health facility. Now? She just felt numb.

When she didn't fling open her door and gallop off into the night, Ty explained his need to drop this bombshell right here and right now. "You're mine, so I had to be the one to tell you."

She should've argued the "you're mine" part of his statement, but she couldn't seem to work up the energy. Without a word, she pulled back into traffic.

"He's telling the truth, Kelly." Q sounded as serious as she'd ever heard him sound.

What were the chances that in one vehicle there'd be two crazy people, an unconscious werewolf, and one sane ordinary human? Right now, she wasn't even sure she could stick the tags of *sane* and *ordinary* next to her name. So she just drove. And if her fingers gripped the steering wheel a little too hard, it was the price she paid for forgetting that if a job seemed too good to be true, it probably was.

She took a few minutes to wash off as much blood as possible in the condo's lounge bathroom before they took the elevator up to Fin's suite. Kelly held on to her silence all the way to his door.

She recognized the man who answered Ty's knock.

Al-with-the-braid, rescuer of women about to be eaten by vampires and all-around good guy. This time she was calm enough to also notice his gorgeous hazel eyes. Were there any ugly men in this group?

"Kelly. Great to see you again." He took in her bloodied clothes. "Run into more killer vampires?" He pulled her into a friendly hug, ignoring Q, who'd already strode past him with Neva in his arms, and Ty, who stood right behind her.

She wasn't fooled for a moment. Al fixed his gaze on Ty as his lips turned up in a sly smile, daring Ty to do something about the embrace. From the angry vibes Ty was emitting, he was about to pick up that dare.

Stepping out of Al's hug, she smiled up at him. "Hey, I know the code now. Ty is for Tyrannosaurus, Q is for Quetzal-something, and Al is for . . ." She held up her hand. "No, don't tell me." Kelly ran through her meager knowledge of dinosaur names. She doubted there were any plant-eaters in this bunch. So Al was probably for . . . "Allosaurus? I know the name, but I can't get a mental picture."

"Right the first time." He was now involved in a stare down with Ty. "Allosaurus was as big as T. rex."

"You wish." Ty's murmur sounded murderous.

Al's smile disappeared, replaced by a savage baring of his teeth. "And just as mean."

Kelly closed her eyes wearily for a moment. What was with these guys? Al wouldn't turn his back on Ty to lead them into the condo, and Ty wouldn't walk past Al because then he'd have to show the other man his back.

She wasn't in the mood for this crap tonight. Scowling at both men, Kelly strode past Al into the condo, then paused to take in everything. "This is spectacular." Across a huge room sparkling with crystal and light was a split marble staircase. "How big is this place?"

Fin seemed to materialize from nowhere. "Three floors with a private pool and sundeck on the roof."

The godlike Fin was dressed for the part tonight. His black leather pants and black shirt were stark contrasts to his sparkly silver hair. Kelly wondered how he'd managed not only to arrive before them, but to change clothes as well.

"Looking good for your company, Fin." *How'd you put the souls of the Eleven into human bodies? And where'd you get the bodies? Did you just hold people up by their heels and shake them until their souls fell out? How'd you keep Ty safe for sixty-five million years? What are you, really?*

"This is my first meeting with a child of the night. I want to make an impression." His smile was friendly enough, but his attention was for the two men still at the door.

She turned to follow his gaze. "They look like they want to tear each other apart."

Ty scowled. "*They* can hear you. And yeah, a little tearing and rending right now would put me in a great mood." He took the steps necessary to pass Al and joined her.

Al threw Ty an angry glare before walking away.

Fin exhaled deeply and for the first time looked a little human. "Don't blame Ty. Being around me ramps up his aggression."

"Being around jerks who want to play games ramps up my aggression." Ty stared at Al's back as the other man left the room.

When Fin turned to lead them to the meeting room, Ty moved close to Kelly. His warm breath skimmed her neck and for a moment she forgot the blood, the violence, and all the weirdness. She stiffened her body against the desire to lean back against all that heat and hard muscle, to sink into his sensual promise, and forget, forget, forget.

"It's been sixty-five million years, Kelly. Ask me how much I want you." Ty's soft laughter suggested all the things he'd like to do to make up for eons of missed pleasure. "I stopped last time. I don't think I could do that again." She understood that if the circumstances were repeated, he'd be a little less noble.

Kelly didn't get a chance to answer Ty because Fin picked up his pace. Probably a good thing; she needed some space right now—to think, to accept.

Fin led them to a media room with elegant furniture and a solid glass wall with sliding doors that opened to a marble-tiled balcony. But the room itself paled in comparison to the men seated around it. All of them were big and beautiful with hard faces and eyes.

"Are these members of the Endeka family? I sort of see a resemblance." She allowed Ty to guide her to a group of three men who sat watching them with eager, hungry gazes. They had to be brothers, because they all had short spiky blond hair and bright blue eyes.

"None of us are related, except for these three." He nodded toward the men as he eased onto the couch beside her. "And *endeka* means 'eleven' in Greek. Fin's idea of a joke."

"Going to introduce us to the pretty lady, Ty?" The spokesman grinned at her while the two others fixed their unblinking attention on her clothes. "Looks like she fought something big and mean. And won. My kind of woman."

Remembering that she still wore her bloodied jacket, she stripped it off. Her top had a few blood spatters, but they weren't as spectacular. Then Kelly moved a little closer to Ty. He wrapped his arm around her waist and pulled her against his side. Under other circumstances, she would have resented the possessive gesture, but just this once she appreciated it.

All three men practically crackled with suppressed violence. No way would she ever want to see them in action. Together. Because instinct told her they weren't solitary hunters.

Ty offered them a warning snarl.

Nope, he wasn't going to introduce her. Kelly jumped into the breach before tempers could explode. "I'm Kelly, Ty's driver. Fin wanted me here at your meeting. I'm having a great time figuring out who you guys are." She didn't do perky well, especially when her nerves were in screaming overload. "So what're your names? You have to be triplets."

The speaker shifted his gaze to Ty for a moment. Must be trying to figure out which he wanted to do most—attack Ty or dazzle her with his predator's charm.

The latter won, because he looked back at her and turned up a kill-on-contact smile. Women would strew his path with lacy panties and indecent proposals in honor of that smile.

"I'm Utah. That's Tor, and that's Rap." He nodded toward the other two men, who sent their own versions of "the smile" her way. "And yeah, we're triplets. We do everything together. *Everything.*" His emphasis on the last word suggested that making love with all three at once would be a life-altering experience.

She believed him.

Ty might not believe the "life-altering" part, but he definitely believed the "making love" part. "Even think about it and you'll be *dying* together."

Oops. Kelly rushed into speech. "Fin wasn't too subtle about your names. You're Utahraptors." *Raptors.* The word made her shudder. *Jurassic Park* had painted a chilling picture of the swift and deadly hunters.

"We frighten you." One of the others spoke for the first time.

She didn't have a clue whether it was Rap or Tor. "Well, yeah. You have terrifying soul forms." Was she being too honest? Did she care? No. Worrying about the hurt feelings of prehistoric hotties wasn't high on her priority list right now.

His smile shifted from sensual to just friendly. "Thank you. Oh, and I'm Tor. I know you can't tell us apart. I'm the kind and gentle one."

Rap snorted. "He's the lying one."

Their banter eased the tension a little. Too bad another hot spot popped up right away.

"What's *she* doing here?" The question was a low angry growl.

Kelly looked up and up and up. Holy colossus. The man looming over her while he glared at Ty had to be close to Fin's height. With wide shoulders and muscular arms exposed by his sleeveless black T-shirt, he made her want to slide between the cracks in the cushions and not come out until he was gone.

Which was exactly what she would *not* do. If she was going to be around these men for even a short time, she couldn't always be in cowering mode. They'd enjoy it too much. "*She's* sitting right here, so *she'll* answer your question. I'm Ty's driver, and Fin asked me to be here."

The man turned his gaze on her. She took a deep breath and ramped up her courage. All the men in the room had a hard edge, but this guy was different. There was a wildness about him that said he just didn't give a damn about anything. She'd seen animals like that. They didn't do well in captivity.

"Why *you*? Why aren't all the drivers here?" He studied her, his eerily pale eyes a startling contrast with his tanned skin and wild mane of dark hair.

She didn't hear Ty move, but suddenly he was standing, crowding the stranger's space. "Get away from her, Gig."

Gig smiled, a predatory lifting of surprisingly sensual lips. "Why? Jealous? Looks like you're a little possessive, the way you had her squeezed up tight against you." He shifted his suddenly hungry gaze back to her. "I wouldn't mind having a driver like her. How'd you get so lucky?"

"Back. Off." Ty's words were a guttural warning.

The room fell silent. Kelly dropped her gaze from Gig's face to slide the long scary length of him past his jeans and scuffed biker boots. His jeans were torn in several places, but she didn't think he was trying to make a fashion statement. God, she couldn't let this come to violence.

Taking a deep breath, she stood. "Look, if my presence here is a problem, I'll leave."

"No." Fin's voice was soft, but it had a cutting edge.

All eyes turned to him. Kelly looked at Fin's expression and understood how he controlled these men. She didn't know what Fin had been before, but he must've been a hell of a predator.

"*I* asked Kelly to be here. She's seen Ty's and Q's soul forms. I want her to know what we are and why we're here. She can help us." Fin narrowed his eyes as he focused on Gig. "Do you have a problem with that?"

For a moment, Kelly thought Gig would challenge Fin, but instead he stalked away.

"Anyone else?" Fin scanned his audience. Finally satisfied with the silence, he spoke directly to Kelly. "Cut Gig and the others some slack. They haven't been around females for a long time. They're hungry."

Kelly nodded, but she hoped her expression let everyone know there wouldn't be any snacking on her. She sat down and pulled at Ty to join her. He stood for a moment undecided, and she hoped he wouldn't go after Gig. Finally, he sat down too.

She was relieved when Q joined them.

"How's Neva?" Kelly kept her voice to a whisper. She wished she could help the other woman. Did Neva have a family? Would she want them contacted? Kelly thought about *her* parents. No, some things were better not shared.

Q shrugged. "Still unconscious. Fin has her in a secure room with a guard. No one knows what to expect."

Fin stopped any further conversation. "Jude is on his way up. He has three guards with him. They can stay. We want him to feel safe." His smile said it would be a false sense of security. "We need allies. So no threats, no attacks. Mess this meeting up and I'll show you violence like you never imagined."

Kelly was duly impressed.

The tension built until the bell rang. Fin nodded at a man sitting near the back of the room. He was bigger than Ty, with a shaved head and the prerequisite hard face. The difference was that Kelly knew Ty smiled sometimes. This man looked like he'd never smiled in his life. He got up and left the room.

By the time the vampires trailed in behind the big man, Kelly felt as if she were drowning in a sea of testosterone gone wild. She expected to see fights breaking out all over the room. Fin was right about his effect on the others. Even she felt a little snarky.

Jude's three protectors entered the room first: two men and a woman. The two men didn't disappoint. They were massive, muscle-bound giants with scary faces, glowing eyes, and fangs on full display. As intimidators, they were awesome.

The woman was a shock: cute in a sweet, innocent kind of way, with big green eyes and curly red hair. You just wanted to take her home and plunk her on your bed next to your fave teddy bear.

Jude entered last.

The two hulking male vampires didn't seem to inspire any interest from Fin and his men. The woman was getting plenty of interest, all sexual.

But when Jude appeared in the doorway, every predator in the room went on instant alert. Kelly didn't have to read minds to understand the reaction of a bunch of alpha males to the vampire leader.

He was one of them—powerful, deadly, and an equal. With his red shirt open at the throat, black pants, riding boots, and that black hair loose and flowing, he gave Fin a run for his money in the notice-me department.

Riding boots. Kelly just bet he had lots of riding skills.

His gaze slid to her, and he smiled—all smooth, sensual invitation. "You'd be surprised how well I ride."

Ty's grip on her tightened. "And you'd be surprised how well I kick vampire butt."

Jude's attention shifted to Ty, and his smile widened. "Ah, the T. rex. You intrigued me last night. Nothing has intrigued me in centuries, so I savored the moment." Even though he sounded almost playful, his dark eyes were watchful.

Kelly stared at Jude with wide eyes, and then she looked up at Ty. "He read my mind. He freaking *read my mind*."

Ty allowed himself a tight smile. He had a feeling Kelly's universe would do a lot of expanding tonight. But he had a question he had to ask Jude before Fin got started. "What'd you do with the body you took away last night?"

The vampire leader raised one dark brow. "Be more specific. Do you mean the part that's in Galveston Bay, the part that's in Lake Conroe, or the part that's floating down Buffalo Bayou?"

Ty couldn't help it, he laughed. He hoped Jude turned out to be an ally, because he wouldn't mind fighting beside him. His smile faded. As long as the vampire stayed away from Kelly.

"Glad you could make it. I saved you a seat." Fin's smile was open and nonthreatening as he gestured to a chair near him. "We're new to Houston, and you're the first guests we've had."

"Do you think Jude will buy Fin's friendly and harmless act?" Kelly braced her hand on Ty's thigh as she shifted into a more comfortable position.

Ty almost groaned out loud. He should take Kelly with him whenever he had to be near Fin. All she had to do was touch him and he forgot about his need for violence.

As if given a silent signal, Jude's three bodyguards moved to different spots in the room, all with good views of Fin and their leader. Jude's smile was slow and very threatening. "I bet you say that to all your guests right before you kill them."

Fin's smile was sincere this time. "That or something similar."

Jude seemed to relax a little as he took the seat Fin offered. "I suppose you want to know about me first."

"If you don't mind."

Ty translated: If you don't want to die. From Jude's expression, he knew it too.

"Vampires have divided the United States into ten territories. I govern the territory that includes Texas. I'm in
Houston now because there's been an outbreak of vampire
attacks on humans. We like to keep a low profile. Multiple
drainings could out us. So I'm here to pick up the trash
and dump it in the compactor." His gaze never left Fin.
"Now who are *you*, and what are you doing in my territory?" Jude showed some fang to emphasize his question.

A low, rumbling growl came from Q. Ty shook his head
at his partner, and Q subsided.

The change in Fin's expression was subtle, almost as if
the angles and planes of his face shifted just enough to reveal something terrifying. Beside Ty, Kelly gasped.

Above the threatening murmurs of his men, Fin smiled
his frightening smile, baring his pointed canines. "I ad-
mire a lot about you, Jude, especially your teeth. Hope you
don't mind that I borrowed the idea." He leaned back in
his chair. "Technology amazes me. One of my people prepared a PowerPoint presentation. Images enhance understanding."

Jude chuckled and some of the tension eased from the
room. "Way to defuse a situation. It's tough to enjoy a good
bloodbath in the middle of a PowerPoint presentation."

Fin's eyes glowed with pleasure. Ty frowned. The bastard was getting a kick out of this. He could make Jude do
anything, say anything he wanted, but he enjoyed the
game. Always had. Again, he wondered why he was so sure
of that.

At some unseen signal from Fin, the lights dimmed, the
big-screen TV came on, and the show began. "We existed
as Earth's greatest predators sixty-five million years ago."

The scene caught at Ty's throat. *His* time. And the

creatures of his time. As they'd really been, not as he'd seen them when he Googled *dinosaurs*.

Kelly must've felt his tension, because she clasped his hand and squeezed. Warmth flooded him, a feeling that had nothing to do with sex.

Fin's voice was flat, emotionless as he continued. "Existence on Earth is measured in time periods. It's been so since the planet formed. And as each time period ends, the same immortals visit Earth once again. Their only goal is to create anarchy by eliminating the dominant life form of that time. When they succeed, the balance the planet has achieved is destroyed and other life forms, weaker or with fewer members, battle for supremacy, and so chaos continues. The immortals have *always* succeeded."

Jude's hiss of surprise was the only other sound in the room.

"But until now, the outcome had fewer ramifications. Forces that exist now didn't exist during the last Dying Time. Humans are the dominant life form now. Their extinction would cause catastrophic destruction on Earth. And those that came after them would bring unspeakable evil."

Ty could feel Kelly shiver against him. He bent close and whispered, "It won't happen. Trust me." He shocked himself with the ferocity of his promise. Before now, he would've said he fought just for the hell of it and because that's what Fin expected. Now it was more personal, more about Kelly surviving.

"The Mayans understood some of this. Their long count calendar ends on the winter solstice, December twenty-first, 2012 at eleven eleven UT. Then time will reset to zero and start again." Fin clicked to the next image. "This is what happened to us when time hit zero."

Ty closed his eyes, shut out what he knew the screen showed. All of his kind dying. The asteroid strike, the volcanic eruptions it triggered, and all the things that had come after. It hadn't happened over one hour or one day or even one year, but it had happened. Slowly, inexorably.

Ty opened his eyes when he heard another click, opened them to the future.

"That is what will happen on December twenty-first, 2012 at eleven eleven to whatever remains of humanity." Fin gazed out over the room. He didn't have to look at the screen.

Kelly gasped. "Omigod."

Vampires, shape-shifters, demons, and some nonhumans he didn't recognize were pictured massacring what was left of humanity. Ty's killing instincts rose on a wave of emotion that forced him to clench his hands into fists, digging his nails into his own flesh. Even pain couldn't distract him from his need to destroy all of them.

Jude looked puzzled. "If these immortals are that powerful, why don't they kill everyone themselves? Why even leave the nonhumans alive? They could have the whole planet. And if they called up an asteroid before, why not do that again? It'd be a lot faster."

"They can't destroy the dominant species directly." Fin shook his head at the vagaries of the universe. "Some higher power must've set the rules, I guess. So they need minions to do their dirty work for them. And they don't want everyone dead. They feed on chaos. Can't have chaos with no one to create it."

Fin's smile was bitter. "The asteroid would be a last resort. No fun. Besides, only their leader can call up that kind of cataclysm. And I'm keeping him busy in my own way right now. But that sort of ties up my power. That's why I need all the help I can get."

"Fuck." Jude spoke for all of them.

Fin shrugged. "From a vampire's point of view, that might look like a bright future. But I promise that civilization will revert to its most primitive state. Earth won't be a comfortable place to live." He clicked off the TV.

Jude leaned forward. "I've always thought vampires have a vested interest in the future of humanity. Besides, I have business interests and a big home in Austin to protect. How do we stop this?"

"There are ten of them, one who leads and nine who carry out his orders." Fin's eyes turned predatory. "I don't know their names, so I call their leader Zero. He's mine. The others are numbers too, and we're working on our own personal countdown to zero."

Then his expression returned to calm neutrality. "Zero has targeted all the major cities of the world. One number per city." He smiled. "Zero is overconfident. A mistake. He thinks it'll take only one of his immortals to bring a city under his control. Once an immortal has recruited enough nonhumans willing to destroy the city's human population, he moves on to the next city. I'm calling the one assigned to Houston Nine. He'll pull together an army ready to rise and kill when the moment comes. He's already gotten to some of your vampires."

Jude curled his lip away from his fangs. "We'll stop that."

"Tell your people to keep their ears open. Nine is finding a way to recruit. Discover how he's doing it, and we'll get rid of him."

"If I find him, I'll kill him." Jude's eyes glowed black with fury.

"That'll be tough. He has no weaknesses. But he can be

flung back out into the cosmos, and once out, he can't return until the end of the next time period."

The vampire didn't look like he thought throwing Nine out into the cosmos was a satisfying ending. "I find him, I try to kill him. I fail, and I turn him over to you."

"Give it your best shot." Fin's smile said Jude would have to learn the hard way.

Jude stood and started to leave. Then he stopped and turned back to Fin. "Notice that I didn't ask you a bunch of questions. Like how you've managed to exist for millions of years just so you could show up at the right moment to save humanity. And how you know so much about these galactic goons. But tell me, what were you before you were dinosaurs? Because you *were* something. I'd guess you jumped into the dinosaur bodies the same way you did the human bodies."

Something about Jude's question tugged at Ty's memory. There was something he should know, but it was just out of reach.

A sudden stabbing pain in his head dragged a grunt from Ty. What the . . . He pressed his palms against the sides of his head to keep his skull from shattering and spilling his brains onto the floor. Kelly's voice asking him what was wrong sounded like it was coming from far, far away.

Through a haze of pain, Ty heard Fin answer.

"Nothing. We were nothing."

The agony went as quickly as it had come. The absence of pain left him feeling weak. He couldn't even remember what he was thinking before it hit. Somewhere in the middle of all that pain, the vampires had left.

"Are you okay? What happened?" Kelly sounded worried as she slid her fingers along his jaw.

He shook his head, trying to shake off the lingering

effects of the pain. Her touch helped. A lot. But not in the way she'd want. The feel of her fingers smoothing across his skin was like striking a match against a stick of TNT. An instant superheated explosion of his senses.

"I'm fine. Just a stab of pain in my head. It's gone now." But the fierce need she'd ignited wasn't even close to gone. *Tonight*. He wanted her warm, naked body beneath him. Wanted her fingers touching his chest, his stomach, reaching between his thighs to cup his balls. Wanted to feel his cock slipping deep inside her.

She nodded but didn't look convinced. "What Fin said, it's true?"

"Yeah." He hadn't lived through the ending of his time because Fin took his soul before it happened. Seeing the images on the screen, even if they were computer generated, hurt. Not that he'd left anyone behind. Ty frowned. Shouldn't there have been something, someone he missed? Had his life been that empty?

Ty looked at Kelly. There was real concern for him in her eyes. Maybe he thought of his past life as empty because this one wasn't. Not as long as Kelly was his driver. He decided that if he lost her, he'd remember, even across millions of years.

Fin started talking, and reluctantly Ty glanced away from her.

"Keep your drivers with you at night. Don't let them go off by themselves. If any of them have a problem with that, tell me and I'll get you a new driver."

"A little late for Neva." Kelly's mutter carried to Fin.

Ty waited for Fin to react. He didn't.

"If you have a confrontation with nonhumans, open your link and tell me." Fin threw Ty and Q sharp glances.

"I'll send help. And you will not turn that help down just because of pride."

Whatever else he might have said was lost as thunderous crashes and wild howls seemed to shake the whole condo.

Q winced. "Sounds like Neva's awake."

Chapter Eight

Kelly hit the stairs running. She was a step behind Ty, Q, Fin, and the big guy from the back of the room. By the time she reached the third floor, she was puffing.

"Fin has an elevator." Ty watched as everyone stopped before a large metal door with bars over a small window.

"Don't. Need. An. Elevator." She punctuated each word with a gulp for air. What she did need was an exercise program.

"Want me to go in?" The big man peered in the window.

Fin glanced at the woman who'd been assigned to keep watch on Neva. "What happened?"

Tall with short dark hair, the woman looked tough enough to take on a few of Fin's men. "She started to come to, so I got out of the room. I was about to call you when she changed. She went crazy in there, trying to climb the walls and then throwing herself at the door."

Fin nodded at the big man. "Go in and see what you can do."

"Who's he?" Kelly worried her bottom lip as the heavy metal door shook under the assault of something heavy and determined.

Ty edged closer to the door, pulling Kelly with him. "Car."

"As in?"

"Carcharodontosaurus."

"What?"

"Big meat eater." He hesitated. "Bigger than me."

"That bothers you, doesn't it?" Ordinarily, Kelly would chalk up to male ego Ty's unwillingness to admit that someone was bigger than he. But she was starting to understand what drove him.

"Size, strength, and savagery meant everything in my world. It was all about survival." He glanced at Car. "Sometimes savagery could trump size, though. The Brothers Grim, better known as Utah, Rap, and Tor, were some of the scariest predators going." Ty smiled at Car's back, his eyes gleaming with the hunger for battle. "I'd bet on me in a straight-up fight." His gaze slid to her. "And that bothers *you.*"

"Yeah, it does." She wouldn't insult him by lying. "I've never been in the might-makes-right camp. But I also know that I wouldn't have survived for five minutes in your world." Left unsaid was that he was in *her* world now. Then it occurred to her that if everything Fin said about these cosmic creeps was true, Ty's take on life might save humanity.

Ty didn't comment as he turned to watch Car slide open the steel door just enough to slip through. The door clanged shut behind him.

"Can I see?" She didn't *want* to see Neva. Kick-butt and badass weren't adjectives anyone would stick in front of her name. But she owed it to a fellow human to help if she could.

Fin moved aside to make room for her. When she looked through the window, her first impression was of an immense space. The room stretched more than two stories high and took up the whole third floor. The rest of Fin's condo had walls of glass everywhere. The windows in this room were narrow and small, set close to the ceiling. Was this a ballroom or a prison? She guessed it could serve both purposes.

"It's a containment room for any of us who feels he's on the edge and needs a cool-down space." Fin answered her unspoken question.

"What's with the human-sized door?" If there was a fire, anything that wasn't fully human couldn't escape.

"No one gets out of that room without his soul form under control." Fin's tone said that any of his men who couldn't get their act together long enough to fit through the door would be on their own. "I can't take a chance of turning one of us loose on the streets while his mind is impaired."

Now that was a scary scenario. Still . . . "You'd just let your own man die?"

"I'd do what I could to save him."

Kelly figured that would be quite a lot.

She forgot any other questions she might have asked as she got her first look at Neva. If Kelly hadn't watched Ty and Q fight the werewolves in Memorial Park, she would have been a lot more horrified. Neva looked like them: She was the size of a small pony, with glowing eyes, gaping jaws and lethal-looking teeth.

But there was something different. It was in Neva's eyes. Kelly tried to get a better look at them, but it was tough because she was in constant motion. Neva must have been out-of-her-mind panicked because she was so busy trying to climb the far wall that she still hadn't seen Car.

Finally, the wolf spotted him. She froze, then crouched. Kelly recognized that position, but she figured Car did too. Neva came out of her crouch in a giant leap that covered half the room. But Car was quicker. His massive form took shape around him in an instant, cocooning him from the werewolf's charge. And yes, he was bigger than Ty. His skull alone had to be at least five feet long.

Kelly shook her head as she glanced up at Ty. "That's so weird. I still don't get it. I can see Car through the animal, but nothing can get to him. . . ." Neva tested that theory as she bounced off the dinosaur's chest, cutting short her killing leap. "I understand the shape-shifter concept. Like Neva. The wolf body completely replaces her human one. But with you guys, it's sort of a layering of forms, one inside the other, both existing at the same time. What I really can't wrap my mind around is how your dinosaur form can be so lethal when I can still see your human form." Neva yelped as Car head-butted her, sending her skidding across the floor.

Ty's smile was slow, sensual, and deadly. All at the same time. "We give true meaning to the term two-natured. When you see us as humans, our soul form still lives in us, only hidden. It comes when we need it, though."

"I've noticed. Strange."

"Yeah, it *is* strange." Ty glanced at Fin.

Kelly understood. Only Fin knew the Eleven's secrets. But she wondered why he didn't share any of them with his men. *Trust* wasn't the first word that came to mind when she thought of Fin.

But Kelly forgot about Fin as she watched Neva fling herself again and again at Car, despite the fact that she wasn't getting anywhere with him.

Finally, Car roared at Neva, sending her into another frenzy of leaping and snapping.

"He's losing his patience." Fin sounded worried as he watched from behind Kelly. "I'll have to get him out of there before he hurts her."

"What exactly was he supposed to be doing?" She finally got a good look at Neva's eyes. Kelly recognized the emotion in them.

"I thought Car would scare her so much she'd cower in a corner somewhere." Fin seemed puzzled that his plan hadn't worked.

"She's out of her mind with fear. Neva's not reacting rationally. You don't help by adding to her fear." Kelly wondered whether Neva would become like her savage pack mates once she accepted her change and lost her terror. Or did werewolves have individual personalities as humans did? So much she didn't know.

Ty put in his two cents. "She must realize she can't get past him."

Angry, Kelly turned on him. "Have you ever been afraid, really afraid?"

"No." He sounded definite about that.

"Well, I have. When I was about five, my dad thought he'd give me an up-close look at a big snake. He didn't think anything of it. The snake wasn't poisonous, and he knew I loved animals, especially the large carnivores. Well, I went crazy. Screamed, fought, and worked myself into a frenzy. Threw up all over the place. Nothing Dad said could calm me down, even after he got rid of the snake. I'm still terrified of them."

"Your point is?" Fin sounded impatient.

"Fear is a human thing. I understand it. And Neva is terrified. Let me go in and try to calm her down." A *human* thing. Kelly realized her mistake three words too late. She'd neatly drawn a line between them. Human on one side, the Eleven on the other.

Ty narrowed his eyes. He'd gotten her point. "You're right. We think like animals. But fear isn't just a human emotion. I never felt it because I was at the top of the food chain. Ask some of the plant-eaters about fear. So what's your plan?" Anger simmered in his voice.

Kelly sighed. "Sorry, guys. I just meant that if you've never been afraid, you don't know how it feels. I can relate, so maybe I can find a way to defuse the situation. Besides, I'm used to the wolves at the zoo." Did that make sense? Probably not to them.

Ty snorted his contempt. "In other words, you don't have a plan."

She dug into her jeans pocket and pulled out her pepper spray. "Fin, do you have anything nonlethal I can borrow to protect myself?"

Fin nodded at the dark-haired woman, who opened a metal cabinet standing beside the door. She pulled out a gun and handed it to Kelly. "Taser. Hit her at about fifteen feet if you think she's coming for you."

"Thanks." Kelly drew in a deep, calming breath. "I'm ready."

Fin didn't comment, just rapped on the door and waved Car out.

When Car's human form was back in the driver's seat, he slipped out of the room, his expression harsh with controlled rage. "I can't stand this world. Don't know how much more holding-everything-in I can take."

Kelly knew better than to say anything. But when Car turned his gaze briefly on her, she got a surprise. She'd thought he'd have black eyes to match his personality and what passed for his heart. Surprise. They were the purest green she'd ever seen. Eyes so beautiful were wasted on Car.

As she reached for the door, Ty put his hand over hers. "I'll go in with you."

The word "no" formed in her head. If she were a heroine in some book, she'd go in by herself and do her calming-the-savage-beast routine. But she wasn't a heroine, and she had enough common sense to know that Neva could rip her apart before she had a chance to get "I'm your friend" out of her mouth.

Ty pushed harder. "I won't frighten her. I'll crouch down and make myself small."

That dragged a smile from Kelly. "Right."

Taking her smile as acceptance, he pulled the door open and slipped into the room with Kelly. As promised, he moved a few feet away from her and crouched down.

Without the solid door between herself and Neva, some of Kelly's courage wilted. She could only hope the woman retained her human understanding inside that big scary wolf's body.

When Car left, Neva raced to the other side of the room. Once again she was leaping into the air, trying to reach windows way too small for her to squeeze through even if she could jump high enough to reach them.

Kelly must have made a noise, or maybe it was just the *ker-thump ker-thump* of her wildly pounding heart that alerted Neva. Kelly swallowed hard as the werewolf swung to face her. Omigod. Was Neva really that big, that ferocious, and was Kelly really that scared? Yep to all three.

With a furious roar, Neva crouched and then launched herself at Kelly. In the time it took to register death racing toward her, Kelly reviewed all the soothing and logical things she'd meant to say to Neva. One problem. No. Freaking. Time.

"Lift your arm and aim the damn taser." Ty's command was a harsh shout.

Lift? Taser? Kelly shook her head, trying to clear it, trying to make sense of what was happening through the fog of sheer, life-sucking panic.

Neva peeled her lips back from enormous teeth as she prepared to make the final leap that would land her on top of her quivering prey.

Kelly raised the hand holding the taser. It was trembling wildly.

Neva crouched low, ready to spring off her powerful haunches. Kelly heard Ty jumping to his feet. She knew that in a few seconds the two would explode into violence while she stood watching them try to kill each other.

Do something. Now. Kelly opened her mouth to speak and only made a gurgling sound. *Way to go, Maloy.* She tried again. "Stop!"

Neva froze and recognition flared in her eyes. Kelly exhaled shakily. Relief made her light-headed.

Ty grunted his opinion of the whole chain of events. "This is why Fin doesn't want humans involved in the battle. You're not prepared for attacks by shape-shifters, vampires, and things like that."

No kidding. If Neva had been a charging lion, Kelly still would have been scared shitless, but she wouldn't have let the fear paralyze her. "Give me a break. I'm not trained for combat." She took a deep breath. "I'll do better next time."

"Forget next time."

Neva's low growl jerked her attention back to the wolf. "Try to calm down, Neva," Kelly said in her most soothing tone. "The werewolves made you one of them, but you'll be able to return to human form. You just have to give it time." She didn't know if that was true, but if it eased Neva's terror, she'd lie all day and all night long. "We only want to help you." That at least was true.

For the first time, Neva's ears pricked forward. A good sign.

Giving Ty a warning glance, Neva crept closer. Kelly tried to convince herself the wolf's walk was just a walk, not a stalk. As she drew near Kelly, Neva bared her teeth again.

Oh, crap. "I'm talking to the human in you, Neva. The part that can reason. Let me help you."

Ty made a disgusted sound. "I'm talking to the animal in you, Neva. Hurt Kelly and I'll rip you apart."

Neva looked as if she was considering both options.

"I know a werewolf—not anyone belonging to the pack that hurt you—who'll know what to do." *Please let her gray wolf friend call.* Kelly fixed her gaze somewhere left of Neva's head. No direct eye contact to signal aggression.

When Neva finally reached Kelly, she sat down with a wolfy whine, misery dimming her amber eyes.

Thank you, God. "I don't know how you turn back to human form. Maybe if you relax a little, it'll come naturally." Or not.

Kelly sensed what she had to do next. It was a symbol of her trust in Neva, even though she wasn't feeling particularly trusting right now. *Just do it.* Trying to look relaxed while wondering if she should kiss her hand good-bye, Kelly reached out to touch Neva.

Ty didn't try to stop her. Chalk one up for his control. But he could also see she had a firm grip on the taser.

Her legs felt like rubber by the time she finally rested her hand on Neva's head. "Ty, Q, and all the other guys here are different." After seeing Car, Kelly figured Neva already understood that. "But they want to help you."

Neva glanced at Ty again. She didn't look convinced.

Kelly rushed into speech. "You'll probably have to stay

in the condo until I find my wolf friend. It's a lot safer here than the apartment."

Neva's panicked expression returned.

"Okay, okay, I'll stay with you."

Neva seemed to accept that.

"I'm taking you out of this room now. I think you're smart enough to know running away won't solve anything. There's no way you could find someone to help you on your own."

Praying she was reading the wolf's expression right, Kelly opened the door. The men on the other side backed away. Ty followed Neva and Kelly out.

"I'll stay the night with her." Kelly hoped her tone sounded calm and unafraid.

"Then I'm staying too." Ty's tone signaled not negotiable. "And don't insult Neva. She's a wolf right now, and she can smell your fear. It's an *animal* thing."

Kelly winced. Payback. She glanced at Neva. The wolf was staring at Ty with new respect.

"Look, she's my driver. I'll stay with her tonight. You guys can go home." Q looked resigned.

Neva's low growl made her opinion perfectly clear.

Q shrugged. "Hey, I'm deeply hurt, but it looks like she wants to stay with you guys."

Silence fell as Fin thought about the situation. Then he nodded. "Ty, Kelly, and Neva, follow me."

Obediently, they all trailed after him. Kelly was beginning to understand a little better how he controlled his men. She for one didn't even consider not following him.

Fin led them down to the second floor. He stopped in front of a double door, threw both doors wide, then stepped aside. "I'll send up something for you to eat. Then get some sleep. You have a busy night ahead of you. If you have to walk Neva, try not to let anyone see her. I'll hang a leash by the door."

Neva looked stricken.

"Sorry about that. But Houston has strict leash laws. Be thankful I don't make Ty carry a pooper scooper." He strode away without looking back.

"Walk Neva?" Kelly looked at the wolf.

The wolf's expression said, *Duh?*

Ty smiled, a slow slide of wicked anticipation.

Kelly thought she knew why. "Fin only gave us one room. Where're you going to sleep?"

"Where do you want me to sleep?" His gaze seared her with the heat of all his sexual hunger.

The answer she *wanted* to give fought a silent battle with the one she *ought* to give.

Neva didn't seem to give a damn about where Ty slept. She wandered past them into the huge room.

Maybe Ty expected Kelly to argue with him, or maybe he wasn't looking beyond a possible night of pleasure. Who knew what he was thinking? Kelly was thinking they could settle this later, because Neva was back at the door whining.

"Neva needs to go outside." Without meeting his gaze, she headed for the stairs with Neva padding beside her.

Ty kept pace with her. He had to admit to a little disappointment. Even though he'd resented Kelly's hint that he didn't think like a human, she was right. Sex was to be enjoyed. Nothing complicated about the process. But he'd learned enough about human behavior to know there were rituals attached to everything people did. So he'd expected, no, looked forward to an argument about sharing a bed where sex might take place. The fight hadn't happened. But the sex still might. That thought cheered him up.

Kelly stopped by the front door. "Wait here. I left my jacket in the media room."

Ty waited until Kelly was out of hearing before turning his attention to Neva. "Look, I know tonight has been rough for you. And if you need any help adapting to your animal nature, just yell." He thought about that. "Or howl."

As promised, Fin already had a leash hanging on a hook. Nothing fancy, just a long piece of rope. Ty tied it loosely around Neva's neck. "It's just for show."

Neva still looked suspicious.

"I need a favor. Kelly and I will be sleeping in the *only* bed. She'd appreciate some privacy. Me, I don't care if you watch or not." He shrugged. "Guess it's the animal in me."

Neva gave him a drop-dead look.

Okay, nice never worked with some people. "Don't come anywhere near that bed. Sleep on the couch. Sleep on the floor. But don't set one paw on that bed." He made sure his smile showed lots of teeth for emphasis.

Neva wilted beneath his threat. She turned scared eyes up to him.

Hell, no. He wouldn't let sympathy for her get in the way of what he wanted. Did he ever think about how pathetic his prey looked right before a kill? Never. If he let Neva's expression bother him, it would be proof that humanity was catching. He couldn't afford to worry about the emotions of others if he expected to help take down Nine.

With a disgusted grunt, he watched Kelly return wearing her still-bloody jacket. Picking up the end of Neva's rope, Ty waited.

Once outside and away from the condo's floodlights, the night wrapped around them. Kelly rubbed her hands together. "Chilly."

"Feels good." If he faced away from the building and stared into the night, he could almost believe he was free again, in the body he missed, with the remembered power surging through him. He glanced at Kelly. But the one thing he wanted to do most, he'd do as a human.

Kelly looked at the big lawn that ended in a small wooded area. "Fin's protected this building, hasn't he?"

He nodded. "The building and probably the land up to where the trees begin."

The words had barely left his mouth when Neva lifted her head, sniffed the air, and took off toward the trees. When she hit the end of the rope, Ty hung on. The rope snapped.

"Hell."

"Tell me she isn't trying to run away. She just wants privacy, right?" Kelly took a few steps toward the woods.

"No on both counts." He knew he sounded grim. "Go back and find Fin. Tell him to get out here."

Kelly dug into her jacket pocket and pulled out her cell phone. "I don't have Fin's number. Do you?"

"Nope."

Ty didn't need help, and he could call Fin just by opening their mental link. But he wanted Kelly safe before he did anything.

"I can't believe you don't have his number." But she turned and ran back to the condo. He waited until she was out of sight before following Neva. The howling started just as he reached the trees. It wasn't an angry howl or even a frightened one. If he was reading it right, the howl was just sad.

So he wasn't surprised when he found the wolf standing over a body, howling mournfully. Shit. One glance confirmed the cause of death. Puncture wounds, blood drained. Vampire attack. The glance also confirmed the victim's identity. Double shit.

He extended his senses, searching for the killer. No vampire. But there was something else close by. Neva responded to that something with a growl. "Yeah, a cat. Maybe we'll go see what it wants."

"I think if we wait, it'll come to us." Fin appeared out of the darkness with Kelly right behind him.

She looked pissed. "I broke speed records getting to Fin, and then I remembered you have instant-messaging capability." Kelly touched her index finger to her forehead. "You just wanted to get rid of me."

Ty exhaled deeply. "It didn't work too well, did it?"

"He wanted to keep you safe, Kelly." Fin sounded like he was on Ty's side.

Ty looked down at the body. "Steve. I guess he didn't make it to Dallas after all. A vampire kill. I hope our new friend Jude isn't involved. We only have his word that he's on our side. He did us a favor last night, but he was helping himself too." He peered into the surrounding trees. "Something else is out there. Not vampire."

The animal scream came right on cue.

"That's a big cat. It's the same cry I heard last night in Memorial Park." Kelly crouched down next to the body. "What was Steve doing here?" She looked up at Ty. "You terrified him. He didn't want to be anywhere near you again." Her words were laced with sorrow.

Ty felt frustration tugging at him. This near-stranger's death was bringing out all kinds of emotions in Kelly and Neva that made him uncomfortable—sadness, regret. He couldn't ever remember feeling loss over another's death. But then he'd always hunted alone, and his matings were fast, fierce, and over.

All he felt now was rage at whatever vampire had killed this man just because he'd worked for Fin. And Ty had no doubt that was the motivation.

"Balan is here." Fin's voice was calm, no hint of tension in it. He didn't even spare a glance at the body.

A cold bastard. The thought surprised Ty. He'd always admired Fin's power to handle any crisis with emotionless efficiency. That made him a good leader. But now that Ty was thinking about emotions, he realized Fin had even fewer than he did. At least Ty could express honest rage. Fin got angry when he wanted to manipulate, but he could turn it off at will. He never burned hot about anything.

Kelly's gasp and Neva's low growl alerted him that their visitor had arrived.

"A jaguar?" Kelly sounded more awed than frightened.

"Balan," Fin corrected.

The large black cat emerged from the shadows, its golden eyes fixed on them. It moved with the powerful grace of its kind. And Ty knew exactly how a jaguar moved because among the millions of bits of knowledge Fin had fed to him had been visuals of earth's animals in their natural habitats. Fin was always thorough.

"What do you want?" Fin sounded politely interested.

Ty was used to hearing only Fin's voice in his head, so the unfamiliar new one startled him.

"It is an honor to meet two Gods of the Night." The cat's gaze slid to Kelly and Neva. *"As well as their minions."*

Both Kelly and Neva looked startled, so Ty knew Balan was including them in the conversation, too.

"Gods of the Night?" Ty smiled. "Sounds like a fancy name for the Eleven."

"Those I serve name you such." His attention moved to Fin. *"You lead them. My masters wish you not to interfere*

with what they have ordained will come to pass." Balan circled Steve's body, his nostrils flaring at the scent of death. *"If you persist in defying my masters, they will destroy all who follow you."*

Fin smiled, that icy smile Ty was beginning to recognize as belonging to the real Fin. No warmth lived in that smile. "I and my . . . minions—" his smile widened a little as he glanced at Kelly, who looked like she wanted to kick the word "minions" around a little and then cover it with dirt—"appreciate your masters passing along their warning. We'll definitely take it under consideration. By the way, do they have names? I've been calling them numbers. The one here in Houston is Nine." Fin was in full sarcastic mode.

The jaguar's tail whipped back and forth. *"My masters do not tolerate mockery. They prefer to be called Lords of Time."*

"Good grief. Gods of the Night, Lords of Time? It sounds like we're living a freaking video game. Can we say pretentious?" Kelly's muttered sarcasm caught the big cat's attention.

Balan glared his annoyance at Kelly before dismissing her. *"Individual names have power. My masters choose not to reveal them."* The jaguar crouched near Neva, studying her with unblinking intensity from those eerie golden eyes. Neva lowered her head and growled at him. *"This is the one changed by my masters' allies."* Balan swung his gaze to Ty. *"The ones you killed this night. You are a predator like no other I've seen. I would find you a worthy hunting partner."*

Ty had to make a real effort not to take pride in the jaguar's compliment. This was his enemy.

"I am no one's enemy. I am merely the messenger of your enemy. I take no sides in battles. I simply observe."

"And report." Ty felt a sense of invasion knowing the big cat was in his head. It wasn't the same as when Fin was there.

"And report."

"It's nice to have a neutral party acting as a messenger. But I wonder exactly how neutral you are, Balan? Why have you chosen to carry messages and observe for them"

Fin sounded as if he couldn't care less about the jaguar's answer, but Ty was familiar with every nuance of Fin's voice. There was tense excitement thrumming through it now.

"How do you know my name?" Balan rose from his crouch to move closer to the trees, where he became one more shadow out of many.

Fin shrugged. "I tuned in to all the mental chatter going on in Memorial Park tonight." He looked faintly bored. "Interesting that *balan* means jaguar in the Mayan language. You're black. I think I read somewhere that the Mayans believed the black of your species was the Jaguar God of the Underworld. Not surprising since you're a creature of the night. Didn't they also believe you were a helper to Bolon Yokte, a Mayan creation lord?" Without warning, Fin's gaze sharpened. "Maybe you're a little bit more than a lowly messenger."

"How do you know all these things?" Balan's voice was an angry hiss.

"I read a lot?" Fin had returned to bored indifference.

"Perhaps we have much to learn about each other." And with something sounding close to a dry chuckle, Balan was gone.

The silence dragged on longer than it should have.

Kelly sighed and ran her fingers through her hair. "I

don't even want to guess what that was about. I'm mentally and emotionally done for the night."

She looked down at Steve, her expression going soft in a way that tugged at a yearning Ty didn't understand.

"We have to take care of Steve. He didn't deserve this." Kelly's eyes hardened. "I never thought of myself as much of a hater, but I'm beginning to think it's because I never had true evil set up shop next door to me. I'm building a mile-high mountain of hate for these guys." She glanced at Neva. "How about you?"

Neva lowered her head, peeled her lips back from a formidable set of teeth, and growled her hatred.

"I'll take care of Steve." Fin sounded matter-of-fact about it.

And why not? Fin had taken care of everything as long as Ty could remember. None of them ever questioned that.

Perhaps we have much to learn about each other. Balan knew as much about Fin as Ty did. Which was a big freaking nothing. That was wrong. Why didn't he know more about his leader? Why hadn't he ever asked questions? Why hadn't *any* of them asked questions?

Ty raised a troubled gaze to Fin. Fin met his gaze, and something dark and threatening moved in his eyes.

"Don't go there, Ty."

With that parting thought, Fin lifted Steve easily into his arms and strode into the darkness.

Chapter Nine

"What're you thinking?" Ty didn't look at her as they stood outside the door to their room.

"Nothing." A colossal lie. Kelly absently swung Neva's broken leash.

"Right." He seemed disappointed in her answer. Opening the double doors, he waited for Neva and her to enter the room.

Suddenly exhausted, Kelly collapsed onto the couch. She noticed someone had lit the fireplace while they were gone. Dully, she watched Neva wander around the room. The werewolf ignored the food waiting for her by the wet bar.

Under other circumstances, the huge bank of windows with sliding glass doors leading to a private balcony, the separate sitting area, and the marble fireplace would have wowed Kelly. But all she could think about was what Fin was doing with Steve's body. Would he put it somewhere for the police to find? Kelly hadn't known Steve well, but the thought of his body being dumped in the weeds somewhere upset her. And how long before the police started to wonder about bodies turning up with puncture wounds and no blood?

Kelly noticed Ty staring at Neva, who'd finally settled next to the windows, head on paws, gazing into the darkness.

"The night calls to me too, Neva. It'll always call to the animal in us. But that's not a bad thing. Your enhanced senses will allow you to experience the world of darkness in ways you never imagined." Something in his eyes spoke of his own longing for the night.

Kelly felt alone, even with Ty and Neva in the room.

Ty walked over and sat beside Kelly. "Still thinking nothing?" He picked up a sandwich from a tray someone had left on the coffee table.

If only. Closing her eyes, she leaned her head back against the couch. "These last three nights have redefined my life."

"Bad."

"Bad," she agreed. "Before you popped onto the scene I was an ordinary student, working part-time at an ordinary zoo, with an ordinary family I loved. I put the 'o' in ordinary."

"Now?"

"Now I don't know. I'm living a you've-gotta-be-kidding life. It's so far out there even my sister Jenna's tabloid wouldn't touch it. And it's dead serious. End-of-humanity kind of stuff."

"I'm sorry I screwed up your life."

There was emotion in his voice. Regret? The depth of it startled her.

"If what Fin says is true, it would've gotten screwed up soon anyway." Kelly wanted her old life back.

Didn't she? Kelly glanced up at Ty's face. He hadn't turned on the lights when he entered the room, but the moonlight shining through the windows bathed everything in a cold glow. It cast his face in shades of light and dark.

Shades of light and dark. Like him. "I don't get you. You're one of the good guys, but you love violence. Out there with the werewolves tonight, you were having a blast."

"Understand me, Kelly. I went to sleep one day and woke up sixty-five million years later. So I'm only about a week removed from being the biggest badass of them all. I lived to hunt, loved the excitement, killed to survive. What do you expect of me? I don't belong to your world, will probably never belong, no matter how much Fin wants that to happen."

"I think you will." Fin and she finally had something in common. She wanted it to happen too. But not completely. It was the wild and dangerous that drew her. Probably that's why she liked working around the large carnivores at the zoo. She smiled. Correction—she liked wild and dangerous as long as it didn't include snakes.

He didn't answer, only stared into the flames.

"I'm going to take a quick shower. I noticed someone left a nightshirt on the bed for me." Only one. Pink. Small. So it was hers. He was on his own. Without waiting for him to respond, she rose, grabbed the nightshirt, and headed for the bathroom.

Once in the shower, she blocked out all thoughts of the room's only bed. Kelly convinced herself she didn't need to think about it. The darn thing was as big as a football field. If they both stayed on their own side, they wouldn't even be within shouting distance of each other, let alone touching. Besides, she wasn't about to make love in the same room with a werewolf. A woman had to have some standards.

Climbing from the shower, she ignored the splendor of the room as she pulled on the shirt, then used the blow-dryer on her hair. No use bringing her bloody clothes back out with her, so she left them hanging from a hook on the back of the door. Then, taking a deep breath, she returned to the bedroom.

Neva had eaten and moved to a darkened corner of the

room. Looked like she was already asleep. Ty was waiting for his shot at the shower. His gaze trailed over Kelly, lingering where the nightshirt ended at midthigh. His smile was filled with heat and promise.

Without saying a word, he went into the bathroom and shut the door behind him.

She grabbed a sandwich and climbed into bed to eat it. Bad habit, but she loved eating this way. Usually she was watching TV or reading while she ate, though. Now she nibbled at the sandwich while she wondered what he'd wear to bed. Probably have to sleep in his shorts. Her lips curled up in a can't-wait grin at the thought.

Two sandwiches later, the bottomless pit lovingly referred to as her stomach was filled. Hey, she'd missed dinner. Imminent death worked up an appetite.

Now her eyelids drooped as she waited for Ty to come out of the bathroom. But no way was she falling asleep before getting a chance to see more of him than she'd ever seen before. She needed to end this totally crappy night with something positive.

Just when she'd started to think he'd crawled out the bathroom window, the door opened.

Kelly's eyes popped open. Whoa. No more droopy eyelids. Naked demigod at twelve o'clock. The reasoning part of her brain sputtered with an overload of logical concerns: Where're your shorts? Do you really want Neva to see you this way? Do you really want *me* to see you this way? Aren't you embarrassed, because I sure am?

A more primitive corner of her brain thought this had to be the highlight of her whole employment by Eleven Inc.

Without even glancing her way, Ty walked over to the wall of windows and stood gazing out.

"Umm, aren't you afraid someone might see you?" His

back was a smooth flow of golden skin from his broad muscular shoulders down to taut, round butt cheeks. She completed her buff-bod scan by admiring his strong thighs and legs.

He glanced over his shoulder. "We're thirty-plus stories up. Pilots of low-flying planes might do a double take, but that's about it."

"Oh." She slid her tongue over suddenly dry lips. "Uh, I thought you'd wear your shorts to bed." Prude. Queen Victoria and her.

"Why?" He turned to face her.

"Because . . ." Omigod. She'd seen his perfect pecs before, with his nipples just begging for the touch of her tongue. She'd seen his hard flat stomach with the shadowed indentation of his navel. But in the darkened room lit only by moonlight, it was like seeing him for the first time. "You don't know me. In this world, men wear their shorts to bed if they're with a woman who's not their wife or lover." True, but she should look at things from his perspective. Clothes weren't high on a dinosaur's priority list. Maybe so, but this was all about her, and his exposed body was weakening the few pathetic defenses she had against all his über maleness.

Ty shook his head. "I don't get it. Why should I hide certain parts of my body?" He looked sincerely puzzled.

Kelly's gaze slid lower. *Because seeing those heavy sacs resting between your thighs and watching your erection grow hard is turning the dial up on my lust-o-meter.* "Exposing your sexual organs is an invitation to have sex."

He raised one expressive brow. "Do you *want* me to wear shorts?"

There it was, the direct challenge. Her brain shouted *yes*, but her senses rose up as one and proclaimed, "No."

His smile was hard and predatory, his lips soft and mobile. She was really conflicted about that smile. Hard or soft? She'd have to touch, taste before making a decision.

"And you're wrong, Kelly. I *do* know you." He moved away from the windows, his movements smooth and fluid. "I know what's in your eyes. Hunger." Ty stopped as he reached the side of the bed. "Recognizing things like that is one of the perks of having a primitive soul hot-wired for sex."

"You really want me to believe in that primitive stuff, don't you?" She gripped her lower lip between her teeth, tension thrumming through her along with the hunger she wished she could deny. And if he didn't move out of grabbing range fast, she'd give in to temptation and slide her fingers the length of his cock. Her Victorian image would shatter into a million shining sexual shards.

When she released her lip, he fixed his gaze on it, his eyes blazing with a need that went way past mere desire. "Never doubt it. Primitive doesn't hide behind pretty words. I want you. I want to touch every inch of your bare body, bury myself deep inside you."

Denial was the coward's way. Her body knew the truth, and her brain, except a tiny cluster of whiny common sense cells, thought it was a hell of a good idea. "Fine, so I want you too. But we're not alone."

His gaze slipped to Neva. "She's out of it. She wouldn't know what we were doing."

"I would."

He nodded. "I'm going out on the balcony."

His eyes burned with his invitation, but he didn't say anything as he strode to the glass doors. The glimpse she got of the foil package clenched in his hand said he expected her to join him.

As he stepped onto the balcony, she silently chanted the rules of the civilized: Thou shalt not make love on a balcony even if it's thirty-something stories up because *someone* might see you. Thou shalt not make love with a dinosaur no matter how sexy he is. Thou shalt not make love on a balcony when a werewolf is in the room, even if said werewolf is asleep. And last but not least, thou shalt not make love outside when it's cold because goose bumps are never attractive.

But the chant was slowly and inexorably drowned out by a voice that wasn't civilized at all, a voice hoarse with need, a voice that urged her to pull off her shirt and expose her body to the night wind, to bare her teeth and rake her nails over his perfect body, and to hell with goose bumps.

Almost in a trance, she climbed from the bed and walked to the glass doors. His back was to her, the wind blowing his hair away from his face. She imagined running her fingers through that hair, reveling in the silky slide of each strand. Placing her hand on the door, she paused to glance at the privacy sheers.

Taking a deep breath, she made her decision. She closed the sheers, pushed the door open, and stepped out onto the balcony.

Ty turned to stare at her, his eyes asking a silent question. He must have seen the answer in her eyes, because he lifted those sensual lips in a smile that was all starving predator. "Decided to cross over to the wild side?"

"It seems so." Kelly lifted her face to the breeze. Even though the balcony was protected on three sides, she'd expected to feel cold. She didn't. Nerves along with anticipation kept her toasty warm.

He took the two strides necessary to enter her personal space. No, make that *dominate* her personal space. Only as he stood inches from her with the wind blowing at his back did she appreciate his size, his power. It was more than a physical presence. She shivered.

Ty reached out to run his fingers along her tightly clenched jaw. "Don't. The part of me you see in battle has no place in what we'll share."

Kelly nodded. "I know that. The shiver wasn't a fear thing." She grinned. "It was just appreciation for the sheer *everything* about you. And anticipation. Lots of anticipation."

His soft laughter was filled with savage joy. He glanced at a nearby chaise. "We won't be able to get too enthusiastic on that."

"Forget the chaise. Standing up. Definitely standing up." There was something deliciously urgent about that. "And soon. Very soon."

Ty's eyes darkened. "Good."

He took that final step and swallowed her world. She absorbed his scent, an exotic mix of the unknown and heated male arousal. And when he grasped the hem of her shirt, she was ready. Lifting her arms, she allowed him to slide it over her head.

The night breeze played across her body, touching and teasing. Something broke free inside her. Probably her inhibitions making a run for it.

Dropping her shirt, he stared. In his eyes blazed the same naked emotion that she'd seen as he leaped into battle. And everywhere his gaze skimmed—breasts, stomach, and finally the spot that made her want to spread her legs and invite him in—fire touched her.

"You're a beautiful woman." He touched one nipple with the tip of his finger and watched it pebble. Then he wrapped his arms around her and pulled her close. Bending his head, he whispered to her, his breath teasing the sensitive skin beneath her ear. "It's been too long, and I want too much." He closed his teeth lightly over her earlobe and tugged.

She shivered again. Reaching behind him, she trailed her fingers up and down the smooth planes of his back. When she felt him take a huge shuddering breath, she looked up into his face.

Ty's eyes gleamed hot, and the shadows cast by the moonlight made his predator past real. "Everything I want to do to you is pushing and shoving at me, trying to be first." His smile brought him back from the primal edge for a moment. "I can't control it all . . ." He reached for the words. "What's dammed up inside."

"Tell me what's inside, Ty." She stretched, wrapping her arms around his neck, brushing her nipples across his chest. Closing her eyes, she felt the friction as a starburst of sensation racing along her nerve endings.

Dropping his hands to her hips, he cupped her bottom, pulling her tight against his arousal. "Wind and driving rain. Booming thunder and jagged streaks of lightning." Tangling his fingers in her hair, he tilted her face up to him. "My time was ruled by hunger and the elements. That's how I still think. You're the center of my storm, Kelly Maloy."

Kelly opened her eyes. His face was close to hers, so close she could see that he didn't have laugh lines. She drew the lines around his eyes and mouth with the tip of her finger.

His gaze never left hers as he gripped her finger and slid his lips over it. His tongue, warm and wet, swirled around and around the finger. And when he finally released it, his sheer intensity convinced her they'd shared their first sexual act. Need, heavy and full, clenched low in her stomach.

"You don't have laugh lines." Was that wispy little voice

hers? At this rate, she'd never make it to the final act. "Why?"

"Guess this body hasn't done much laughing." Ty's grim expression said there hadn't been much to laugh about in his life either.

Too bad she wouldn't be around long enough to add a few of those lines to his face. Kelly's regret surprised her.

He didn't give her a chance to obsess over it, though. He lowered his head and took her mouth. And it *was* a taking.

Ty's lips moved against hers. No softness. Only the predator's need to possess. Once again, his immense erotic energy pushed at her; all heat, power, and demand.

And she wanted him right back, with an intensity that almost scared her. Where had it come from? What layer had she peeled back from the tepid emotion she'd always thought was passion? Had this primal hunger always been there?

Kelly opened to him, met his tongue, and tasted all he'd been, still was.

Ty's body shuddered against hers. He abandoned her mouth with a harsh gasp and stepped away. "Not working. Run, little girl. I can't hold back what's coming. And I can't make this the kind of mating you want. I don't know how." His chest was sheened with sweat even as cold wind whipped his words away. Every muscle in his hard body was tight with tension.

She applauded him. It took guts to give his prey a chance to escape. Kelly recognized how much it cost him. But he had no idea what he'd unleashed.

"I'm no one's 'little girl.' We might be in the middle of Houston, but I just yanked open a door and walked into your world. And you have no idea what kind of 'mating' I want." Kelly reached out and dragged her nails the length of his torso from nipples to stomach.

Shock widened his eyes as he glanced down to where the red imprint of her nails stood out against his body. Then he smiled. It was a savage baring of his teeth. "See, now that attitude is guaranteed to put all kinds of happy lines on my face."

Before she could open her mouth to respond, he scooped her up and carried her to the side wall of the balcony. Setting her on her feet, he stood breathing hard, but not from exertion.

Pressing her back to the wall, Kelly stared up the length of him. His body blocked out the moonlight, and he was all dark menace. She watched his chest moving with each harsh breath he took, and she was sure if her own heart wasn't pounding so hard she'd be able to hear his.

He moved closer, so close she could feel his cock hard against her stomach. Desire was hot, heavy, and definitely wet between her thighs.

"I can't wait." His voice was a harsh apology. "I can't freaking wait."

"Now." They had a meeting of minds for once.

Ty didn't say anything. He retrieved his little foil packet from where he'd dropped it on the chaise, ripped it open, and slipped the protection on with a minimum of cursing.

Kelly understood. She clenched her fists to keep from reaching out and helping him hurry the process along. Taking a deep breath, she tried to gather together the old familiar parts of herself, the parts that didn't think they'd shrivel and die if she didn't lick every inch of his yummy body, the parts that enjoyed sex but didn't drown in it. Deep breathing didn't work. There was a whole new gang in town, and they were ready to turn loose the tsunami if something didn't happen damn soon.

Something happened. Finally ready, he slid his hands

under her bottom and lifted her. She grabbed his shoulders, then wrapped her legs around him.

He slowly lowered her onto his cock.

Her breaths came in moaning gasps as he nudged her open. And then bit by deliciously excruciating bit, he allowed her to slide over him. She made whimpering noises as he stretched and filled her. Then when she was completely impaled on him, she clenched around his long hard length. Ripples of the coming orgasm teased her each time she tightened her muscles. She licked her dry lips and focused on those ripples.

Kelly's senses reached overload and exploded. His scent was an extension of the night. For the rest of her life, when November rolled around with its smell of fall and wood smoke, she'd remember this.

And touch was a pleasure-pain. Kelly burned for him. "Keep up with me, Endeka, if you don't want me to lap you."

He laughed, a dangerous sound that had more to do with challenge than humor. "Oh, I'll keep up with you. I'm greedy. I don't just want my cock buried in you. I want your flesh touching mine everywhere, so all this heat can melt us together. I never want to stop feeling this." His husky murmur was thick with suppressed hunger.

Kelly made an unintelligible sound as she wrapped her arms around him and pressed against his body. The scrape of her supersensitive nipples across his chest drew a moan from her. "Move. Now." She emphasized her demand by sliding her tongue across his collarbone. His taste was a memory to be savored on nights when she was running short of great memories.

He built slowly, lifting her off his cock and then driving back into her. Their rhythm caught and quickened. Kelly groaned as she slammed down onto him. Digging her nails into his back, she braced herself against the wall as he arched, burying himself deep inside her again and again and again. She cried out. So good, it felt so damn good. That rising sense of fullness, of heaviness, of something awesome about to happen moved closer and closer.

Now, now, now. She had to move faster, harder. The flesh-on-flesh friction, the pounding, the filling and emptying drove her wild. Coming, coming, it was freaking coming.

With a last powerful drive upward, Ty lifted her, and she froze in that moment. That soul-shattering, unbelievable moment when she couldn't move, couldn't breathe as wave after wave of spasms shook her seemed to go on and on. Somewhere in the background she heard Ty's cry join hers.

As her orgasm gripped her at the peak of sensation, of emotion, it seemed as if a door inside her was flung open and she *saw*. Ty's confusion when his essence first became aware deep beneath Newgrange. His fury when he'd thought the vampire would kill her. His battle with the beast that was a part of him.

She plunged past all those emotions to reach deeper, so deep she thought she might never find her way back. *There.* At the center of his being she touched something magical, brilliant, and savage. Her mind didn't recognize it, but her soul knew. For one blinding moment she *felt* his soul. And then she spiraled back through an endless tunnel. The door inside her closed.

Kelly didn't know what had just happened, but she did know it was beyond explanation. She somehow felt as though she was *more* that she'd been a few minutes ago, as if she'd taken something of that brilliant and savage part of Ty and made it her own.

When she finally tumbled out of the moment, she could only cling to him weakly, the thud of her heart loud in her ears. Oh. My. God. That wasn't making love. She'd made love before, and it'd been a pale shadow of what had just happened. This was a whole new life experience. What to name it? Ty. For the rest of her life, whenever she felt this way—not that it was ever likely to happen again—she'd say she was having a Ty moment.

Limp, with her breaths still coming in harsh rasps, Kelly barely noticed when he carried her over to the chaise and lay down with her on top of him.

The cold breeze cooled her back while the heat of his body warmed her front from breasts to still-curled toes. With her head on his chest, she could hear the pounding of his heart, feel the rise and fall with each deep breath.

When had she felt like this after making love before? It was a bone-deep satisfaction. She was like a big old cat lying in the sun, knowing that life didn't get any better than this. She sighed her contentment.

He smoothed his fingers over her tangled hair. "I had so many things planned for you. Shot. I didn't get to tease your nipples until they were hard and so sensitive you were ready to scream. I never got the chance to kiss a path over your stomach and along your inner thighs. And then I was going to spread your legs and—"

She put her finger over his lips. "You're handing me a shopping list after I've already been to the store."

"Next time." It was a whispered promise.

Would there be a next time? Yes. In just a few minutes that had rattled and shaken her nice neat concept of what lovemaking should feel like, he'd become her addiction. *Should* there be a next time? Kelly didn't know.

Ty's gaze never left her face. His eyes were too close to

her, their expression too deep. What was he thinking? She rushed into speech.

"So you guys are pretty much immortal, huh? I mean, it's tough to kill you, and your essence, soul, or whatever has survived sixty-five million years?"

He looked puzzled for a moment, and then he smiled. "What brought that question on? I was hoping you'd want me to expand on my future plans for your body." His smile widened. "I even hoped you'd have plans for mine."

"Well—" She glanced away. "What we just shared was pretty much a major wow, and I'm having trouble expressing my overall awe of your lovemaking skills." Kelly shrugged. "So I'm making small talk since you're not saying too much."

His laughter vibrated through her and she wiggled a little to maximize the sensation.

"I have no words for what just happened." His laughter died. "Thank you."

A few over-the-top adjectives would have made her happy, but she knew he wasn't a multiple-adjective kind of guy. And that was fine with her. "What about the immortal thing?"

Ty nodded. "Yeah, we don't have an expiration date as far as I know."

Kelly made a real effort not to frown. Sure, she was happy for him. It must be great not to worry about growing old and dying. But there would never be a happily-ever-after for a woman with a man like him. She'd watch herself grow older and older while he stayed the same. And then she'd die while he went on. Not a happy resolution for either of them. *Reminder to self, don't get attached to Ty Endeka.*

Her eyelids were beginning to droop. He was warm and

comfortable, and she wouldn't mind sleeping this way forever. "After you get rid of this Nine, I suppose you'll move on."

"Once Houston is safe, we go wherever the other Lords are." He didn't sound happy about that.

Good. Sleepily, she wondered what it was about him . . . The ultimate dangerous male? Not a wise attraction. He'd be moving on while she was setting up her life in Houston. Now that thought really made her sad.

At some point during all those deep thoughts, she fell asleep.

Chapter Ten

"The Gods of the Night are hunting for you, Mr. Wyatt. They know you're recruiting." The vampire laughed. "Gods of the Night? Who came up with a dumb-ass name like that?"

"The 'dumb ass' who leads us chose that name, Lee. He has a flair for the dramatic and a passion for truth in advertising. They are what their name implies." He frowned. "He also has little patience with those who mock his creative efforts."

Lee stopped laughing. "I guess he can call them whatever he wants. But they're reaching out to other nonhumans for help. That's bad news for you."

The immortal hated having to explain himself to things like this vampire, but he needed help running his organization. "I'm more than all of their combined powers. Let *me* take care of the heavy lifting. You just do your job. That means bringing back information I can use." He paused to listen to the sweet sounds of rage, fear, and violence coming from the room below. "Now, was there anything else?"

Lee watched him from eyes black with hunger. "You promised me a hunting territory."

"Ah, yes, the ever popular hunting territory. It's truly sad that someone with your predatory nature has been denied the right to kill humans. I can give that right back to you." He shrugged. "But you understand, I'm a businessman.

The news you brought me tonight wasn't really worthy of such a valuable reward. Perhaps if you hear something that leads to the death or capture of an enemy, I might reconsider." He rose from behind his desk. "Now, if you'll excuse me . . ."

Lee nodded, but the vampire's fury and frustration coated the room in dark energy.

He tried not to smile. This was what he existed for. This was what he'd waited millions of years to enjoy. All of those roiling emotions multiplied tens of thousands of times would create savagery on a scale Earth had never before experienced. And the gods knew Earth was no stranger to barbarism. This vampire, along with untold numbers of other paranormal beings, would tear apart the fabric of the society humans had built, and evil would stalk the world. He couldn't help it; he smiled.

"I'm going down to check on my newest enterprise." He knew his smile was insincere, but he really didn't give a damn. "I'd invite you to join me, but I know the scent of fresh blood is an unbearable temptation. I wouldn't want you to leave here and indulge your need in a weak moment. It would horrify me if your clan executed you. That would be a terrible waste of an excellent spy. But once you have your own hunting territory, I'll protect you from them." He made a shooing motion. "So run off now and bring back good news."

"Basil died last night. You gave him his own territory, but the T. rex found him and killed him anyway. I saw it happen. Where was your protection then?"

He shook his head in mock sorrow. "So sad. But Basil hunted outside his territory. I can't protect any who choose to freelance. When you get your territory, remember Basil's fate."

Looking unconvinced, the vampire left his office.

Dissatisfaction? If Lee dared to express it, the vampire'd have to be eliminated. He hoped things wouldn't come to that. A spy on the inside of an enemy's camp was always useful.

Pushing aside thoughts of the vampire, he locked his office door and walked down the hall to the storage room. Sounds of voices and music filtered along the hallway from his club. Business was good.

He unlocked the storage room and slipped inside and relocked the door behind him, shutting out the sounds from the front of the building. Punching in a code on a panel hidden behind boxes of paper supplies, he watched a door slide open in the opposite wall. The opening revealed a darkened stairway leading to a large room beneath the back of the club. A room that was winning him lots of new recruits.

He paused at the top of the steps to soak up a totally different sound from those coming out of the club: a savage roar of bloodlust. A happy sound. He smoothed his palm over his Armani jacket, stepped through the doorway, pressed a button to close the door, and descended the stairs.

His manager met him at the bottom, a sorcerer with a delightful talent for black magic. A wonderful find.

"How're things going, Thadeus?" He scanned the crowd.

Thadeus—tall, thin, and perpetually bad-tempered—frowned. The sorcerer hated anyone using his full name. He preferred Thad. So, of course, using Thadeus's full name was a perverse pleasure.

"Lots of enthusiasm tonight, Mr. Wyatt." Thadeus nodded toward the large and rowdy crowd surrounding the circle the sorcerer had cast in the middle of the room.

The circle with its attendant barrier of energy contained

two naked fighters. The naked part was his idea. Thadeus disapproved. But then Thadeus didn't understand the type of clientele that came to his nightly entertainments. The sheer level of violence along with all the blood drew the most vicious members of Houston's paranormal community to this room. And blood looked so much more dramatic against bare skin.

He eyed the demon and ghoul in the circle. It was almost over. The ghoul had brute strength, but the demon had the brains. Intelligence was trumping strength this time. Blood smeared the bodies of both males and trickled down stomachs and legs to pool on the floor.

The ghoul tried frantically to escape, but Thadeus's circle was impervious to physical or magical attack. The ghoul was doomed.

Even as he watched, the demon fought through the ghoul's weakened defenses and simply ripped his head off. The resultant spray of blood sent the watching vampires and werewolves in the crowd into a frenzy.

Interesting. He'd approach the victor with a job offer. The ones who fought in the circle were, for the most part, volunteers. He awarded tempting prizes to the winners of his little contests.

But once in a while he'd throw a captured enemy into the circle. They didn't come along too often, though, because his growing number of minions enjoyed killing a lot more than they did capturing. Perhaps he'd lay down a few rules so he could feed his circle.

While Thadeus took care of the body and the winner showered, he'd talk to the audience. That was the price he demanded for his free show. He waited until the clamor stopped and then he reached out to them.

"Houston, you have a problem. For hundreds of years

you've been told you can't kill freely, you can't call attention to yourselves."

A rumble of anger told him he was right on the mark.

"Your natures are to kill, to feed, but for too long your leaders have told you that humans are off-limits." The rumble grew louder.

"Told you that you couldn't drink from the living, the only blood that truly nourishes you." The vampires in the audience shouted their hatred of that rule.

"Told you that you couldn't hunt the prey you were created to hunt." Werewolves and a few other carnivorous shape-shifters joined their voices to the din.

"Told you that you should hide from a species that could never be your intellectual or physical equal." The fae in the audience just sat and looked dangerous.

"And so you've hunted in secret, hoping your leaders wouldn't find out." Silence fell. He was treading on thin ice now.

"But that's okay, because I'm on your side. The world is about to change. Humans will be wiped from the face of the earth." He felt the uneasy silence. They didn't quite believe him. "Except for sorcerers and those willing to work for our cause."

"And I haven't forgotten my demon friends. No one will ever again deny you access to Earth or try to send you back into the abyss." He didn't promise demons the right to kill, because they already thought of murder as their right. Besides, they were a varied race with many different agendas.

The fae? Who knew what they wanted. Like the demons, they were too varied for him to address their individual needs. But he'd assume that all lusted after power, particularly the Sidhe.

He paused for a moment to scan the minds of his listeners. As usual, he found what he was looking for. There were a few in every group. Three werewolves—a woman and two men—sat in the back near the stairs. They were planning to return to their pack and tell their alpha about him. Earth's inhabitants, whether human or nonhuman, were so predictable.

He smiled at everyone. Now for a demonstration, because lesser beings always required proof of power. "I'm sad to announce that we have three members of our audience who are contemplating telling their leader what they've seen and heard here." He sighed his fake regret. "I'm afraid I can't let that happen."

Mentally leafing through his termination Rolodex, he chose a method that wouldn't be instantaneous, one that would be rare and impressive, one that would, in the common vernacular, scare the shit out of everyone.

Presentation was everything in this part of the show. It was his favorite part. Extending his arms out in front of him, he pointed at the three werewolves. "You would betray us to our enemies. For that sin, your lives are forfeit." Yes, he sounded a bit overdramatic, but it added to the impact of the whole thing.

The three jumped up and tried to race for the stairs, but they were too late, much too late. It took only a thought to stop them. They stood frozen.

Unfortunately, to do what he intended, he had to reveal his true form. Oh, well, the audience wouldn't be able to say they didn't get a spectacular show tonight.

He changed.

There were gasps of disbelief followed by a babble of voices.

The first scream silenced them.

And then for the next fifteen minutes, he meticulously

took the werewolves apart cell by cell. It looked as if an eraser were smudging them out little bloody bits at a time. Their mouths were the last to go, still stretched wide even though their screams had ended five minutes before.

When he'd finished, the audience still stared wide-eyed at the spot where the werewolves had stood. He quietly returned to human form.

Someone finally broke the silence. "Uh, who'll we feed from?"

He blinked and turned to face the demon that had fought in the circle. Cleaned up and dressed in jeans, shirt, and a leather coat, the demon looked bigger than he had in the circle.

"What?"

The demon shrugged. "I mean, if you're going to wipe humans from the earth, then what'll we hunt?"

One another, you idiot. He pasted a smile on his face. "I'm sure no one will mind if you raise a few humans for your own use." It wouldn't happen. All humans would die, along with any nonhumans who supported them, and those who were left would fight for supremacy. It was all about creating chaos.

Turning back to his audience, who had at last recovered from their shock, he smiled. "Each of you has a form listing the rewards for joining us in this great crusade. Fill out the bottom and Thadeus will collect it as you leave. Someone will be in touch with you later."

He narrowed his gaze. "If you choose not to join us, please hand in a blank form." He had no need of the scribbled information on the papers. All he needed was something each of them had touched with their bare skin. With the papers, he would call them to him when the time came.

None could resist. And those who handed in a blank form? His smile widened. They'd be dead by morning.

He turned back to the demon that still stood behind him. "You did well in the circle tonight. I could use someone smart and powerful to help eliminate those who would stand against us. Your rewards would be great."

The demon watched him from icy blue eyes. "Sounds like fun."

"What's your name?"

"Seir."

"Once everyone has left, Thadeus will explain your first assignment, Seir. I'm sure you'll find the work satisfying and the rewards even more so."

Seir nodded before joining Thadeus.

He'd keep an eye on this one until he was sure the demon could be trusted, as much as demons could ever be trusted.

Then he forgot about Seir as he made sure every member of the audience handed in a form. Their minds spoke of eagerness to slaughter, fear that they might be killed like the three werewolves, or lust for power. All perfectly good reasons to join him.

It was only when he returned to his office that he realized Seir had never turned in a form.

Kelly woke to the sound of her cell phone and the sensation of something heavy crushing her legs. She lay with eyes closed, trying to figure it out. Random thoughts skittered around her brain before finally settling into a memory of last night. She was at Fin's. Neva was a werewolf. She'd made love with Ty.

On that last thought, her eyes popped open and then

widened. At some point while they'd slept, Neva had joined them. Her massive bulk was hanging off the bottom of the bed. Pulling her feet from beneath Neva, Kelly rolled over and met Ty's steady gaze.

He smiled, a slow sexy grin that said he was thinking about last night too. "Your phone is ringing."

"Right." She glanced down. "Naked."

"Beside the bed."

Rolling over again, she spotted her nightshirt on the floor where Ty must have dropped it last night.

She snatched it up and pulled it over her head. Then she climbed out of bed and stumbled into the bathroom. Closing the door behind her, she fumbled around in the pocket of her jacket, which still hung on the hook.

"Hello?" Probably Mom or Jenna. She hadn't called them yesterday.

"Is this the woman who was in Memorial Park last night?" A deep male voice. Sounded cautious.

"Maybe." Kelly was just as cautious. Okay, and nervous too. Considering all the scary stuff that had gone down last night, she wasn't saying more than necessary to a stranger.

There was a long, uncomfortable pause. Long enough for Kelly to wonder whether she should end the call.

"You met a wolf last night. You gave him your number. I'm his pack leader. We need to talk."

He sounded all nice and polite, but Kelly got the feeling this meeting was on the level of a royal command. Mr. Pack Leader wouldn't take no nicely.

"Where?"

"Parking lot across from the Museum of Natural Science. Midnight." He didn't sound like any of that was negotiable. "The guy you met last night will be there. Look for him. He'll bring you to me." He didn't offer a name.

Okay, she was meeting a werewolf outside a museum tonight. Was that surreal or what? "I'm bringing a friend with me." No way was she going to meet a werewolf by herself.

There was another long silence. "One friend. No one else." And the line went dead.

While she was in the bathroom, she freshened up and tried to decide what to do about tonight. Fin had supplied a few basic cosmetics, and Kelly wasn't proud. A little cheek cream and some lip color gave an impression of life. Then she left the bathroom.

Good things had happened while she'd been gone. Someone had brought breakfast and left some of her clothes on the bed. Ty sat on the couch eating his meal.

He wore a clean pair of jeans. She had a brief but intense underwear moment. Was he wearing any? She forced herself to move on. A fresh shirt hung over the back of a chair.

Neva was tearing apart a huge piece of raw meat set on a platter. Ugh. Still in wolf form.

Kelly grabbed the clothes and ran back into the bathroom to change before settling down next to Ty on the couch.

"Who brought breakfast?" Technically it was afternoon, but for this job, afternoon was the new morning.

"Shen."

Worry didn't affect her appetite. She helped herself to eggs, bacon, and toast. Making love was tough work.

Kelly nodded. "Fin's secretary, or whatever. He hired me. What about the clothes?" His knee touched hers, but she didn't move it away. Yesterday she would have chosen a chair, but now being near him felt natural. Her reaction to the bare expanse of his chest still tensed her up, though. His low-level erotic hum never let her forget the sexual animal part of him or her reaction to it.

"Shen said they went to your apartment this morning."

After a fortifying gulp of coffee, she told him about the call.

While Ty thought about what she'd said, Neva padded over to sit next to Kelly. The rest had evidently done the werewolf good, because her eyes were bright and—thank God—sane. Her wolfy expression said she was ready to take an active part in determining her destiny.

"You know, I think Neva should go with me to meet this pack leader. After all, it's her future we'll be bargaining for." Kelly hoped he wouldn't fight her on this.

"I agree." Finishing his coffee, he stood. "I need to talk this over with Fin." He retrieved his shirt, slipped into it, then pulled on a pair of boots. "Relax until I get back."

"Just a thought, but if I've got this straight, you can communicate mentally with Fin. So why do you have to tell him in person?"

"Fin's mental power is pretty much tied up right now with distracting Zero. When you're psychically blitzing the enemy, you can't be bothered with a minor communication unless it's an emergency."

"Oh." Kelly watched him leave. She glanced at Neva. "Relax. Right. Vampires, werewolves, and the ultimate big bad are after our behinds and he wants us to relax. Feeling relaxed yet, Neva?"

Neva shook her massive head and offered Kelly a wolfy grin. Her expression looked hopeful, though. Kelly sort of liked Neva's can-do attitude.

"I just realized that you only know bits and pieces of what's going on. Let me fill you in."

Kelly had just finished her explanation when someone knocked. Now what? She walked to the door and then hesitated. No peephole. But her hesitation only lasted long enough for her to remember where she was. No unfriendly monster waited on the other side of the door. They were all friendly monsters here.

She opened the door to Shen. "Hi, haven't seen you for a while. Come in." Kelly stood aside to let him pass.

A second after she said it, she remembered Neva. Oops. Shen strode past her and then stopped. Neva crouched by the couch, a low rumbling growl warning of bad things to come.

"It's okay, Neva. You remember Shen. He hired you."

Neva wasn't impressed. Her growl grew louder.

Shen wisely backed out into the hall.

Kelly frowned. "I don't know why you upset her."

He held up his hands. "Hey, it's okay. I'm a shape-shifter. Her animal senses my other form. No biggie."

Shen smiled. About six feet tall with dark hair and eyes, his quick grin might've fooled her into thinking he was friendly and uncomplicated. But that was before. Now she knew that no one who worked for Fin was uncomplicated and a smile could hide any number of agendas.

"Shape-shifter? So what's your other form?" Behind Kelly, Neva's growling died away.

Shen glanced at his watch. "I'd love to hang and talk, but I need to get you down to the office so I can update some of your employment info before you run off for the night."

"Sure." She frowned. "What about Neva?"

"Ty will be back in a few minutes. She'll be okay alone until then."

Kelly glanced at Neva. "Do you mind staying by yourself for a short time?"

Neva didn't go all wild-eyed on her. Instead, the wolf jumped back onto the bed and spread out. Kelly took that as an *I'm cool with being alone.*

Stepping out into the hallway, Kelly pulled the door closed and followed Shen to his office. Grabbing a chair on the other side of his desk, she waited for him to leave the doorway and sit down.

Mesmerized, she stared out the floor-to-ceiling windows behind his desk. Night was falling, and the Houston skyline was lighting up. "Wow, Fin sure likes windows. Can't say that I blame him. This view is spectacular. I think I get it. He came from an environment where he was never enclosed, so I guess claustrophobia could be a problem when he's in a building."

"Very insightful, Kelly." Fin's voice was blandly approving.

Uh-oh. Kelly turned her head and watched Fin walk toward the desk. Shen had skipped out on her. This could not be good.

Fin lowered himself to Shen's chair behind the desk and smiled at her.

If Helen of Troy's face launched a thousand ships, then Fin's smile was good for the launch of at least a million rockets. And yet Kelly sensed no emotion behind his expression, nothing to connect her to the man.

His silver hair gleamed, and against the backdrop of the sparkling Houston lights, he looked like some cold, beautiful Christmas tree.

Fin's bark of laughter was the first really sincere reaction she'd felt from him.

"A Christmas tree? That has to be a first. Now you've put me in a good mood for our meeting."

He really was a gorgeous man. But he also made her mad as hell. "Stay out of my mind."

"How can I do that when you're so entertaining?" He held up his hand to forestall her tirade. "Okay, I'll try."

"Why the bait and switch?"

"I knew if Ty showed up while I was trying to drag you off to my lair, he'd insist on coming too." Fin's expression turned thoughtful. "He's getting all protective with you. I don't know if that's a good thing. He doesn't need any distractions."

Her stomach dropped about four floors at the thought that Fin might assign her to another one of the Eleven. And immediately after that, she had an oh-no moment. She cared too much.

Three nights did not a relationship make. Sure, she had impulse issues at times, but she'd never made love with a man after knowing him only three nights. And she'd certainly never done it naked on a balcony. The truth? She'd do it hanging upside down from a tree limb if it kept her close to Ty. A dangerous admission. Dangerous to her emotions. He'd be moving on soon. Dangerous to her health. Caring would make her more likely to follow him into scary situations.

"I have a favor to ask," Fin said.

Favor? That snapped Kelly back into the moment. "What?"

"I'd like to record your brain waves."

Okay, that was officially weird.

Chapter Eleven

"*Brain waves?* Mine?"

"Hear me out."

"I wouldn't miss it."

Fin leaned back and idly tapped his finger on the arm of his chair. "I can see the distant future. I see the problems, the potential solutions, but not the outcomes. Two out of three is a start, though."

"How distant?" Three nights ago she would've dismissed what Fin was saying as idiocy. She knew better now.

"Sixty-five million years." He was staring at her, but his eyes had that unfocused look that meant his thoughts were elsewhere. "I saw that Zero and his crew would return to Earth and try to raise an army of nonhumans so they could wipe out the human race in 2012. I saw what measures could stop them." He shrugged. "I didn't see if anything worked."

"Is that how you were able to save the Eleven from the extinction event?"

"Yes." He watched her with those strange silver eyes.

"And my brain waves have something to do with your master plan?"

He grinned. "Not *my* master plan. This is more like the universe's master plan. Not to fall back on a cliché, but it's bigger than both of us."

"Right." Kelly's thoughts were in turmoil. Her first

instinct was to walk, because there was something insanely creepy about Fin targeting her millions of years in the past.

"You want to run from me." Fin captured her gaze and held it. "But you won't be able to run from what's coming. No one will. Not you, not your family."

She hated him. Because he was right. Because he didn't hesitate to bludgeon her with the truth. Because there wasn't one speck of warmth in him. He didn't care about her or her family, just his fight against the Lords of Time or whatever they wanted to be called.

She forced her gaze away from him and focused instead on the Houston skyline behind him. "You know, this is one time I hate the messenger more than the message. What do you love, Fin? What do you have a passion for other than this battle?"

"Nothing. Love is a weakness. I can't afford to have weaknesses. Now can we get back to the brain waves?" His voice was cold, flat.

"Sure. Explain." She fought down her anger. Anger would bounce right off that hard shell he called a heart. Of course, just because he had a human body didn't mean he had the emotions to go with it. Ty *felt* human. Fin was alien.

"I believe in synchronicity. I believe that we were meant to rise at the same time as Zero and his crew. And I believe it's our affinity for numbers that makes us the right choice to save humanity. There are no coincidences in the universe."

"And what does that have to do with brain waves?"

"I saw *you*, Kelly, and everything you were. I saw you playing a melody on your flute. No, I didn't hear it. But I knew it wasn't composed by you or given to you by someone else.

It was a *part* of you. And I saw the possibility that you would defeat Nine. Unfortunately, that's all I saw."

"Not too helpful." He'd targeted her from the beginning. Shen's story about talking to someone who said she might be interested in a job had been a lie. The outrageous salary was bait, and she'd bitten.

"But I finally figured it out. I read an article about people who're using electroencephalograms to record their brain activity and then having it translated into music. They think listening to their own brain music helps with anxiety and insomnia."

"Or with kicking galactic goons out of Houston." Kelly didn't bother asking what this had to do with numbers. She understood the relationship between numbers and music. But there was something terrifying about knowing that the fate of humanity might rest on her and her flute. *Eat your heart out, Pied Piper.* "Are you sure this is the solution?"

Fin hesitated.

"You're not."

He swiveled his chair around to stare into the night. "I don't know what else it could be. But, no, we won't know if that's the answer until you play the tune for Nine."

"So it's possible that I could play my brain music and then Nine would do lots of giggling right before he splattered said brain all over some wall."

"Hypothetically. Although, since he can't touch you directly, one of his helpers would do the splattering."

The ball was in her court. "Uh, maybe we could make a CD of my brain music and just mail it to him."

Fin shook his head. "I *saw* you playing the tune."

She could say no. She *should* say no. She said yes. "Okay, where do I get an EEG? And before you begin to celebrate, this isn't a promise that I'll play my flute in the face of certain death. I have strong survival instincts. I reserve the right to run like hell if the odds are wrong."

He spun his chair to face her. "Understood. I have all the equipment here. It'll take five minutes to record your brain activity, and then you'll be free. I'll get the tune to you as soon as the lab finishes up. Memorize it, and then make sure you don't go anywhere without your flute."

She stood, and Fin stood with her. "I have a question now that we're alone. Why haven't you told your men that they were something else before they were dinosaurs? It's obvious to me, and God knows I'm not the perceptive type. Why isn't it obvious to them? Why don't they ask questions about their past?"

He stopped and stared at her. Kelly felt his stare as a sudden stabbing pain that threatened to shatter her skull. Gasping, she pushed her palms against the sides of her head to hold it together.

"What's your name?"

She opened her mouth . . . and nothing came out. Her name? Her freaking *name*. Her mind raced in panicked circles, searching for the word. Gone. She didn't know her own name.

Fin looked away, and her name was back. *Kelly.* She said it over and over in her head to make sure it was really there.

"Sometimes forgetting is kinder than remembering." His voice grew harder, colder. "Imagine the worst nightmare you could possibly create, magnify it a hundred times, and it still wouldn't come close to the horror they've forgotten."

"You've wiped their memories." The enormity of what he'd done to his own men sickened her. And then it made her mad. "Where the hell do you get off playing God? Why are you the only one with a right to remember?"

Fin looked back at her, his expression shutting her and

everyone else out of his world. "There are just so many memories anyone can handle. How would the memory of something unspeakably evil help their concentration now when they need it most?"

"That's not the point."

"That's exactly the point." He turned toward the door again. "Get this straight, Kelly. We're going to defeat Zero and his nine buddies one damn number at a time. And I won't let anyone or anything distract my men from that goal."

"And if I decide to tell Ty?"

"Do we have to see if you can remember your name again?"

Fin wasn't subtle about his threats. She'd back off and re-group. Then when she had time to think, she'd decide what to do. The part of her brain in charge of self-preservation thought she should keep her big mouth shut, that this was an internal affair and none of her business. Maybe she'd listen to her brain on this one.

"There are other distractions beside the past. What are you going to do if one of your men falls in love with a hu-man?" Now where'd that question come from?

His harsh laugh managed to sound ominous. "No chance of that. Once she knew what was involved, no woman alive would be willing to claim one of our souls for her own."

Well, that sounded scary but intriguing. She joined him at the door. "So what does Fin stand for? I can't think of any carnivores beginning with those letters."

"Infinity." He led her toward another room at the end of the hallway.

"I should've thought of that. It goes with your number obsession. And since you chose the names, you got to call yourself anything you wanted. But what kind of dinosaur *were* you?"

Fin paused in front of the closed door. He closed his eyes for a moment. "How does Ty stand all your questions?"

She was getting to him. Good. "It's part of my charm."

He pushed the door open, then turned to face her. "I was huge and horrifying, and I don't have a name because there were only two of us. Scientists haven't found our fossil remains." Fin waved her into the room, where a woman in a white coat waited, and then he escaped.

Coward. While the EEG was recording her brain activity, she wondered about the other one like Fin. A mate? Interesting.

Ty was about ready to go looking for Kelly when she finally returned. Instead of dropping onto the couch, she walked over to the wall of windows and stared out.

"It's amazing. Houston looks just like it always did, but knowing what's happening below the surface makes it a place I don't recognize anymore." She sighed and turned to stare at him. "Do you think it'll ever go back to the way it was?"

She'd caught him by surprise. "When Nine is gone." *When I'm gone.*

Without answering, she got a bottle of water from the wet bar's small fridge and sat on the couch. "I was with Fin. He wanted to record my brain waves so he could have them made into music." Neva wandered over, and Kelly absently scratched behind her ears.

"Music?" Why hadn't Fin told him about this? Once again, he got the feeling there were lots of things Fin didn't tell any of them. And that bothered him. *Why? It never bothered you before.* He shook his head to clear the fog that seemed to roll in whenever he tried to think about Fin.

"Yeah. He said he can see into the distant future. One of the things he saw was the possibility that I'd defeat Nine by playing my flute. The weird part? He thinks the melody will come from my brain waves."

Ty knew he was glowering, but he couldn't help it. "Forget it. You'll never get close enough to Nine for him to hear you playing your flute. I'll make sure of that."

Kelly smiled at him, and he could almost hear cracking sounds as something hard and brittle inside him developed a few more fissures. Dangerous stuff. He'd have to make sure he didn't get to like that smile too much, because she'd be gone as soon as they took care of Nine.

"I guess Fin knew how you'd react, because he sent Shen to drag me off to his office before you got back."

He'd talk to Fin later. Not now, because even Ty's short meeting with him had triggered all kinds of aggressive impulses. Like the urge to plant his fist in Fin's face for sneaking around behind his back to get to Kelly. "Fin insists we take plenty of help with us tonight. Neva goes, and we have to pick up Q. Someone dropped him off at his apartment last night, but he still doesn't have a driver. And another one of the Eleven is going with us, too. His name is Spin."

"Spin? This won't work. The alpha said I could only bring one friend with me."

Ty nodded. "I'll be with you. Neva stays in the car until we're sure she's welcome. Q and Spin will be in the wind. Fin isn't a trusting kind of guy."

"What if the pack leader senses them?" She shuddered. "I'm tired of being afraid. I need some mental downtime between werewolf wars."

He dropped onto the couch beside her and tilted her face up until she met his gaze. "I'll protect you. Do you believe me?"

"Yes." No hesitation.

Ty's relief was way out of proportion to her answer. But his protection was all he had to offer. No money. No shared interests. Hell, he couldn't even talk to her about movies or TV shows. He was all about brute strength and a past she couldn't relate to. *And why are you getting so intense about this anyway?*

He glanced at his watch. "Oh, and we got an invitation while I was talking to Fin. Jude owns a club in the Montrose area, Eternal Pleasure. He wants us to stop by tonight about ten. Maybe he has information we can use. I thought we could hit the club first, then get something to eat before meeting your pack leader."

"Eternal Pleasure?" Kelly looked doubtful. "I'm not dressed for a place with that kind of name. I'll change when we stop at the apartment."

He dug Neva's rope leash out from between the couch's cushions and dropped it over the werewolf's head. "Sorry. Have to keep up pretenses."

They left the room with a sulky Neva and headed down the stairs. A man stood by the front door. Spin. The guy with the all-black outfit and long blond hair. Ty felt the familiar need for violence, but not quite as urgently as usual. Maybe Kelly was having a calming effect on him after all.

When they reached the door, he stuck out his hand. "Ty."

The man smiled and shook his hand even as his gaze slid to Kelly. "Spin."

They both tightened their grips. Spin grimaced but refused to back down. Ty felt like the bones in his hand were being crushed. He bore down harder.

"Oh, for crying out loud." Kelly sounded disgusted. "Call it a draw, guys, and get over it."

Ty grunted and dropped his hand at the same time Spin did. He controlled the need to flex his fingers. After considering his chances of getting away without introducing her, he came down on the side of a grumpy intro. "This is Kelly." He glanced down at the werewolf. "And this is Neva."

"Hi, Spin." Kelly offered her hand, and Spin took it in both of his. "What's Spin short for?"

She shot Ty a warning glance that stopped his growl before it reached the top of his throat.

"Spinosaurus." He slid his gaze to Ty, and his grin widened. "Big meat eater like Ty, but with a lot more style and charm. T. rexes were long on attitude but short on personality."

"I bet I could tear your head off with lots of style and charm." Ty glared pointedly at where Spin still held Kelly's hand.

The other man maintained his grip a few seconds longer just to establish that he wasn't afraid of Ty, then stepped back. "So what're we doing tonight?"

Ty carefully avoided Kelly's gaze. She'd be pissed that he'd challenged Spin. Once again, their worlds clashed. In his time, Spin would've expected Ty to warn him off his mate. *You're not her mate, and she'll hate that you went all possessive on her. Again.* He clenched his fists. Would he ever adapt to this era?

Kelly answered for him. "We're stopping by our apartment to pick up Q, and then we're hitting Jude's club to see what he has for us. Finally, we're meeting the alpha of a werewolf pack. Maybe he can help Neva."

Spin took the time to meet Neva's gaze. "Sorry I ignored

you. Must be tough to go through the change alone. Hope this guy can help you."

Ty was impressed. Spin granted Neva human dignity instead of treating her like an oversized dog. Maybe the Spinosaurus did have more style and charm than a T. rex.

He thought about that once they were on their way back to the apartment. Ty again had the seat next to Kelly. A brief glaring match with Spin had warned Mr. Style and Charm not to try to claim it.

Winning those kinds of minor skirmishes wasn't enough, though. Ty understood that claiming Kelly's respect would be a lot tougher than claiming the seat. Oh, she trusted him to protect her, and she'd enjoyed his body last night. But he'd have to step away from his primal past and into her civilized present for respect to grow. And, yeah, he was admitting it. He wanted some of those things that brute force couldn't get him. He'd start by trying to sit on his aggressive instincts.

As Kelly pulled into the apartment parking lot, she glanced at all of them. "Stay here. I won't be long. I'll just make a quick change and then get Q."

"Why change? You look great." Ty couldn't conceive of her ever not looking great.

Kelly smiled her appreciation. "It's a girl thing. We're hitting a club. I want to dazzle."

Ty wasn't sure he liked the idea of her dazzling anyone except him. But he made a real effort to beat down his jealousy.

Spin put in his two cents. "Hey, I'm all for dazzling, but remember we're meeting an alpha wolf. Don't want to stir up the old savage heart."

Kelly tried to keep from laughing. "Uh, guys, look in a mirror. I think you have the savage-heart market cornered." She climbed from the SUV before either of them could answer her. It felt good to get in the last word for a change.

She guessed there was just so much fear a person could absorb, because she wasn't thinking about the wolves. Instead, Kelly was actually looking forward to the club visit. It'd be a brief chance to act normal again. *Act* was the operative word, because normal wasn't in her present vocabulary.

After letting Q know they'd arrived, she stopped in her apartment long enough to make a quick change. Not much to choose from, but she slipped into some silky black pants and a sexy purple top with a deep vee plunge that teased and taunted. Kelly didn't for a minute try to fool herself about where she was aiming that teasing. She added some dangly earrings and a pair of shoes with heels way too high for running. Maybe no running would take place tonight. A girl could hope.

Satisfied, she refreshed her lip color, swept a little shadow across her eyelids, grabbed a jacket to replace the bloody one still hanging back in the condo, and headed down to join the others.

A woman would always feel like a woman around the Eleven. As Kelly settled into the driver's seat, she could sense an explosive blend of testosterone and sexual energy bouncing off every surface.

She hadn't put on her coat, and she handed it to Ty to hold. Okay, she'd purposely left it off to impress. So sue her. As she pulled out of the parking lot, she chanced a quick glance at Ty.

He met her gaze, and something so sensual gleamed in his eyes that she wanted to park the car and climb all over him. She took a deep breath and looked away. Wow. Just wow.

She thought about him all the way to Montrose and Eternal Pleasure. It took more time to find the club than she'd expected. That was because it was tucked into the top floor of a small two-story building. An antique shop took up the first floor. And the sign with the club's name was so tiny, Kelly missed the place the first few times she drove past.

Jude had chosen a great spot for his club, though. The Montrose area had a unique flavor with its eclectic mix of boutiques, restaurants, and small galleries. But the area's residents had no idea exactly how unique their neighborhood really was.

She got lucky. Someone pulled out of a parking spot right in front of the club.

Ty climbed out and looked around. He turned to Spin. "Maybe you should take Neva for a walk. Keep your eyes open for anything suspicious while you're at it."

Kelly glanced at the werewolf. "It's funny, but ever since she calmed down, Neva hasn't acted like I'd expect a werewolf to act. No violent rages, no bloodlust. What's with that?" Kelly spoke to Neva. "Too bad you can't talk."

Neva looked frustrated that she couldn't express herself.

Spin opened the door so Neva could jump out, then slipped on her makeshift leash. "This is so cool. I'll feel like the biggest badass on the block walking a werewolf." He paused to think about that. "Oh, right, I'm already the biggest badass." He stared at Ty and Q, daring them to claim the badass crown.

Ty ignored Spin as he headed toward the outside stairs that led up to the club. Kelly followed him, and Q brought up the rear. She was breathing hard by the time she reached the second floor, but it wasn't because of exertion. Talk about an adrenaline rush. She was with two hot and dangerous men and about to meet with the city's head vampire. An excitement high like this could trigger a nosebleed.

Kelly heard the music before Ty opened the door. A woman was singing something slow and so erotic it took her breath away. Images pushed and shoved to be the first to trail across her memory. A naked Ty looking out the window, his smooth back tapering down to the most perfect ass she'd ever seen. Ty pressing her to the balcony wall, his cock hard against her stomach, his eyes . . . She shook her head. Later. She'd indulge her memories when she had the time to do it right.

As Ty pulled open the door, Kelly felt Q tense behind her. Some of her euphoria faded. Danger came with this kind of excitement. Could you become addicted to the constant pulse-pounding uncertainty of what would happen in the next few minutes? Would life seem boring once she settled back into her normal routine?

Pushing that thought aside, along with all its potential for emotional disaster, she stepped into Eternal Pleasure and its low throb of sensual music.

Sensory impressions swirled around her—shadowed interior, dim atmospheric lighting, rich fabrics, expensive scents, and a sense of silent watchers just out of sight. The quiet murmur of conversation died as the three of them stood just inside the door.

Kelly shivered. This didn't feel like a normal club. No loud music, no noisy drunks, just the feel of all those eyes. Oh boy.

But there was sex. Wow, was there sex. The female singer stood on a small stage and crooned about the pleasure a man brought to a woman. With dark hair that tumbled over her bare shoulders and down her back, large dark eyes that almost glowed, and a mouth that even Kelly recognized as a dangerous weapon, she put the "c" in carnal. Her body was all lush curves. Kelly knew this for sure because only a few strategic spots were covered. Kelly felt her own sex appeal oozing out of her even as she stared.

From a woman's point of view, though, the singer wasn't the main attraction. Three men with hard, muscled bodies and gorgeous faces wound themselves around the woman, demonstrating for those unable to visualize the creative ways to bring a woman to orgasm. Wearing only G-strings, they looked really . . . persuasive.

Kelly stole a quick glance at Ty and Q. Yep, they were totally into all that sexual excess. As her gaze slid back to what the men were doing, she noticed the piano player and the bar almost hidden behind the stage.

And then Jude was there. He materialized out of the shadows, his appearance just as impressive as the first time she'd seen him. Tonight he was in pirate mode—black pants, high boots, billowing white shirt open to his navel, dark hair pulled back and fastened at the base of his neck, and gold earrings. No eye patch.

"Does the sensuality shock you?" His smile was merely a sly lifting of his sexy lips.

"Nope." Kelly had no compunction about lying.

Ty dragged his gaze from the singer. "I like it."

She frowned. Of course he liked it—he was male. But jealousy was an insidious thing. Not admirable, but almost impossible to dislodge.

Ty nodded toward Q. "I don't think you were ever officially introduced to Q."

Q never took his attention from the singer. "Jude."

"And this is Kelly."

She smiled her approval at Ty. He hadn't snarled at

Jude when he introduced her. Tough for him. Of course, she still felt a shimmer of terror. She was probably reacting to the grumbling of his inner beast. Or maybe this time she was reacting to the strange vibes she was getting from Jude's club.

The vampire's gaze glided over her, pausing where her neckline plunged. He took the plunge with her and didn't come up for air until Ty shifted closer.

"I remember. You had a strong opinion about my riding skills." Jude's smile widened.

"She had *no* opinion about your riding skills." Ty had evidently reached the limit of his tolerance for sexual banter.

"Uh, I'm here, and I get to answer questions directed at me." Kelly tried to hold on to her temper, tried to remember where Ty had come from and why he acted the way he did. She bit her lip to keep from making any more snarky comments.

Then she glanced into his eyes. They were dark with frustration. He exhaled and ran his fingers through his hair. Kelly clenched her hands into fists to keep from reaching up to touch the tangled strands.

"I keep forgetting. Instincts are out, control is in. I can't be what I was before. I guess the rules just aren't sinking in yet." He met her gaze. "But I'm trying."

Wait for it.

"For you."

Yes. His last two words had been a low murmur, but she'd heard them. He'd admitted he was trying to change for *her.* That was worth celebrating. "Why don't we sit down so everyone can stop staring?"

Jude nodded and led them to a table in a darkened corner. "Can I get you something to drink?"

Q and Ty asked for water. Good. The thought of going to war with two drunken dinosaurs was pretty scary. "I'd love a Diet Coke."

While Jude went to get their drinks, Ty slowly scanned the room. Then he stared at Q. "You think?"

Q nodded.

She was left out of their communication. "What?"

"Everyone in this place is a vampire." His tone didn't exactly say, *Run for your life,* but it definitely hinted they might be wise to cover their necks.

Jude returned with the drinks. "I wondered how long it'd be until you realized this was a vampire club." He sounded amused.

"You heard that?" Kelly calculated how far away from the table Jude had been when Ty spoke. Nope, he shouldn't have been able to hear what Ty said.

"We have enhanced senses." Jude's expression said it was a miracle that humanity was still around with such poor survival skills.

After just a few days among nonhumans, she was beginning to think he was right. "So no humans come in here?" She scoped out the vampires at the nearest table. A woman waved at her. Now where . . . Then she remembered. One of the bodyguards who had come with Jude when he visited Fin's condo.

Jude shrugged. "They wander in now and then."

Q snorted. "Question is, do they wander back out again?"

"Always." Jude sat down between Ty and Q. He pointed at the menus on the table. "They can buy drinks and food. Everyone around them may look a little hungry, but they leave none the wiser."

Kelly reached for a menu. "We were going to eat before we went on to our next meeting anyway. I think I'll order now." She remembered Spin and Neva. "And I'll need two to-go meals when we leave."

Q and Ty looked wary. Kelly took a leap of faith that Jude wouldn't serve them human hearts sautéed in blood. "I'll take the lamb and . . ." Someone stop her. Too late. "Garlic mashed potatoes."

Jude's laughter was deep and sexy. "I love garlic. And since we're shattering beloved stereotypes, crosses and holy water don't bother me either. Sunlight's a problem, though."

Taking their cue from her, Q and Ty ordered the same thing.

While Jude called someone over to take the order, Kelly looked around the room again. A few vampires had left their tables to dance in front of the stage. They all moved with the same sinuous rhythm that screamed, *We are sexy*.

Her gaze drifted back to the vampires at the tables. They looked so normal, drinking and talking. *Drinking*. "What're they drinking?"

"Not blood drained from the little old lady who runs the store downstairs." He leaned back in his seat and studied her. "Although the temptation is always there."

Kelly felt Ty tense beside her. "I wouldn't be sitting here if I thought you couldn't control temptation."

Jude nodded. "We run our own blood banks. Volunteers are paid well."

"You never drink from the source?" Q sounded disbelieving.

The vampire smiled at Q, a slow taunting expression that exposed impressive fangs. "Once in a while we allow ourselves a treat. But the donor is always willing, and we never take enough to kill." He leaned toward Q. "Did you enjoy killing all those wolves the other night? Had lots of fun, didn't you?"

Q couldn't quite meet his gaze.

Jude leaned back, satisfied. "Except for Kelly, we're all predators. But my people have suppressed their hunting instincts for the survival of the species. Vampires don't reproduce often, so humans outnumber us ten thousand to one. Not good odds, even if you have strength and ferocity on your side."

Kelly thought Jude was sounding a little unfriendly. "In other words, if you weren't outnumbered, you'd be slaughtering humans?" Talk about being outnumbered . . . Hmm. She gauged how far they'd have to run to escape the roomful of vampires.

"Not in this time. Life is good in the here and now. We don't need to kill to survive. And if blood from a blood bank isn't as exciting as the hunt—" he shrugged—"we deal."

The waiter arrived with their meals, and they put the conversation on hold for a while. Surprised, Kelly realized the lamb was fantastic. Or maybe it was just that she was starved.

While she ate, she watched the men on the stage. After a few minutes her imagination replaced them with Ty's image. The fantasy felt way too good. So she turned to Jude. "You're a pirate tonight."

"Tonight's the three hundred eleventh anniversary of my turning. I lived and died a pirate."

While she was trying to wrap her mind around his age, Ty got down to business. "You wanted to talk to us."

"My people are turning rogue or getting killed in record numbers. I've checked in other parts of the country, and they report the same thing. When I talked to Fin, I didn't know the full scope of the problem. Now I do."

Ty nodded.

"Last night I found a friend I'd known for two hundred years dead in his home. His body was on the bed, his head under it. I tracked down his killer. He was a Houston vampire who'd disappeared off the radar a few months ago." His face became all harsh lines and angles. "Before he died, the killer confessed to working for a Mr. Wyatt in exchange for being granted his own hunting territory." Jude's lips peeled back in a snarl. "Hunting license revoked."

"Hunting territory?" Kelly put down her fork. Somehow she knew this wouldn't be an appetizing disclosure.

"This Wyatt guy gave him a small area in Houston where he could kill and feed from humans. He said Wyatt guaranteed his protection as long as he stayed in his own territory. In exchange, he murdered for Wyatt."

Kelly stared down at her lamb. Ugh. After listening to Jude, she was feeling seriously lamblike herself. Couldn't eat a relative.

Q wasn't having that problem. He only paused in his eating long enough to throw a question at Jude. "What's your plan?"

"You got lucky when you found that vampire at the club. It won't happen again. They've been warned. You won't find any of the ones you're looking for at clubs where humans go."

"Makes sense." Ty's appetite wasn't suffering either.

"You don't know the secret clubs in the city that cater to nonhumans. I do."

"And?"

Kelly didn't think she'd ever seen anyone enjoy a meal as much as Ty was enjoying his.

"I thought I could handle this by myself, but it's too big

for me. Especially when I don't know which of my people I can trust."

She knew what was coming.

"I want to hunt with you." Jude's smile was beautiful and totally deadly.

Chapter Twelve

"Is this it?" If not, Ty decided, he'd get out of the SUV and walk the rest of the way. He wasn't used to sitting in small enclosed spaces. And he was tired of the lamb smell from the meals Spin and Neva had eaten in the car. Besides, being close to other predators ramped up his aggression. It wasn't uncontrollable, but he had to work at keeping it to a low growl.

"Yep. There's the Museum of Natural Science on the other side of Hermann Circle Drive. And this is Hermann Park." She pulled into a parking space and stopped. "If it wasn't close to midnight we could visit the museum and you could say hi to the skeletons of your peers."

Just what he needed. A bunch of skeletons to remind him of what a dinosaur he really was. Dinosaur as in out of date and obsolete. He'd spent most of the time they'd been at Eternal Pleasure concentrating on his food so his other hunger wouldn't embarrass all of them. Kelly's silky pants and sexy top had made him want to drag her onto the floor and . . .

She looked over at him, eyes wide and startled.

Damn, he was broadcasting again. With a grunt of disgust, he climbed from the SUV, stretched, and tried to focus on the wolf they'd be meeting.

Kelly glanced back at Neva. "Stay here and keep your head down. No one will be able to see you in the dark. If this guy's willing to help, we'll come get you."

Neva gave a wolfy sigh and put her head on her paws. She filled most of the back of the SUV.

Ty scanned the area. No other cars. "Looks like we got here first."

Q joined him. He lifted his head and sniffed. "Yeah, we're alone."

"So we just hang in the woods in case you need some muscle?" Spin looked like he was hoping for an all-out werewolf attack.

Ty sympathized. None of them was used to sitting around. Sometimes he thought if he didn't get more action, he'd explode. "You got it. Probably just showing yourself will work. Fin's still pissed about what happened in Memorial Park."

He watched Kelly get out of the SUV. Those shoes didn't look like they'd take her far.

She closed the door. "I'm not locking it. Cars with werewolves inside rarely get stolen."

Ty grinned before turning to the two men. "We got here early and lucked out. No one else has arrived. Get into the woods and just stay close enough to hear what's going on."

With their enhanced hearing, Q and Spin wouldn't have to risk discovery by getting too close. And they were hunters. They knew enough to stay downwind of the pack leader. Ty didn't have a clue whether werewolves retained their keen sense of smell when they were in human form. He hoped not.

Ty watched the men fade into the darkness. Then he turned to Kelly. "Let's stand a short distance away from the SUV. When whoever is coming shows up, we don't want them even thinking about looking inside."

She nodded, and they walked away from the car in

silence. Once they stopped, the silence continued. The memory of last night filled Ty with a ton of conflict. He wanted to talk about it, but he wasn't sure what Kelly's expectations were. Maybe going into graphic detail about how she'd blown him away would make her uncomfortable. Fin had dumped a lifetime of knowledge into his head, but he'd missed the finer points of human emotions. Probably because emotions weren't important to Fin.

"Jude gave his club an interesting name. Eternal Pleasure. What a great concept." Kelly didn't look at him as she spoke.

"Yeah. Great concept." Eternal sex with Kelly. He couldn't even begin to . . . Ty stopped. No, last night hadn't just been about having sex, at least not the version he was used to.

"What're you thinking?"

Ty wished she hadn't asked that question. "I was thinking that last night was the first time I'd made love. Yeah, I mated back then, but it was one dimensional. A physical release. The end. But that was okay, because my animal mind was one dimensional too. Tired—rest. Hungry—kill. Last night had layers. All my senses got into it. And I never had that kind of . . . reaction before." Must be something in his male DNA that wouldn't let him say the word "emotional" out loud.

She looked puzzled. "Well, yeah, me too. But you were bound to have an intense experience. I mean, sixty-five million years is a long time."

Should he mention that time wasn't a factor in a T. rex's mating urge? A minute or a month apart, his enjoyment of sex was always the same. But last night had been different.

He never got a chance to say anything because a pickup pulled into the parking lot and stopped next to them. A man got out. Looked pretty ordinary to Ty.

The guy stopped in front of Kelly. "I still don't know your name, but I'm Travis."

"Kelly. And this is Ty."

Travis smiled, but his eyes looked wary. "I'll take you to the meeting place." He turned and started walking toward the woods.

"Where's your leader?" Ty didn't like surprises.

Travis glanced back. "He'll be along in a few minutes. He's not too trusting. Wants to make sure you followed the rules."

Ty understood that. He'd take the same precaution. His gaze slid to Travis's hand. The one he had shoved into his jacket pocket. "Got something in your pocket you want to keep your fingers on?"

"Panic button. Anything goes wrong and I press it."

"And then?" Ty figured there might be a gun in one of those pockets too. He glanced at Kelly. Did she have Q's gun in the coat she'd slipped on? He had to start thinking like a human. Bringing a weapon had never occurred to him. He *was* a weapon.

Travis shrugged. "Help comes."

"Smart idea. So you're like the canary in the coal mine. If you go down, your leader knows there's danger."

"Yeah. Something like that." Travis didn't look too happy about Ty's comparison.

Travis didn't know that *he* had a panic button too. It was in his head and it was called Fin. Ty hated keeping his mental link open, but he understood why Fin had demanded he do it. If things ever got out of hand—read Memorial Park—Fin could channel some of his power to Ty. And Fin didn't give a damn that he was trampling all over Ty's pride by hinting that there might be a situation he couldn't handle by himself.

Travis turned away and continued walking.

Kelly elbowed him in the ribs. "Did you have to antagonize him?" Her voice was a whispered hiss.

"Yes. People say things when they get mad. Things they wouldn't say if they were thinking straight."

She stared at him as though she'd discovered something new about him. Not something good either. "You approach every stranger you meet as a potential enemy, not a friend."

"It's kept me alive. With what's happening in Houston, you'd be smart to cultivate a healthy dose of suspicion too."

Kelly looked troubled. "I hope I never get that cynical."

Ouch. More proof that they came from different worlds. She took everyone at face value. He never would. A good example was this Travis guy. She'd given him a chance to talk to her back in Memorial Park. Ty would've killed him before he got his mouth open.

They fell silent as they followed the werewolf. This wasn't real woods, just a stand of trees. Travis stopped at the first clear space they reached.

Then they waited.

Ty sensed his coming. And he wasn't alone. Ty hadn't expected him to be. Wolves were pack animals. Their leader wouldn't hold an important meeting without the pack. Ty didn't see any reason to object. He hadn't come alone either.

A man strode from the shadows a few moments later. Dressed in worn jeans and a sleeveless black T-shirt, he was big, muscular, and walked with the confidence all predators had. His tangled mane of dark hair lifted in the light breeze.

He stopped in front of them. Travis backed away, giving his leader lots of room.

Ty did a quick scan for obvious weapons and found none. The man met his gaze. "Macario. And you are?"

"Ty." He met Macario's stare and held it.

Kelly coughed. "When you guys are finished with your stare down, maybe we can get on with things? And aren't you cold with just that T-shirt?"

The pack leader shifted his attention to Kelly and simultaneously slid into a different persona. "Werewolf blood runs hot." His voice was a husky murmur, suggesting things that no one could mistake. "Travis said you were beautiful."

Ty's inner beast woke up and paid attention.

"I've been looking forward to meeting the woman who wasn't afraid to battle the red wolves." Macario leaned closer to Kelly.

Ty's inner beast contemplated the fun of tearing this guy's head off.

"I love a woman who's willing to fight beside her mate. Tell me your name."

"Kelly." She looked impressed. At least she didn't deny Ty mate status in front of Macario.

"Look, you called Kelly, so I assume you had a reason." Ty tried to keep the jealousy out of his voice.

Macario looked at him then, all business. "Actually, Kelly told Travis to contact her. But after hearing what you did to the red wolves, I wanted to meet you personally. What are you?"

Now that the pack leader's attention was off of Kelly, Ty relaxed. "We're otherkin."

"I've met your kind. But none of them could manifest their souls in a physical way, and their souls weren't dinosaurs."

Ty grinned. "We're different."

"Different enough to wipe out the red wolves. No big loss there. What brought you to Houston?"

Ty kept it short. And when he was finished, the other man didn't speak for a moment.

Finally Macario exhaled deeply and nodded. "Three of my pack didn't return last night. We can't find them. Two of them left mates behind. There's no way they'd walk away from their families. And a week ago we found Sara dead. She'd been murdered. If this immortal's responsible for their deaths, I'll help you get rid of him."

"We have something else to talk about." Kelly looked a little nervous. "The red wolves bit one of our friends at Memorial Park. She was unconscious for a while, but when she woke up, she changed. She's still in wolf form. How can she take human form again?"

"Where is she?"

Kelly glanced at Ty. He nodded.

"In our SUV."

"Go get her."

Ty listened to the small rustles that meant the pack was moving closer. "Will your pack let us through?"

Macario grinned. "Your senses are as good as ours."

Better. Because you haven't sensed Q or Spin yet.

"Pack?" Kelly looked startled.

"They're all around us. Let's get Neva." He turned away from Macario and guided Kelly back toward the car, breathing more easily once he sensed they'd cleared the waiting pack.

Kelly's gaze darted left and right. "Are they in wolf form?"

"Yeah." The parking lot was still empty except for Travis's truck and their SUV. That meant the rest of the pack had parked elsewhere and walked in. He watched

Kelly let Neva out. "Okay, Neva, we'll see what this guy can do for you. His name is Macario."

All the way back to the clearing, Kelly imagined malevolent yellow eyes peering at her from the darkness. She was more nervous than afraid. After all, how scared could you be with a werewolf on one side and a T. rex on the other?

Kelly stepped into the clearing and froze. The pack stood facing her, at least twenty gray wolves. And standing in front of them was the biggest of them all, a massive black wolf. His yellow eyes were fixed on Neva.

Kelly put a steadying hand on Neva's back. "Okay, work your charm, do your thing, and know we're here for you."

Neva stepped away from them, but Kelly could feel her fear. Somehow, you just didn't think of a werewolf being afraid of anything. But then, Neva hadn't shown any real aggression since her first spurt of panic. Showed what Kelly knew about werewolves.

The black wolf circled Neva, sniffing and studying her. Neva had enough sense to stand still and look unconcerned.

Finally, the black wolf moved away and turned his back to them. Then he changed. It was so fast that the twisting and lengthening of bones and replacing of fur with skin were only a blur. Kelly clapped a hand over her mouth to stifle her amazed gasp.

As Macario walked to where he'd left his clothes, Neva's gaze followed him. And if her interest seemed a little too intense, hey, Kelly understood. That was one fine male body.

This time when the terror hit Kelly, she understood. She turned to Ty. "What?"

Ty's eyes were dark with emotion. "I want to tear him apart."

"Why? Is this a predator thing?"

"This is a jealousy thing." His voice was almost a snarl.

Startled, Kelly glanced at Neva.

"Over Neva?"

"Over *you*." He took a deep breath and looked away. "Yeah, I know. Stupid. But when I saw you staring at his body like that, my instincts went into overdrive. Don't worry, I've got control."

Kelly didn't smile. She really didn't. A little jealousy was okay. Too much could destroy a relationship. Not that they had a relationship. But he was jealous over *her*. That counted for something. *She* counted for something with him. So she smiled inside.

"I can help Neva." Macario walked over to a small first-aid kit that rested beside a pile of clothes belonging to one of the other wolves. Opening it, he took out a bottle and syringe. After filling the syringe, he returned to Neva.

He ignored everyone except her. "When you become one of us through violence, your awakening immediately triggers a change to wolf form. The trauma plus all the stress and fear make it almost impossible for you to return to human form until you relax. And yes, you might relax during sleep, but the change must be willed. You can't will it while you sleep." Macario glanced at Ty and Kelly. "Or when you're dead. That's why none of the red wolves regained human form after death."

Kelly frowned. "Relax? You're kidding. Who could relax after waking up to find that Little Red Riding Hood is now the enemy? Neva probably has the willing part down, though."

"That's where this comes in." He held up the syringe. "We have a pack member who's a chemist. He came up with a relaxant that works on us." Turning his attention back to Neva, he moved closer. "It'll make you a little loopy and free a few inhibitions, but it'll also relax the hell out of you. Do you trust me to do this?"

Whatever Macario saw in Neva's eyes, he took it as a resounding yes. Kelly bit her lip as he injected Neva with the relaxant. Then everyone waited.

After a few minutes, Neva sat down and opened her mouth in a wolfy grin. Looked pretty relaxed to Kelly.

"Okay, now it's up to you." Macario retrieved a plastic bag from the ground behind him. "We all bring clothes for after the change. These are extras. I don't know your size, but let's hope they fit."

Oops. Kelly hadn't even thought about clothes for Neva.

The pack leader put his hand under Neva's chin. "Now concentrate. Visualize yourself in human form."

For a moment nothing happened. And then the change began, slower than Macario's, but a transformation nonetheless. Kelly couldn't tear her gaze from the wonder of it, incredible and terrifying at the same time. Neva had to be in agony as everything, even her skull, shifted and changed shape. And where'd the fur go when the skin appeared? Kelly searched for a scientific explanation and found none.

"There's untapped magic in all of us." Macario had read her expression correctly.

Kelly shook her head. "Not in me."

"You'd be surprised." There was laughter in his voice.

At last the transformation was finished. Neva seemed a little disoriented. Kelly rushed forward, scooped up the clothes, and helped her dress. The top was for a smaller woman, so Neva filled it to overflowing. At least the pants fit. The shoes were too small, but since they were going right back to the apartment, that wouldn't be a problem.

Something else *was* a problem, though. Neva was at her uninhibited best. She tottered over to Macario and just stared at him. Then she ran her hand down the middle of his chest. "You're so hot I can feel my fantasies starting to sizzle, pack daddy." She giggled. "Thank you." Neva traced an *S* on his chest. "You're my superhero."

The pack leader laughed as he reached out to steady her. "You'll feel normal after a good sleep. Then I can teach you what you need to know."

The rest of the pack went suddenly still. Without warning, one of the wolves returned to human form. She was tall, naked, and spitting mad.

Without worrying about clothes, she strode over to Macario and glared from him to Neva. "She isn't pack. We don't know anything about her. We don't know anything about *them*."

Kelly figured she and Ty were *them*. She glanced at Ty. He looked as if he was enjoying the exchange.

The woman swung around to face the rest of the pack. "These guys killed the whole red wolf pack. How'd they do it? I don't believe the crap that Travis told us. I think we need to kill them all before they try to take over our territory too."

Macario's expression said, *You're in a world of shit, woman.*

But she wasn't paying attention. She was too busy trying to work the other pack members into a frenzy. "How many are with me?"

The pack shifted restlessly.

"Guess I need to stop this now." Ty turned toward the trees and whistled.

Startled, the pack stared at him. But not for long.

Kelly heard Spin before she saw him. First there was the *thump, thump* of something really big coming and then the sound of branches breaking. He must be doing major damage to some of the small trees she'd seen along the path.

The pack moved back as one.

Then Spin appeared at the edge of the clearing. Even Kelly, who knew what to expect, gasped. Ty muttered something like, "Showboat."

Kelly wasn't good with size, but Spin looked almost as big as Ty's T. rex. He walked on huge, powerful back legs like Ty too. But unlike Ty, he had a long narrow snout and a bunch of skin-covered spines sticking up from his back. Each one had to be at least six feet tall. In the shadows, it was tough to see the man at the heart of the beast. She swallowed hard.

Spin didn't come closer; he just stared at the pack and then roared. Kelly winced. God, she hoped no park security or late-night joggers heard that.

The wolves flattened themselves and stared from terrified yellow eyes.

Macario studied Spin for a few minutes before looking at Ty. "What are you?"

"A T. rex."

The pack leader rubbed a hand across his forehead. "And the red wolves attacked you?"

"Two of us."

Macario shook his head. "The red wolves never did have any sense." He turned on the woman. "Are you satisfied, Yvette?" Macario didn't give her a chance to answer. "You challenged my leadership with the pack a minute ago. Does that mean I have to kill you?" He didn't raise his voice, but the woman visibly wilted.

She shook her head and looked around for support. The other wolves avoided her gaze. "But I'm the alpha female."

"If you die, there'll be another."

"But alphas belong together." Yvette sounded more whiny than wicked right now.

Kelly could connect the dots. Yvette saw Macario's offer to teach Neva as a sign of sexual interest. Evidently Yvette had already staked her claim on the pack leader.

"I choose whom I take as mate. No one makes that choice for me. And last time I looked, I hadn't chosen anyone."

Kelly winced. Talk about a public putdown. She almost felt sorry for the bitch. Almost. She watched as Yvette picked up her clothes and hurriedly dressed. Yvette didn't say anything to anyone as she left.

By the time Kelly stopped watching Yvette, Spin had disappeared and the other wolves were human again.

Ty grabbed her hand as he walked over to join Neva and Macario. He fished a card out of his pocket and handed it to the pack leader. "This is Fin's card. He's our leader. Call him and maybe we can coordinate efforts."

Macario nodded, then looked at Neva. "Why don't I drive you home?"

"Sure, pack daddy. Hey, I don't know what was in that shot, but wow—" She glanced around. "Don't wanna go home right now. Why don't we sleep right here on the grass, and I can go all earth mama on you?" Neva offered him a silly grin and did some serious wobbling. She managed to stay on her feet, though. Barely.

The pack leader looked worried. "Forget your home. You need someone watching you until the relaxant wears off. I'll take you to my place."

Kelly had opened her mouth to offer to watch Neva

when she looked at the other woman's face. Glazed eyes and all, Neva's focus was only on Macario. She wanted the pack leader. Alpha girl hadn't scared her off. Kelly closed her mouth.

Neva glanced at Kelly and gave her a finger wave. "Thanks for the save, girlfriend. Owe you. Talk to you tomorrow night."

Kelly nodded and turned to Ty. "Ready to go?"

"Yeah." He still had her hand as they walked away.

She savored his touch all the way back to the car. It was a different kind of pleasure than the intensity of last night. It was a kind of claiming, an act of admitting that you wanted contact with your lover's body.

Q and Spin joined them halfway back to the SUV. Spin looked smugly satisfied.

"Did you see the looks on those wolves' faces?" He grinned. "I would've come closer, but they were ready to bolt. Then that Macario guy would've had to chase their furry butts all over the park to get them together again. Didn't want him pissed at me. I was hoping they'd be like those red wolves, dumbasses who thought they could take us."

"Be glad they weren't. Too many battles and we're going to run out of luck. Someone will see us who shouldn't." Ty returned his grin. "But yeah, I enjoyed it too. You put on a good show."

As they emerged from the trees, the guys were still talking about what had just happened. Everyone saw the man leaning against their SUV at the same time.

Ty and the other men grew still, that eerie quietness only a predator could manage. God knew, Kelly couldn't do it.

"Oh, shit." Kelly gripped Ty's hand tighter. More weirdness. Because no one could mistake this man for human. He also couldn't be mistaken for anything other than a dangerous hunter. It was something sensed, a dark coiled energy that thrummed with quiet power. She shivered.

Since meeting Ty, she'd been tripping over gorgeous men. But except for Fin, they'd all had an earthy realness to them. Like Fin, this guy was so beautiful he brought tears to your eyes just looking at him. She was too far away to see eye color in the darkness, but the total impression was mind boggling.

"Who are you, and what do you want?"

Ty's voice sounded relaxed, but Kelly sensed his readiness to spring if the man gave the wrong answer.

He skipped Ty's first question. "Wanted to talk to you." He lifted his hands to indicate their surroundings. "This looked like a good place to do it. By the way, great show back there with the wolves."

Ty exhaled on a quiet hiss. "Why didn't we sense you?"

The man looked puzzled. "Because I didn't want you to." Then he grinned. "And you can come closer. I'm just here to talk. If I was going to do something, I would've done it by now."

Kelly watched Ty make his decision. He glanced at Q and Spin. Once they both nodded, he moved closer. Under normal circumstances, she would've demanded a vote, but they were the experienced ones when it came to fighting.

Ty tried to push her behind him, but that was a little too much for her pride to accept. Yanking her hand from his grip, she moved up beside him and the others. "Why would he waste time taking me out when you guys are the dangerous ones?" She thought for a moment. "What are the chances he wants us closer because he's planted a bomb under the car?"

Ty shook his head. "I would've sensed it."

"Like you sensed *him*?"

The man focused his attention on her and smiled. "Hey, I'm harmless. But I wouldn't be surprised if you were their secret weapon, sweetheart."

If Fin were to be believed, that's exactly what she was. And if she wasn't busy lusting after everything Ty, that smile would've knocked her down and danced on her heart. Kelly's motto: when rattled, say something. "And whose secret weapon are you?" Ulp. Maybe she should screen her comments before they came out of her mouth.

He chose not to answer. Instead he pushed a few strands of long blond hair away from his face. Blond hair that seemed a blending of shades from intense to pale. If he wasn't so scary, she'd find the tendency of his hair to curl in a mad tangle kind of endearing. But endearing wasn't a term that fit him.

He pushed away from the SUV and approached them. Ty's tension didn't increase. Evidently he'd chosen to believe that this guy just wanted to talk. She sure hoped his instincts were right.

Up close, Kelly got her first look at his eyes. She couldn't see too much in the darkness, but she'd swear they were a light color. As tall as Ty, he wore leather pants and a leather jacket that only added to a sensual aura that was way too potent. Once again, she thought of Fin. He and this guy didn't look alike, but they had the same *feel*, whatever that meant.

"I'm here with a proposition." He seemed relaxed. Even after seeing what Spin could do, he didn't act worried. That either made him very powerful or very stupid.

"Name?" Q moved so he was slightly behind the stranger.

"Seir. That's S—E—I—R. I know you'll want to Google that as soon as you get home." His lips turned up in a mocking smile.

"Let's hear your proposition." Spin moved away from Ty so they had Seir semi-trapped in a half circle.

Seir's smile widened. "I know you're searching for the immortal who's recruiting nonhumans. I can lead you to him. For a price."

"Maybe we don't have to bargain. Maybe we can make you want to tell us."

Obviously Q thought threat-of-violence was always a good place to start negotiating.

Seir shook his head in fake sorrow. "So predictable. If I thought you could beat the hell out of me, I wouldn't be here. What next?"

"How do we know you're telling the truth?" Ty was moving beyond options that involved violence.

"Well, let's see. I know that the immortal you're after has a gambling thing going that pits two nonhumans in a fight to the death. He's getting lots of recruits that way. I also know he destroyed three werewolves at a fight last night because they were going to tell their alpha what they saw." Seir shrugged. "That enough?"

"What's your price?" Ty seemed to force the words from his lips.

Seir looked relaxed, almost as if he didn't care what Ty decided, but Kelly felt a sudden tension in him she hadn't sensed before.

He met Ty's gaze. "I want to possess your soul for one night."

Possess? Soul? *Demon?* That was the only thing she knew that possessed souls. Images of exorcism rituals and swiveling heads made her own head want to rotate a few times. No, definitely not. Seir couldn't have Ty's soul.

Ty's smile was bitter. "You might find my soul more trouble than it's worth. Why do you want it?"

Seir's expression didn't change. "I've possessed plenty of human souls and a few not-so-human ones, but I've never ridden the kind of raw physical power I saw tonight. It'd be the ultimate thrill. And, hey, I'm all about testing limits."

"Why just a night? Why not forever?"

"You wouldn't agree to forever."

"I won't agree to a night either." Ty looked at the others. "Are any of you takers?"

Q and Spin just looked murderous.

Ty turned back to Seir. "I'd say that's a no."

Seir shrugged. "Well, if you ever change your mind, come around midnight and stand beside old Sam Houston's statue in the middle of Hermann Circle Drive." He nodded toward the dim outline of the statue across from the museum. "I'll find you."

And then he was gone. Kelly blinked. Without saying a word, she climbed into the SUV, slammed the door shut, and leaned her forehead on the steering wheel. Then she closed her eyes. What had happened to the Houston she knew? She wanted it back. Without vampires, werewolves, demons and . . . Ty? No, she definitely wanted Houston with Ty in it. Too bad he and the others were a package deal.

When everyone was in the car, she picked up her head and turned the key in the ignition. Kelly pulled out of the parking lot and drove toward home in silence. Finally, she couldn't stand it anymore. "I didn't think demons existed." Or vampires, or werewolves, or men with the souls of dinosaurs.

Q leaned forward in his seat. "Celia, she of the incredible Mexican food, is otherkin, but her soul is demon."

That didn't make much sense to Kelly, but she was beyond wanting to know one more freaky fact tonight. They were home, thank God. She parked, got out, and didn't look back as she let herself into the building.

She climbed the stairs, then stopped in front of her door. There was an envelope taped to it. She pulled it off and unlocked the door. She could hear Ty coming up the steps.

No, tonight she wanted to be alone to come down from the emotional high of these last few nights. If he came in, he'd stay the night. She knew that. She slipped inside, closed the door, and locked it.

Kelly heard him stop in the hallway. She held her breath. Then she heard his door closing, and she went weak with relief. He was giving her some space tonight.

Making her way to the bedroom, she turned on her bedside lamp, stripped and climbed into bed. Only then did she open the envelope.

A single piece of paper fell out. Across the top was a simple message: *your brain music.*

Chapter Thirteen

Ty shut down his laptop and sat thinking. If Seir was the demon he said he was, then he was legit. That's if you believed in demons. Ty did. A little research had turned up that Seir was a Prince of Hell with twenty-six legions of demons at his command. Not too shabby.

As demons went, Seir wasn't one of the über evil entities. One of his major powers was finding hidden treasures. Ty tended to believe that Seir was the real deal. The description fit—unearthly beauty, blond hair, ice-blue eyes. The only thing missing was the silver winged horse he was supposed to ride. Probably had it tied to a tree somewhere.

Ty wondered why the hell Seir wanted his soul for just one night. He'd never know, because no way was he giving a demon any part of him. Then Ty dismissed Seir from his mind. He wouldn't need a demon to get his job done. Standing, he stretched. After sleeping late, he'd gotten a few things out of the way.

One of those things had been reporting to Fin. Ty frowned as he grabbed his jacket. Fin hadn't sounded good over the mental link. Sure, the news that he could count on the local werewolves to help fight Nine had made Fin happy, but Ty had a feeling the psychic battle with Zero was taking a lot out of him. Fin wouldn't be able to put Zero on hold if the rest of the Eleven needed him.

Ty tried not to feel too excited as he left his apartment,

locked his door, and went across to Kelly's place. He'd wanted to go to her as soon as he'd climbed out of bed this afternoon, but he'd reined in that need. She deserved some space after all that had happened.

Besides, no matter how much he wanted to be with her, he couldn't fool himself into thinking their relationship would end well. When Nine was gone, the Eleven would leave Houston. What woman would choose to go with them, putting herself in constant danger as the Eleven moved from city to city? The fact that he was even considering it said a lot about his feelings for Kelly.

But that didn't stop him from ringing her doorbell. And it damn well didn't stop him from picturing her long bare legs wrapped around his hips. He heard her on the other side of the door and carefully schooled his expression to match what she expected, a prehistoric killing machine.

Kelly was smiling when she opened the door, but her eyes were red.

Ty stepped into her apartment and slammed the door shut behind him. "You've been crying?"

"No." She widened her eyes, refusing to blink.

Trying to hold back tears? He glanced at the crumpled tissue she clutched in her hand.

"Yes." Panic settled in the pit of his stomach. He didn't understand, didn't know how to deal with tears. Crying was a human reaction to emotion, alien to him in every way. Emotion scared the hell out of him. "Why?"

She gave up and blinked. Tears filled her eyes. "I was just thinking."

A dangerous activity, thinking.

"Fin sent over my brain music, and I was trying to memorize it." She nodded to where her flute lay on the couch. "And I panicked. What if I forget the melody when I get my one shot at Nine? I mean, stress can make your mind go blank." Kelly swiped at her eyes with her tissue. "So I made it the ring tone on my cell phone, and I put it on my iPod." She raised her hands in a helpless gesture. "Last week I was shoveling lion poop, and now I'm responsible for saving humanity. I don't know if I'm up to the challenge." She waved her hand to stop him from interrupting her. "Just ignore the rant. This is my crisis-of-faith moment. I'll be okay."

"Let's sit down." He led her to the couch, moved the flute, and sat. Then Ty drew her down beside him and pulled her close.

Kelly rested her head against his chest. "My sister, Jenna, called. Mom and she were worried because they hadn't heard from me. She said she's working on a story about vampires in Houston. She's put together a few facts and built it into this big exposé. By the way, she still thinks you're a vampire. She doesn't have a clue how close she is to the truth, and how much danger she and everyone else in Houston are in. I'm terrified for my family and afraid I might not be able to save them." Tears clogged her voice. "Everything depends on me and my freaking flute."

"I'll keep you safe." An overwhelming surge of protectiveness shattered any illusions he might have had that he really didn't care about this woman.

"But what if I fail? I listened to Jenna talk about a date she had with an ordinary guy she met at some club. And it was like she was talking about this whole other world, a normal world, while I'm going to war alongside vampires, werewolves, and the Eleven to defeat some cosmic menace." She gave a hiccuping laugh. "Good God, I sound like a comic book character."

Ty gripped her shoulders and forced her to meet his gaze. "You will *not* fail, and I *will* protect you. Always. And

I won't let Fin force you to do something you don't want to do. If you believe nothing else, believe that." For the first time, something that might have been a human soul stirred within him.

Kelly nodded and gave him a watery smile. "I believe you."

He felt his tension ease. "You don't have to go with us tonight if you're not up to it. Fin can get someone else to drive us."

She shook her head. "I'm fine. I'll be ready to go as soon as I put my flute away." Kelly reached for her instrument. "Want to hear my brain music?"

Not really. He wanted to pick her up, carry her into the bedroom . . . No, that would take too long. He wanted to strip off the short, sexy black dress she was wearing and spend the night making love right on the couch. No walking involved. "Sure, let's hear it."

She picked up the flute, put her mouth to it, and played. The melody was simple and haunting, but Ty had other thoughts going on besides the music. Her mouth. On him. Playing her special tune over every inch of his bare body. And he had no doubt his mouth on her would create notes never before heard.

When she finished, he grinned and tried to keep it light. "Love it. I bet Nine will be humming it as he floats somewhere out in space."

"Hold that thought." She disassembled and cleaned the flute.

He watched her place it carefully in its case. "Not that I want you anywhere near Nine, but if you were, wouldn't having to put the flute together slow you down?"

She frowned. "Well, yeah, but I don't have a choice. This is what Fin saw in his vision, me playing a flute and maybe defeating Nine. If we're someplace where I expect to come face-to-face with him, I'll make sure the flute is already assembled."

"Fin is wrong. The future isn't set in stone. The *Eleven* will send Nine's ass back where it came from with no flute playing needed." Ty suspected he sounded vicious about that, but he would never let her put herself in danger. Screw Fin. And he didn't care if their great leader was listening.

"How? You can't kill him. So tell me how, Ty?" She sounded calm, reasonable.

And he hated it. "I don't know. There must be a way." He raked his fingers through his hair. The need to break something pounded at him.

She closed the case and walked back to him. Putting her hand on his arm, she smiled. "It might never happen. I might never even get near him. And Fin will probably come up with some brilliant alternative to my flute. After all, isn't he your godlike leader? Maybe he needs to earn his title."

Startled, Ty stared at her. "You sound kind of bitter. What brought that on?"

Sighing, she walked over to get her coat and purse from a chair. "I've got to get a new jacket. My other one is pretty much ruined." Then she picked up her flute case. "This is going to be clunky to carry around. I wish Fin had seen me playing a harmonica instead."

"You're not answering me." He kept his voice quiet even though he wanted to shout his frustration to the world.

She paused by the door. "He manipulates everyone."

"You don't have to play the flute. You could say no."

"Could I? He's made it clear what'll happen to humanity if I don't play the damn thing. He's counting on my conscience to carry the day for him." Her laughter was no laugh at all. "And he's right."

Sensing she had more to say, he kept quiet.

"I'm not really ticked off about what he's done to me. I mean, he needs to do what he needs to do for humanity." She fiddled with the strap of her purse. "It's about you guys." Kelly looked as if she were trying to make a decision. "Don't you ever wonder about him? Why is he the big boss? How can you be so smart if you were only dinosaurs before? And why don't you ever ask him questions about things?"

"I don't know." He frowned. "I just never do." Why not? He tried to move past the fog that always rolled in when he thought about Fin, but he couldn't fight his way free. "Look, maybe we can discuss this when we get back. I talked to Jude after I got up. He wants us to meet him at Eternal Pleasure. We'll eat there, and then he'll take us to a few clubs that cater mostly to nonhumans. Law of averages says we'll get lucky at one of these places and find out where Nine is operating."

She nodded, but he could sense her disappointment. "Sure."

As she pulled the door open, he put his hand over hers. "By the way, I want you again." Okay, he hadn't planned on saying that, but since he had, he might as well elaborate a little. "I want you in every possible position and on every possible surface in Houston. From this time forward, I want tour guides to point out that Kelly and Ty made love here, and here, and here, and here." He wouldn't put any time limit on his desire for her either. The way he felt right now, this could be a never-ending thing. And that was the scariest thought he'd had since . . . since ever.

She closed the door softly. "How about a peek at coming attractions to raise my spirits?"

Leaning in, Ty trapped her between the door and his body. He lowered his head and paused a breath away from her mouth. "You touch my soul, woman. You touch what I am, what I once was, and what I will be."

Ty wondered at the words, even as he recognized how right they were. They were from something half remembered. Not his words, but the *perfect* words for what he felt.

She had no idea how much he'd just admitted. And only he knew how close he was to the final question. *Will you walk into the heart of my beast and share my soul?* But he didn't ask. It wasn't time. Yet.

Instead he traced her soft sensual lips with the tip of his tongue, tasting the female in her, the essential "one" he'd always remember. Her scent was of all things human: vanilla soap, spearmint toothpaste, and female desire. When he deepened the kiss, she opened to him.

He lost himself in the exchange, exploring the heat of her mouth, welcoming the intense pleasure of his erection pressed against her stomach . . .

And fumbling for his damn cell phone as it demanded his attention. He broke the kiss and stepped back. "Let me shut this off."

She stared at him from wide wondering eyes, her lips swollen from his kiss. "Answer it. You can't afford to miss something important."

Trying to still his rapid breathing, he flipped it open. "Yeah?" Ty hoped whoever was on the other end understood how close to death he was.

"Oops. Sounds like I caught you at a bad time."

"No shit."

"Just thought I'd let you know it's time to go. Oh, and Neva got back this afternoon. She knocked on my door. Wants to go with us."

Ty didn't honor Q's reminder with an answer. He shoved the cell phone back into his pocket. "Q. It's time to go." Sliding his fingers along the side of her face, he kissed her lips one last time. "And I'll bounce his head off a wall for interrupting."

"Make it twice. One for me." She smiled. "But there'll be another time. Believe it."

Out in the hallway, Ty knocked on Neva's door.

"Is Neva back?"

Ty returned to Kelly's side as they waited for the others. "Yeah, Q said she got back this afternoon. She knocked on his door and said she wanted to go with us."

"Well, another mouth full of big teeth has to be good for our side." She didn't look as flip as she sounded. "Sorry, that came out pretty insensitive. I wonder how she's coping emotionally."

Just then Neva's door opened, and she stepped into the hallway. She wore a short dress covered with sparkly things, and heels so high that Ty figured no woman could stand in them without keeling forward onto her face. Her hair was piled onto her head with more sparkly stuff woven through the strands.

"If looks are anything to go by, I'd say she's handling the emotional stuff pretty well." Ty watched Neva actually walk toward them on those shoes. Go figure.

Neva hugged him and planted an air kiss on Kelly. "Don't want to smear my lip color." For a newly turned werewolf, she was in a great mood. "You know, I never believed in all that soul-mate crap, but I do now. Honestly. Macario and I just fit. But before I go on about that, I want you guys to know how much I appreciate what you did. I'll never forget it."

Neva looped her arm through Kelly's. "When all this

first went down, I wanted to run and keep on running. But after last night, I got to thinking about how you took care of me. I owe you. Without you I'd be dead, and I never would've met Macario. That's why when Fin called a while ago offering me the job of Kelly's bodyguard, I jumped on it. Hey, I can out-bodyguard anyone. So you and I'll be inseparable, girlfriend."

"Bodyguard? Did I miss the part where Fin and I conferenced about this?"

Ty bit his lip to keep from laughing at Kelly's panicked expression. His need to laugh vanished though as he realized exactly what Neva had said. "I can take care of Kelly. She doesn't need a bodyguard." He and Kelly were on the same page about that.

His glare didn't intimidate Neva. "No one's saying you're not the biggest badass on the block, but Macario told me how Travis was able to drag Kelly off when you were fighting the red wolves. What if that happened again?"

What if it did? She was right. And that made him even madder. Ty didn't know what he would have said if Q hadn't joined them.

"Fin said he's going to have to get me another driver." Q's glance slipped and slid from Neva's bright red hair down over her many curves highlighted by the sparkly dress and ending at her long, long legs. He smiled.

"Neva's found her soul mate. Macario." Ty admitted his meanness to himself. He was in a rotten mood on a lot of different levels, so he wanted to take away Q's fun. Did he feel guilty? Hell, no.

Q grunted at him as he led the way down the stairs and out to the SUV. Once on their way, Ty filled them all in on what Jude had said.

"He lost two more vampires last night. Found their

bodies down by Buffalo Bayou just before dawn. Heads were missing. Didn't look like they were killed there. Word is in the wind that the number of humans dying each night is increasing too. He thinks if we lean on the right people, someone will talk. I'm not sure that's going to happen." Ty glanced at Kelly, but her gaze was fixed on the road. What was she thinking? Was she wishing she'd never laid eyes on him? That was probably a big freaking yes.

"Why not? If Nine's expanding his operation in Houston, someone is bound to know something. And there're always people willing to talk." Q grinned. "If you give them the right motivation."

"I don't know." Ty hoped he was wrong. "From what Fin has said, I can't picture this Nine letting anyone put his organization at risk. If you kill enough people and scare the crap out of the rest, there's no one left who'll take a chance on talking."

Great. He'd doused everyone's party spirit. Not that there'd been much to begin with. No one said anything until they got to the club. They parked the car behind Eternal Pleasure this time. And as he walked into the place, Ty wondered if the same woman would be singing. That might raise Q's spirits.

Kelly was ready to go back to the apartment. Since leaving Eternal Pleasure, they'd hit enough clubs to leave her wishing to be any place not filled with loud music and people. Sure, the "people" had been entertaining. Just knowing most of them weren't human had given her a rush. For a while. Now she was just tired. She was glad she'd decided not to lug the flute case into the clubs with her. What were the chances she'd bump into Nine in one of these places?

They were standing in front of still another club, The Full Moon, waiting for the vampires. Jude and his ever-present henchmen, or to be technically correct two henchmen and a henchwoman, were in a separate car. Jude said the two cars were necessary to lower the risk of all of them being wiped out in a single attack. Kelly thought his real reason was that he wouldn't be caught dead or undead in a SUV.

Without warning, the vampires materialized out of the darkness. Kelly hated when they did that.

Jude didn't waste time on small talk. He nodded toward the club. "Let's go. This place is owned by one of Macario's pack, so you might meet a few friends, Neva."

Neva looked fresh enough to hit a dozen more clubs and still be good to go. If she was an emotional wreck from her sudden lifestyle change, she was hiding it well. "This has been a blast. I was feeling a little down that I wouldn't be able to see my sweetie until after work, but all this has perked me right up."

Kelly smiled as Ty took her hand, and they followed the others into the club. *Sweetie* wasn't exactly the word she'd use to describe the pack leader.

Once inside, Kelly separated from everyone except her faithful bodyguard. Neva was taking her new job way too seriously. Hovering nearby, she shot glares at any man who even looked like he might be dangerous. And no amount of pleading or threatening by Kelly would keep Neva from her appointed duties. She was superglued to Kelly.

It got worse. Every time the crowd parted, she spotted Ty, his gaze fixed on her. Why didn't they just pack her in bubble wrap and be done with it?

Ignoring both Ty and Neva, she went into mingling mode, trying to pick up pieces of helpful conversations.

And because the nature of the club beast was to hook up with others, she endured the requisite number of semi-drunk men. Although she had to admit that nonhumans seemed to hold their liquor better than their human counterparts. Even though a guy's eyes might look glassy, he usually didn't show any other signs of being drunk. Not so her. That was why she only bought one drink at each club and then just took a few sips.

They'd been at this club an hour, and so far nothing. Ty was hanging near the door, watching her from half-closed eyes. Wait. Someone was missing from the picture. Where was her bodyguard?

Kelly had just finished dancing with a guy who'd filled her ears with whispers of how much he loved humans. He'd left her with the impression that his love extended only as far as her neck.

Looking around, she spotted Neva by the bar talking to another woman. Kelly looked closer. Yvette? That surprised Kelly. Not that Yvette was here, because a werewolf owned the club, but that Neva would be talking to the alpha female after last night. It was a relief, though, to have one less layer of bubble wrap.

Sighing, she moved on to more mingling. This routine didn't seem to be getting them anywhere, though. Evidently Nine didn't choose people with loose lips.

After another half hour, Ty approached her. "We're leaving. Jude has only one other club he wants to hit. Hear anything?"

"Nothing." She walked with him to where Q and the others stood. "Everyone's here but Neva."

Jude frowned. He nodded at one of his men. "Ed, go find her."

The vampire returned a few minutes later. "She's gone."

Something that felt a lot like fear tugged at Kelly. "Last I saw she was talking to Yvette, one of Macario's wolves."

"Would she go off with this Yvette without telling anyone?" Jude scanned the room.

"Never." Kelly might not know Neva well, but her bodyguard couldn't be that stupid.

"Fin hired her to be your bodyguard, so what was she doing talking to someone?" Ty's face was a thundercloud of disapproval.

"Uh, she's the victim here, Ty. Besides, I begged her to leave me alone. So she did. And weren't you the one who said I didn't need a bodyguard because I had you?" Kelly was building up lots of outrage on Neva's behalf.

Ty recognized her warning signals and didn't say anything.

"Let's search the place." Jude turned and disappeared into the crowd. Everyone else followed his lead. Ty stayed with her as she peered into corners, back rooms, and the parking lot. But she was too worried about Neva to complain. Ten minutes later they regrouped.

"We didn't see Neva or Yvette. Ty picked up their scents together in the parking lot, but they dead-ended at an empty parking space." Kelly glanced at the others.

One by one they shook their heads.

"Then we can assume she's gone." Ty got that intense expression on his face that made Kelly think he was talking to Fin.

Jude looked about as dangerous as she thought any vampire could look. "I talked to the manager. Nothing."

Ty nodded. "Let's get out of here." He glanced at his watch. "Neva was meeting Macario after work. He'll probably be at her apartment when we get there, but if not I need his number."

Jude looked at his I'm-too-cute-to-hurt-anyone body-guard, and she immediately produced a PDA that she handed to him. He found what he wanted. "Here's Macario's cell number."

Kelly wasn't paying close attention. She was terrified for Neva. If Neva were with Yvette, that had to be bad news for Neva. She didn't for a minute believe Yvette was anything but a vicious bitch. She glanced at Ty. His expression said he thought the same thing.

While Ty and Q talked about possibilities all the way home, Kelly thought about Neva. Was she even still alive? Was she terrified or just plain pissed? Neva seemed like a survivor. They had to reach her in time.

As Kelly pulled into the parking lot of their building, she saw Macario get out of his car. Parking the SUV next to him, she grabbed her purse and flute before climbing out.

She let Ty tell the story. As she watched Macario's face, she wondered how anyone could ever mistake him for anything other than the alpha wolf he was. Aggression rolled off him in waves.

"No one touches my chosen mate."

After just one night? Well, that told Kelly where Neva stood in his affections. She didn't think Yvette would be rejoining the pack anytime soon.

"I'm calling the pack together. We'll start searching places Yvette might take her. And when we find Yvette . . ." He didn't finish.

"Why don't you call the police?" She suggested. "It wouldn't hurt to have more people searching."

"This is pack business. We take care of our own." Then he got into his car and left with a squeal of tires.

No one said anything as they climbed the stairs.

"If anything new comes up, call me." Q turned away and went into his apartment.

Ty and Kelly stood in the hall between their two doors.

"Tired?" Ty looked worried.

"Yeah." She pushed her hair away from her face. "But I can't sleep until I get some word about Neva. I should've gone over when I saw her talking to Yvette. I should've been there for her."

He evidently made a decision, because he unlocked his door, pushed it open, and stood aside. "We might as well wait together."

No use playing games with herself. She wanted to be with him. Walking past Ty, she entered his apartment.

He closed the door, pulled off his jacket, and strode past her into the kitchen. "Want something to drink?"

"Water's fine." She set her purse and flute on the coffee table.

Ty returned with two bottles of water. He handed one to her before dropping onto the couch beside her and letting the silence gather around them.

They could talk about Neva, but Kelly knew that would achieve nothing except to increase her feelings of guilt and helplessness. But the silence was suffocating her.

So taking a deep breath, she tiptoed out onto thin ice and asked the question her subconscious had known she wanted to ask all along. "When you get rid of Nine, you'll be moving on to another city, right?"

He nodded.

"Will you be taking anyone from Houston with you?" Did she want to pursue this? Was she hinting at what she thought she was hinting?

"I think Fin wants to take Shen and Greer with us." He grinned. "We'd all pitch in to keep Greer. He grills a mean steak."

There was nowhere to go with this conversation that wouldn't send her crashing through the ice, so she tiptoed back to shore.

"I guess you'll go back to school and the zoo when we leave." Something in his voice sounded almost angry about that.

"Probably." She thought about her future, really thought about it. "But, you know, as scary as most of this has been, I've never felt so alive in my whole life. The threat of death will do that, I suppose."

He went to the window and stood staring out. "What're we really talking about, Kelly?"

She never had a chance to decide what she'd say because his cell phone rang.

Impatiently, she waited through the conversation, which consisted of a bunch of "yeahs" interspersed with long silences on his end. Finally he shoved the phone back into his pocket.

"Let's go." He put on his jacket.

"Where?"

"Fin's place. I'll explain on the way."

"Aren't we taking Q?" She picked up her purse and flute, thinking that dragging it around could get old fast.

"Not this time. He gets to sit this one out."

As she drove out of the parking lot, Ty filled her in.

"That was Fin. He's conserving power to throw at Zero, so he used the phone. He thinks we're close to finding Nine, and he wants to keep Zero occupied so he doesn't pay much attention to what's happening in Houston."

"What did Fin want?"

"Macario called him. That card I gave Macario had Fin's number on it. He found someone in his pack who was close friends with Yvette. The friend said Yvette had been trying to get her to go to some club where they had great fights. She didn't know the name of the club, but she did say Yvette told her they could eat at a restaurant near the club."

"What restaurant?"

"Brady's Landing. Macario said it was by the Ship Channel's turning basin. Know it?"

She nodded.

"Macario is bringing his whole pack. Fin notified Jude. He's coming with some of his vampires. Fin says even if we find the club and Neva's there, we probably won't find Nine. He thinks chances are good that both Jude and Macario have spies in their midst. If so, someone will warn Nine. Both leaders refuse to believe it. So this is strictly a mission to rescue Neva. Fin is sending Shen and Lio with us. That's who we're picking up."

"Why Shen? And who's Lio?"

Ty shrugged. "I guess Shen will have to explain why he's coming. Lio's one of the Eleven. You haven't met him yet."

When Kelly pulled up in front of Fin's condo, two men were waiting for them. Shen grinned at her as he climbed into the back of the SUV. The second man was just as gorgeous as all the Eleven were, but there was a stark difference about him.

He looked like he belonged in a corner office. His great-looking brown hair had definitely known a stylist's touch. Expensive pants, expensive shirt, and expensive suede jacket. She glanced at his shoes before he got into the car. Expensive. He could have stepped off the pages of *GQ*.

When she smiled at him, he didn't smile back. He stared at her from cold dark eyes. Well, if he didn't want to be friendly, that was okay by her.

"You know Shen, and the one with the great attitude is Lio." Ty grinned back at Lio. "And this is Kelly."

The other man acknowledged the dig with a chilly smile, but he didn't say anything.

Kelly rose to the challenge. "So what are you, Lio, and why does Fin think you'd be useful?"

There was such a long silence before Lio answered that Kelly thought he was going to ignore her.

When he did respond, it was in a surprisingly deep voice. "I'm a Liopleurodon."

Kelly mentally ran through her list of known dinosaurs. "Never heard of you."

"Naturally." His tone suggested that she was one dumb duck. "I was the prehistoric equivalent of a great white shark."

Wow, he'd managed to surprise her. "How big?"

"Eighty feet long. Eight-inch-long teeth."

She could see him fighting the desire to brag. He lost.

"I read a book that said I was the biggest known flesh-eating vertebrate."

"Did you cut the article out and paste it in your scrapbook?"

"Yes."

She laughed. Kelly wouldn't have pegged him as having a sense of humor. She looked in the rearview mirror. He wasn't laughing. Oops.

Kelly decided to leave Mr. Gorgeous and Grumpy alone. She turned her attention to Shen. "Why did Fin send you, Shen?"

Shen made up for what Lio lacked in good humor. "I'm the official spy. I sneak into places and check them out."

"How do you do that?"

He was quiet for a moment. When she glanced in the mirror, he avoided meeting her gaze. "I guess I just have a knack for getting in and out of places."

Kelly didn't waste time wondering why he'd side-stepped a direct answer. She had other things to think about.

I've never felt so alive in my whole life. Her comment to Ty had been replaying in her subconscious since she'd made it.

Amazing where revelations struck. This one hit her on a dark road heading toward the Houston Ship Channel.

It wasn't the threat of death that made her feel alive. It was Ty.

Chapter Fourteen

"We have a full house tonight, Mr. Wyatt." Thadeus didn't quite smile, but the sorcerer looked a little less sour than usual.

"I find the paranormal community's love of violence eminently satisfying. In fact, after a few more nights I think we'll be ready to move to a larger venue for our final event. I want it to be a major happening that Houston will never forget."

He studied the two wolves stalking each other in Thadeus's circle. Yvette, the large gray, would probably make quick work of the smaller red wolf. But one never knew with werewolves. He'd held up the fight until he made sure the red wolf, Neva, understood exactly what was at stake. That hadn't made Yvette happy. But even though she was one of his most popular fighters, Yvette had to understand he was a businessman. The audience got no enjoyment out of a quick kill. And he was all about keeping his audience happy. An unhappy audience was far less receptive to his sales pitch afterward.

He rubbed at a tiny spot on the sleeve of his gray silk jacket. That spot would nag at him all night. "Have you found a place large enough to hold all our Houston recruits?"

"I've found the perfect building, Mr. Wyatt. Big, empty, and centrally located. We'll be meeting late at night, so the area will be free of humans. I can take care of any security people who come nosing around. After everyone is inside, I'll ward the entrances."

He nodded absently as the fight engaged his attention. "This might not be over as quickly as I feared. Neva seems highly motivated."

Thadeus shrugged. "Neva was furious when Yvette dragged her in here. She was screaming about being tired of all this shit. I saw lots of rage."

"Ah, yes, rage. Lovely, lovely rage." Blood was already flowing from both animals, but he noticed something that warmed his heart. "Neva fights dirty. I like that in a combatant." He believed that no trick was too underhanded when dealing with an enemy. All that mattered was who remained standing at the end.

"Neva will win." Thadeus was usually right about these things. "Yvette has become overconfident. Besides, the red wolf is in better shape."

Thadeus had no sooner made his prediction than Neva crouched and rolled under a leaping Yvette. She struck at the gray wolf's soft underbelly with teeth and claws. Blood flowed, and Yvette screamed in shock and pain. Neva wasted no time. As Yvette fell to her side, Neva ripped out her throat. Then she stood shaking over her dead enemy.

Detached, he watched the drama to its gory conclusion. "Very good. I want Neva on our team. See that it happens."

He barely noticed when Thadeus left to disperse the circle and release Neva. His plan was unfolding right on schedule. Soon he'd be on his way to Dallas. Maybe he'd leave Seir in charge of Houston when he left. The demon had shown himself to be coldly efficient.

He was preparing to address the audience when his cell phone rang. Annoyed, he pulled it from his pocket. "Yes?" After listening to the brief message, he calmly returned the phone to his pocket. He walked over to where Thadeus was giving orders for the disposal of Yvette's body and pulled the sorcerer aside.

"Plans have changed. Our enemies are on their way here." He watched Neva, still in wolf form, glaring at everyone in the room. "Throw another wolf in with Neva. A new fight will keep the audience distracted. We're leaving. Now."

Thadeus paled. "Which enemies?"

"Jude's vampires, Macario's wolves, and even a few of the Gods of the Night." Absently, he rubbed at the spot on his sleeve again. "I truly regret I can't stay here to pit my powers against theirs. But sometimes one must forgo pleasure for duty. Our leader is a big-picture type."

Thadeus's gaze skittered around the room. "But we can't leave. We—"

"The humans upstairs can tell them nothing. The non-humans here for the first time also know nothing. I have no information in my office that will provide any clues." He glanced over the audience, which was starting to get restless. "There are some here who have already commit-ted to us, but they still can't help our enemies. What can they say? All they know is that my name is Wyatt and I'm recruiting an army to kill all humans." He shrugged. "Our enemies already know that."

Thadeus drew in a deep, gulping breath. "So what will happen?"

"They'll charge in, scare the shit out of the people upstairs—have I mentioned how much I enjoy your hu-man colloquialisms?—and probably kill most of the non-humans who try to leave the building. Even those down here who aren't involved in our endeavor will fight just for the joy of it all. If we're lucky, they might even kill a few of our enemies."

"Why don't we close the place down and send everyone home?" Thadeus had gained some control of his fear.

"No time. Start the next fight, and then meet me upstairs. And do it fast." He glanced at his watch. "We'll give them a half hour. That should put them in the middle of their attack. Then you'll notify the police." As he climbed the steps, he wondered how they'd found him. But he shrugged the thought away. It didn't matter. He was almost finished in Houston.

"There." Ty pointed to the building that squatted on a small patch of land at the tip of Brady's Island. "That's it. I feel wrongness there."

The building faced the Houston Ship Channel and showed the only signs of life on the small island. On one side, a narrow strip of water separated the island from the mainland. And on the other side, was the Channel with its constant flow of large ships.

It seemed strange to locate a club in the middle of all this heavy industry. Everything about the area made Ty uneasy. The darkness revealed an alien landscape filled with shadowy silhouettes—warehouses, large storage tanks, refineries, terminals, docked barges, and big empty parking lots.

"The restaurant's been here a long time, but I didn't know there was a club too." Kelly stopped the SUV in the restaurant's huge parking lot, which looked like it also served whatever industries shared the island. She got out of the SUV and peered around. "Jeez, talk about depressing. Not my fave place to be late at night."

Ty, along with Shen and Lio, joined her.

"The restaurant is closed. That's good. The only people we'll have to deal with are the ones in the club." Ty didn't want a bunch of panicked humans stampeding across the bridge to the mainland, carrying their tales to God knew where.

He took time to study the other cars. Some had people sitting in them. As he watched, Macario and Jude got out of two vehicles and walked over.

Jude smiled at Kelly, triggering Ty's automatic primal response. He allowed himself a silent snarl.

"I suppose it'd be too much to hope for a bloodbath." Jude looked resigned.

Macario bared his teeth. "I intend to rip out a few throats. Call it werewolf therapy."

Lio glanced at Kelly. "Am I likely to run into any ships in the water?"

Kelly looked startled. "Why would you be in the water?"

"Fin sent me, so obviously he expected me to be in the water." Lio took patronizing to a whole new level. "I assume if you surround the place, anyone trying to escape with this Neva will take to the water." His smile was all wicked anticipation. "I'll be waiting."

"Who's he?" Macario didn't try to hide his suspicion.

Ty did the introductions. "This is Lio. He's one of the Eleven." He nodded at Shen. "This is Shen. He's a shifter. We can use him tonight."

"What's the plan?" Jude's eyes had a hungry shine. "I'd be lying if I said I didn't have a taste for this kind of thing."

"Maybe you guys should call your people over so I don't have to repeat everything." Ty waited as the vampires and werewolves joined the group.

Jude's vampires deserved a second look. There were five of them, all male. Tall, muscular, and dressed completely in black, they should've been vampire clichés. They weren't. These men absorbed the darkness, and only a primitive soul like his could appreciate the flood of primal power flowing from them. Ty sensed no humanity in them, no souls, nothing to connect them to warmth or kindness. They would kill with passionless efficiency.

Just like you. It hit Ty then. That was what he'd been millions of years ago. But now he was something else, a hybrid, and he wouldn't be as he once was ever again. *But will you ever be completely human?* No, but if he could balance yesterday and today, it would be a beginning. Jude's soft laughter pulled Ty's attention back to their leader.

"Impressive, aren't they?" Jude's pride echoed in his voice. "They belonged to a very old, very powerful clan that was destroyed a few hundred years ago. No one else would take them in because of their clan's reputation for viciousness. I took the chance, and I've never regretted it. I only call on them for special occasions. Feel honored that you'll see them in action."

Ty nodded at the vampires, and they nodded back. But their expressions never changed. No smiles, nothing but hard stares. So much for extending the hand of friendship.

Ty switched his attention to Shen. "Fin said to send you in before we did anything. So I guess you change into something small that no one would notice." He frowned. "That'll make you pretty vulnerable."

"Do you change into a mouse?" Macario looked hopeful. Shen's gaze shifted back and forth between Ty and Kelly. "Not a mouse. Something . . . different."

Ty frowned. What the hell was wrong with him? It didn't matter what he changed into as long as he could find out what was happening inside. "Okay, change."

"Do you remember when you filled out all those papers for Fin, Kelly?" Shen wasn't smiling.

Puzzled, she nodded.

"In the blank space that asked what you feared most, you put snakes."

Uh-oh. Ty watched Kelly's eyes widen to saucer size.

"Oh, shit." Her words were breathed out on a shiver.

"Yeah."

Lio looked interested. "What kind?"

Shen's gaze never left Kelly. "Inland Taipan."

Lio whistled low. "There was some show on TV about you. Most toxic venom of any snake on earth. A single bite has enough poison to kill up to one hundred humans."

"Or two hundred fifty thousand mice." Shen sounded proud of that. "So you can forget about me being vulnerable."

"Yeah, yeah, this is all really impressive, but let's get on with it. If Neva's in there, I want her out. Fast." Macario looked ready to charge the club.

"Shit, shit, shit." Kelly watched Shen with unblinking horror.

Shen sighed. "Sorry, Kelly." Then he stripped off his clothes and shifted.

Ty grabbed Kelly before she could bolt. He wrapped her in his arms. "He's Shen. No matter what he looks like, he'd never hurt you."

"Dammit, I know that. In my head I know that." Kelly shuddered as she watched the six-foot-long snake slither away. "Stupid. I'm so freaking stupid. I know he won't hurt me, but what's inside me doesn't listen to reason. I can't control the fear."

"It's okay, it's okay." Ty wasn't a comforter, didn't know how. But he stroked her hair as he murmured encouragement.

And by the time Shen slithered back, Kelly had pulled

herself together a little. She watched with outward calm as he returned to human form and slipped back into his clothes. But Ty could feel her heart still pounding out a terrified rhythm.

Once dressed, Shen faced the group. "Okay, here's the deal. The room in the front is a regular club for humans. Only about twenty people. In back there's an office and a storage room. Both doors were closed, and I couldn't find any cracks to slither through. While I was there, a guy came along and went into the storage room. Just before he closed the door I got a glimpse inside. Looked like a regular room with boxes and stuff. Thing was, nobody was in there, and he didn't come back out. My guess is there're stairs leading to a basement or something." Shen paused. "And I think we'd better hurry. There was lots of noise coming from down below, howls and stuff. Something's happening, and wolves are involved."

Macario's low, rumbling growl said it all.

Ty nodded. "Lio, go down by the water and get ready to bare your soul if anyone heads your way. Make sure it's the enemy, though, before you chomp." He still didn't rule out the possibility that this was a dead end, that it had nothing to do with Nine or that Neva wasn't here at all.

Lio snorted his opinion of Ty's word choice. "Right. I just hope no ships come along while all this soul baring is going on." He walked away, and once beyond the parking lot faded into the shadows.

Jude looked worried. "How do we do this without scaring the crap out of the humans? We don't need mass hysteria getting in the way of our operation."

"And here I thought for a moment you had a heart." Kelly shook her head in mock disappointment.

Jude grinned. "Hey, the Tin Man and me, babe."

Macario paced. "I'm going in and killing anything that gets between Neva and me."

Ty exhaled wearily. "I know how you feel, but we can't just rush in. Fin seems to think Nine will be gone, but we don't know that for sure."

Kelly glanced around at the shadowy outlines of nearby buildings. "From what Fin has said, if Nine is inside, then he already knows we're here."

Ty made sure he had their attention. "And if that's true, then he's just sitting back waiting for us to come through the door. I don't want any of us to end up dead." The fear that Yvette had taken Neva elsewhere or that she might already be dead looked like a phantom ghoul in the darkness.

"There's a fire alarm in the club. Set it off and it'll clear out the humans." Shen was careful not to stand too close to Kelly.

"Good thought. Where is it?" Ty watched Kelly watch Shen.

"Near the restrooms."

"Come on, come on. We're wasting time." Macario's patience was at an end.

Ty nodded. "Someone needs to go in there, trip that alarm, and shout fire. The humans will run out the front door."

"I'll leave some of my pack out front. They'll make sure the humans keep on going to their cars." Macario smiled for the first time.

"Good. A few vampires should stay out here too. Make sure none of the nonhumans try to get out with the humans. Lio will take care of anyone who makes the mistake of trying to swim across the channel." Ty looked at Kelly. He knew she wouldn't stay out here where she'd be relatively safe. Not while Neva was possibly inside and still alive. So he'd give her the safest job he could think of. "You and Shen go in as a couple. Then you can set off the fire alarm when we're ready. I'll call your cell phone to let you know." *And Shen can make sure you stay out of trouble.*

Kelly's gaze skittered to Shen, then away again. "Sure." She took out her cell phone to set it on vibrate.

Shen made a disgusted sound. "Stop looking at me that way. I'm human, Kelly." He held his arms away from his body. "See?"

She nodded, but Ty recognized the shame in her eyes.

"Everyone else will go in the back entrance. We'll wait at the door to the storage room, and when the alarm goes off, we'll catch the rats abandoning ship." He opened his mental link to Fin. If something went wrong inside, Ty might need whatever help Fin could channel his way.

Macario didn't look happy. "Why wait at the door? Why not just go in and get the bastards?"

Jude answered that. "Impulsive werewolves." He cast the pack leader a derisive glance. "How do we know what's waiting for us? We're not even sure Neva's there. And if by chance Nine is in the building, I want some maneuvering room."

The pack leader snarled at Jude. Ty stepped in before a fight broke out. "We don't have time for this kind of crap. Save it for the enemy. Let's get moving."

A few minutes later he watched Kelly, clutching that stupid flute case along with her purse, walk into the club with Shen a good five steps behind her. Shen was letting her have her space. Smart man. And if anything happened to her . . . His soul stirred. Nothing would be left standing on this island. And not even Fin would be able to control Ty's rage.

Or his despair. Here in the darkness, he admitted that.

His feelings for her had been there from the beginning, growing stronger with each hour, but he'd mistaken them for instincts from another time. The urge to mate was all he'd ever known.

Well, what he felt now was unmistakably human—fear for her safety and the need to keep her close forever. Love? If so, it was a hopeless emotion; what woman in her right mind would go through the ordeal Fin had described just to claim him?

He pushed those thoughts aside as he waited for all the werewolves except Macario to change. Then he crept to the back of the building.

Jude held up a hand and whispered, "Shen can slither through small openings. We can't. This door will probably be locked, so—"

With a muttered curse, Macario pushed in front of Jude and calmly kicked the door down. Everyone froze.

"Son of a bitch." Jude muttered his opinion of that approach.

As an alarm blared the news that some idiot had taken out the door, Ty pulled his cell phone from his pocket and punched in Kelly's number. Almost immediately they heard the fire alarm sound. The music stopped, and Kelly shouted, "Fire!" Then pandemonium erupted from the club.

Macario led the charge into the hallway. He barely paused to kick down the first door he came to. "Office," he flung over his shoulder.

"He could've checked to see if the damn door was locked first." Jude's tone held nothing but contempt for Macario's primitive breaking-and-entering skills. "What ever happened to sneaking in and catching the enemy by surprise?"

"Jude and I will make sure none of them try to escape out the front with the humans. If they get past you, herd them out the back. Lio will take care of them if they hit the water. And for God's sake don't kill everyone. One of them might have information about Nine." Ty ignored the grumbling around him at that order. He placed himself in the middle of the hallway, blocking the path to the front of the building. The human screams were fading into the distance, where they mixed with the howls of wolves and the sounds of cars peeling out of the parking lot. Ty hoped the werewolves weren't having too much fun.

Jude joined him just as the door to the storage room burst open and a rush of nonhumans tried to force their way out into the hallway.

They hadn't counted on an enraged werewolf. Macario's change was almost instantaneous. He was already in midleap as he became wolf. And then he slashed his way through the howling mob with teeth and claws. They gave way before him, and he disappeared into the storage room.

Ty shouted above the noise. "Some of you go in and help him."

He didn't get a chance to see if anyone obeyed him. The nonhumans from the storage room poured into the hallway. Within seconds, the narrow hall was filled with leaping, snarling wolves and battling vampires.

Ty, along with Jude, turned back anyone who tried to fight past them. No immortal with incredible power seemed to be among those rolling around on the floor and bouncing off the walls. In fact, as far as Ty could tell, there were only werewolves and vampires in this bunch. And not especially powerful ones at that. Time to put this show to bed before Jude's vampires ripped out everyone's throats.

"Freeze." He put all the power of his other soul into the command.

They obeyed. For a moment.

Ty spoke before they could get their second wind. "You can all walk away from this. We just need some information. You—" He pointed at a sulky-looking vampire. "What was going on down there?"

The vampire shrugged as he cast Jude a nervous glance. "We'd heard you could bet on some good fights at this club. Real fights. We just got through watching two werewolves mix it up. This was our first time here." He aimed his comment at Jude, who didn't look impressed. Then he nodded at a woman who stood beside him. "We were waiting for the next fight when the alarms went off."

Ty looked over the group. "Is this everyone? Anyone else left?"

Another vampire spoke up. "There's a bunch downstairs. I think they work for the guy running this show. He ducked out about fifteen minutes ago."

"Why didn't they come up with you?" Jude's expression promised instant death to any vampire who lied to him.

The same vampire shrugged. "They heard the door alarm go off before the fire alarm and figured the fire alarm was just a distraction to cover up the break-in. They thought we were under attack. I thought there was a fire." He glanced around. "Guess they were right."

Ty looked at Jude. "We have to get down there to help Macario."

Jude nodded. "I want all of you to go out this back door, get in your cars, and never come back here. This club is closed." He pulled out his cell phone, spoke to one of his men, then put the phone away. "No one will bother you when you leave."

A few seconds later, only Jude, his three vampires, and Macario's wolves were left in the hall. Ty thought they all looked disappointed. They hadn't gotten to kill anyone.

Pushing into the storage room, Ty headed for the still-open door leading down to the basement. The others crowded around him. Sounds of fighting rose from below. "Here's where we do some serious damage."

One of Jude's vampires smiled for the first time, his fangs on full display.

"Don't kill any wolves unless you're sure they're the enemy. Remember, we're here to find Neva, and I don't have a clue what form she'll be in."

As he crept down the stairs, Ty wondered where Kelly was. God, he hoped she'd had enough sense to go outside where she'd be safe. Then he pushed all distractions aside as he leaped the final few steps and burst into the room.

Chapter Fifteen

Kelly liked feeling safe. She felt that way now. Sort of. Or at least as safe as she could feel with a bad-tempered vampire on one side of her and a hyperactive werewolf on the other.

All the humans were gone, even the bartender and barmaids. And if the werewolves chased them to their cars with a little too much enthusiasm, it wasn't her problem. Macario could address that issue.

But safety didn't translate into comfortable. Through the open front door, she could hear the faint sounds of battle. Ty was in there. Was Nine there too? If so, Ty would find it tough to survive the fight with only a few vampires and werewolves to back him up. With no space for his T. rex to take form, he'd be vulnerable. And what about Neva? Was she still alive?

She tallied up the reasons to go back into the club. Ty was in danger. She had the flute, and if Nine was in there, she could play her tune and stop the madness, at least in Houston. Ty was in danger. If Neva was still alive, Kelly might be the only one who could care for her because everyone else would be busy trying to kill one another. Ty was in danger.

And in the end, Kelly knew she had to go back inside. She didn't try to fool herself into thinking it was a heroic decision. It was fear. Fear that she wouldn't be there if Ty should need her.

The vampires and werewolves wouldn't try to stop her.

Their leaders hadn't ordered them to keep an eye on her. Shen? She glanced over to where he stood talking to one of the vampires. No, Shen wouldn't care if she left. He didn't even like her.

Kelly faded into the shadows and made her way to the back of the club. The front was too exposed. In the darkness by the back of the building, she opened her case and assembled her flute. Then she hung the instrument around her neck by the cord she'd tied to it. She let it hang down the back of her neck. It was going to bounce against her butt when she walked, but at least it would be handy if she needed it.

Taking a deep breath, she peeked in the back door. Nothing leaped out at her. She unzipped her purse and pulled out her pepper spray. She left the purse hanging from her shoulder unzipped so she could reach the gun Q had given her. Then she edged down the hallway.

Kelly paused at the open door to the storage room. She could hear the battle raging loud and clear from below, lots of shouting, snarling, and the thuds of bodies hitting walls.

Think. What would happen if she walked down the stairs with a gun drawn? As far as the werewolves went, she wouldn't know friend from foe. And what if she distracted Ty at a critical moment? She leaned against the wall. What the hell was the right thing to do?

The decision was taken out of her hands. She heard something big leaping up the stairs. It didn't sound like human footsteps. Backing down the hall, she pulled the gun from her purse.

Everything happened too fast. The werewolf charged out of the storage room, skidded on the tile floor as it turned toward the back door, and saw her. Bloody and torn, its eyes glowed with insane bloodlust. In just one leap it was on her.

Her reaction was a second too slow. Her shot went wild and she fell backward, putting her arm up to protect her face from its teeth.

In the second before Kelly knew she would die, Shen struck. She saw the snake slither past her head and drive his fangs into the wolf's leg.

With a howl of pain and surprise, the werewolf forgot about Kelly. It bit the snake before slamming him against the wall over and over until Shen released his grip. Then the wolf raced out the door and onto the deck that backed up to the Ship Channel.

Dazed, Kelly stared at the wolf. "Dead wolf running." If it somehow escaped the vampires and wolves surrounding the club, the snake's venom would kill it.

The wolf glanced left, then right. Trapped, it opted for an escape by water. Mistake. It ran to the end of the lit deck and leaped toward the Ship Channel. Lio was waiting.

Kelly's breath froze in her throat as Lio rose from the water propelled by eighty feet of massive body and opened gigantic jaws filled with eight-inch-long teeth. He took the wolf in midleap and dragged him down. Kelly was glad it was too dark to see details.

Shen. He still lay limp at the foot of the wall. Was he alive? Fear rose, clogging the back of her throat, trying to tell her this was a snake, a *snake.* She wanted to scuttle away from the body.

She didn't. He'd saved her life, and if he was dead, it was her fault. If she hadn't come in here, he'd still be outside talking to the vampire. And good intentions didn't count. Dead was dead.

Kelly pushed herself to her feet. Fighting the unreasoning terror that made nausea clench at her stomach, she stumbled over to where he lay. *Pick him up.* She couldn't; she just couldn't.

The biggest battle of her whole life took place as she stood swaying over Shen's body. It lasted about thirty seconds. Conscience triumphed over fear. Crouching, she lifted him into her arms. Then, shaking with terror, she carried him out of the building.

Her heart felt like it was going to burst from her chest with every beat, and her breaths were coming in hard, short gasps by the time she reached the first vampire. "Shen. I don't even know if he's alive. Help him."

The vampire stared at her from cold black eyes before shifting his attention to Shen. He touched the snake. "He's alive. If that bite hasn't killed him already, it won't. Get him to change, and he'll heal himself." Then the vampire turned his attention back to the club.

Kelly felt awful. She wasn't sure which was worse, her worry about Ty and Neva or her guilt over Shen. After finding the spot where Shen had put his neatly folded clothes on the ground, she laid the snake on the pile. She pulled the cord holding her flute from around her neck, and sat beside him.

Her fear was still babbling away in her head, but it was more of a background noise now. Maybe it would help to talk to him. "God, I'm sorry, Shen. I should've stayed out here. And what can I say about your saving my life except thanks. I'll owe you for as long as I live. Which won't be long if I keep doing stuff like that." She wiggled into a more comfortable position and tried not to notice that she was talking to a snake. "One of Jude's vampires said you have to change back to human form so you can heal. If you can hear me, please try. Look, I'll go get a blanket I

saw in the back of the SUV and give you some privacy."
Okay, so she was the one who needed privacy.

Rising, she walked slowly to the car, thoughts whirling
in her mind. Where was Ty? Was he okay? The werewolf
that had attacked her was one of the bad guys, right?
Macario's wolves knew her. They wouldn't try to kill her.
Or maybe they would. Crazy and irrational could equal
dangerous no matter which side the wolf was on.

She took her time getting the blanket and even went to
retrieve her flute case before returning to Shen. To her relief, when she got close, she saw that he was back in human form. He was weakly trying to pull on his clothes.

Maybe she had some maternal instincts after all, because
she hurried over to help him. "Here, don't strain yourself."
She helped him put his shirt on. "Where're you hurt?" Kelly
draped the blanket around him. "Let's get you into the
SUV."

Shen just nodded as she helped him to his feet. Half sup-
porting him, she finally got him into the passenger side of
the car. He leaned his head back against the seat. "My
thigh's a little chewed up, but it's not bleeding too much
anymore. Once I get back to Fin's condo, I'll take care of
it. I heal fast." He studied her. "You know, you impressed
the hell out of me when you picked me up. Must've been
tough."

Kelly didn't sense any sarcasm in his comment. She
wouldn't try to downplay her fear. "You think? I was
scared witless. I would've followed the wolf into the Ship
Channel, but I noticed that it didn't end well for him. So I
decided picking up the snake made more sense than swimming with Lio." Here came the important part. "And the
snake was *you*, Shen. The friend who'd just put his life on
the line for me."

Kelly didn't get to hear his reply because suddenly a vampire and two werewolves burst from the back door. They glanced around, saw they were surrounded and threw themselves into the Ship Channel. She looked away just as Lio rose to meet them. As she tried to shut out their final screams, she bit her lip to keep from screaming herself.

Where was Ty? Where was Neva? By the time Ty and the others emerged from the front door of the club, Kelly was an emotional slice of burnt toast, ready to crumble into brittle bits.

She flung herself from the SUV and raced to meet him. Without considering the consequences, she slammed into his chest hard enough to draw a startled ummph from him. At the same time, she wrapped her arms tightly around his waist. Vaguely aware that he'd put his arms around her too, she babbled her fears into his shirt. "I was afraid Nine might be in there. I was afraid you might be hurt. I was afraid . . ."

The silence finally registered. She turned her head. Everyone was staring. They were smiling. A lot. Oh, jeez. Had she embarrassed him? Trying to look casual, she dropped her arms and stepped out of his embrace. "I, um, was worried about everyone."

When she met Ty's gaze, he wasn't smiling. Thank God.

"Women from this time aren't used to violence. They get overemotional," he said matter-of-factly.

Kelly narrowed her eyes. "What?"

Ty missed the warning sign. Too bad. "Q's watching this video about women. It explains why modern females react the way they do. So I know what you're thinking." His expression said he expected her to be grateful for his understanding. He started to turn toward Jude.

"Whoa. Wait just a minute." She stepped forward and poked him in the chest. "Don't ever presume to know what I'm thinking." *I'm thinking I love you.* And that one thought shut her up.

A rusty laugh emerged from the back of the crowd. "You tell him, sister. No man has ever figured out what a woman's thinking. Shouldn't even try."

Kelly's eyes widened. "Neva?" Pushing through the crowd, she found the other woman tucked firmly against Macario's side. Her red hair was standing on end, and her clothes were stained and torn, but she was smiling.

Neva reached out and gave Kelly a surprisingly strong hug considering how she looked. She had bruises and cuts, but other than that she seemed okay.

"God, I'm glad you're safe. Was it bad?" Defiantly, Kelly wiped tears from her eyes.

"Yeah." Neva's gaze darkened. "But I found out what I was made of. I'm tough, and I fight dirty, and I survive." Then she leaned close to Kelly's ear. "Tell him, sister. Take him home tonight and tell Ty you love him. If he'd stop long enough to really look at your face, he'd see it. But men miss things like that."

"Neva is coming home with me tonight." Macario sounded definite about that. "And she's not going back to work for Fin."

Neva's eyes got a little teary, proving she wasn't so tough where the pack leader was concerned. "This guy saved me. He was the first one down the stairs. Nine's sorcerer had cast a circle, and I couldn't get out. I'd already fought Yvette and killed her. The bitch." She paused to savor that moment. "But then they put another wolf into the circle."

Macario picked up the story. "When I saw Neva fighting in that circle, I went crazy. I got lucky because the circle's energy was almost gone." His lips lifted in a savage grin. "I tore that wolf into so many pieces, they could use him for a jigsaw puzzle."

In the brief pause, they heard police sirens.

"Shit. Let's get out of here." Ty grabbed Kelly's arm and ran for the SUV.

She ran with him, only pausing long enough to scoop up her flute. Already, the remaining cars were leaving the parking lot. "But what about all those bodies inside the—"

"I'll take care of that." He practically threw her into the driver's seat.

Lio raced up and flung himself into the back. He was dressed, but he was still dripping water. Kelly couldn't meet his gaze.

Ty glanced at the front seat, then climbed into the back beside Lio. He rolled down the window while she started the car. As he stared intently at the club, it suddenly exploded into flames.

Her jaw dropped. "What the—"

"Drive."

The sirens were getting closer, so she took his advice. A block away from the club, she glanced back. All she could see was the fire's glow in the sky. "How'd you do that?"

"I kept my mental link to Fin open. He supplied the power."

Kelly wondered what else Fin could do. Considering that he shared none of himself with anyone, she'd probably never know.

"I think I deserve a bonus for tonight. The whole time I worried about going head-on with a ship." Lio was back to being Mr. Morose.

Kelly glanced in the mirror. "You impressed me, Lio." *I might never go in the water again.*

Lio grunted at her, but he looked pleased.

"What happened, Shen?" Ty's voice was quiet.

Shen was huddled into the blanket Kelly had given him. "I went back into the club. In snake form. Thought I could help. A werewolf left your party early and caught me in the hallway. He tried to chew me in half. I bit him and then Lio finished him off."

"He's lying. Shen's covering for me." She threw Shen a warning glance. "Ty should know what you did."

Shen sighed and closed his eyes.

"I knew you wanted me to stay outside where I'd be safe, but I couldn't just stand there and wait to see who came out. I was worried about Neva." She refused to meet his gaze in the mirror. "And you. And everyone." *But mostly you.* "I had the gun and pepper spray. I had my flute in case Nine was down there." Kelly held up her hand to keep Ty from interrupting. "And, yes, it was stupid. I sort of realized that once I got as far as the hallway."

Her rising terror told Kelly that Ty's primal personality was making a cameo appearance. "Anyway, all of a sudden this werewolf came barreling out of the storage room. I had my gun out, but he was too fast for me, and my shot went wild. I thought I was dead."

Kelly realized Ty must be totally ticked to cause the kind of fear churning in her stomach. "Put a cap on your mad, Ty, because you're scaring me." She spoke through clenched teeth. Her fear immediately eased. "That's when Shen slithered past me. He bit the wolf. The wolf bit him back and then banged him against the wall until Shen let go. By that time, the wolf had forgotten about me. It ran outside and jumped into the water. Lio finished it."

"Is that all?" Ty's voice was softly dangerous.

"No." Shen opened his eyes. "After the wolf was gone, Kelly picked me up and carried me outside."

Shock widened Ty's eyes. "You picked up a *snake*?"

"He saved my life." What else was there to say?

"Took guts for her to do that." Lio sounded approving for a change.

"Yeah." Ty didn't elaborate.

The one word didn't give Kelly a clue what he was thinking. Silence settled into the car for the rest of the drive to Fin's condo. Lio and Shen fell asleep. She could feel Ty's gaze on her. He probably had his anger to keep him alert and glowering. Kelly wanted to ask him what had happened, but maybe now wasn't the time.

They were just pulling into the condo's driveway when Ty finally spoke. "Fin wants us to come up with Lio and Shen."

She nodded. What would it be like to have your boss able to pump orders directly into your head? Couldn't check caller ID for those calls. Bummer.

Kelly dropped Lio and Shen at the front entrance and then drove the SUV into the parking garage. Considering his mood, she wished Ty had gotten out with the others. He hadn't. He was determined to be her personal storm cloud, a dark looming presence wherever she went.

"You could've died tonight." Ty forced the words out in a quiet, calm voice. He watched her collect her flute and purse before turning to face him.

"Yeah. And so could you." She tipped her chin up in a defiant gesture.

He felt his fury building, at the werewolf he wished were still alive so he could kill it all over again, at the situation that prevented him from guarding her, at himself for feel-ing so clueless when it came to this woman.

Ty reached out to touch her shoulder. "You. Could have. Freaking. *Died*. Tonight." He shook under the force of his emotion.

Her face grew pale as she drew in a breath and stepped away from him. Damn. He forced his fury back into its cage where it howled and rattled the bars. He rubbed his hand across his face and exhaled sharply. "Sorry."

She stared at him, her eyes wide and filled with an emo-tion he didn't recognize. "You big, dumb doofus. You don't have a clue, do you?"

While he tried to figure out her secret code, she calmly put down her flute and purse, then reached up to tangle her fingers in his hair. She yanked his head down and kissed him. No doubt about who was the initiator here. But no one could accuse him of being a slow learner.

He wrapped his arms around her and deepened the kiss. Her lips moved over his, soft and tempting.

His tongue explored all the warmth and wanting she of-fered. The small sounds of pleasure she made excited him almost beyond his control. He wanted to drag her down between the SUV and the Lexus beside it, rip her clothes from that lush body, and bury himself deep inside her.

Only the thought of how he'd feel afterwards, knowing he'd made love with her in the parking garage, gave him the strength to break the kiss. She deserved a soft bed, tons of comfort after the way he'd lost control on the balcony last time. His breaths came in hard gasps. "No. Not here, not like this. We'll finish this later when you're warm and relaxed." There. He'd done the civilized thing. But, damn it, being civilized was going to kill him.

Her laughter was shaky. "You think warm and relaxed

will make it better? There's a lot to be said for spontaneity."
She looked like she was remembering the balcony too. But
she picked up her things and started toward the elevator.

A few minutes later, Fin was leading them up the stairs
to the suite they'd shared before. This time without Neva.
"Stay here for the rest of the night. You're exhausted. And
I need a report about tonight, Ty." He glanced at Kelly. "I
won't keep him long. You can take a hot shower and un-
wind."

The look she sent Ty's way said she had the perfect plan
for unwinding. "No problem."

Ty waited until the door closed before turning to Fin.
"This couldn't wait until tomorrow?"

"Tomorrow will bring other crises." He led Ty to his office. "So we deal with this one tonight."

Once settled in a chair on the other side of Fin's massive desk, Ty reported everything—the fight and what
he'd learned from Neva about Nine.

"Good. Very good." Fin braced his elbows on the desk
and steepled his fingers as he thought. "So Nine has taken
on the persona of a middle-aged businessman. And he's
sponsoring fights between nonhumans. The violence and
opportunity to make bets are drawing in exactly the kind
of soldiers he's looking for. He rewards those who join
him with hunting territories and kills anyone he thinks
might be a spy. Ruthless and effective."

Ty thought those words could describe Fin too.

"We won't catch him by surprise. He's too smart for
that. So when we find out where he is, we go in knowing
it's a trap. We'll just make sure we have our own trap in
place to counter his."

Ty was about to ask if he could go back to Kelly when a
completely different question occurred to him. He asked

before he could think about it. "I know you've said we were nothing before we were dinosaurs, but that doesn't make sense. Are you telling us the truth?"

Fin stared at him, his eyes showing no emotion beyond their shining surface. "No."

For a second, Ty didn't think he'd heard Fin correctly. He almost shook his head, expecting the familiar fog to roll in and blur his thoughts. Nothing happened.

"No? Just like that? *No?*" Ty fought back his instinctive anger. Now was not the time to lose his temper. "Explain."

Fin shrugged. He didn't look concerned that he'd just shaken Ty's life to its core. "No, I haven't been telling you the truth. And, no, I'm not going to explain."

"Why?" Waves of fury alternated with the suffocating knowledge that Fin had lied to them. He wrapped mental arms around his animal soul, holding it down.

"I've blocked your memories of the time before, and I've done some minor fiddling to keep you from asking questions. It was my choice. Some things are best not re-membered."

"You don't have that right."

"I have more right than you'll ever know." For a moment anger flared in Fin's eyes and then was gone. "You couldn't change what happened or what came after. You wouldn't have been able to function with your primitive soul if you'd had those memories. And now? Those memories would get in the way of what we have to do. Saving humanity is all that matters."

"You're a cold son of a bitch."

Fin's smile would've frozen fire. "Oh, yes. Only a cold son of a bitch could have guarded our secrets for two hundred million years."

Two hundred million years? "Why admit this now? Why

not just keep messing with my mind?" His head would explode if he didn't take a shot at Fin.

"Because you're in love with Kelly, and you have to understand how your past will affect her."

Ty stilled. "What do you mean?"

Fin laughed, not a kind laugh. "No, I didn't get that revelation from your mind. I didn't have to. It's written all over your face."

Love Kelly? The truth hit Ty so hard, he almost forgot his fury at Fin. "You already told us what a woman would have to do if she made the mistake of falling in love with us." He didn't bother hiding his bitterness.

"I told you she'd have to walk into the heart of your beast and claim a piece of your soul. And you'd have to let her." He met Ty's gaze. "I didn't tell you the rest. I think I have to tell you now."

This was going to be bad. Ty could sense it coming.

"Before she claims that piece of your soul, she'll *see* all that you were in your previous life . . . and all that you were before. And the before is almost more than a human mind can bear. I won't have the power to spare her that." Fin spun his chair to face the bank of windows that showed Houston still cloaked in darkness. "Even if she keeps her sanity, I can't guarantee she'll come out the other side of the experience still loving you. And beyond that, there'd be the problem of her immortality."

"Immortality?"

"After surviving that peek into your soul, she'd be immortal like us. Think about how that would change her life. Think about what you'd be asking of her love."

Ty wasn't able to wrap his understanding around everything Fin had said. "So what you're saying is that no woman can ever survive loving us."

Fin's voice held a touch of humor this time. "Well, it wouldn't be a good start to the relationship. And, no, I'm not saying *she* couldn't survive. I'm saying she'd have to love you a hell of a lot for her feelings to survive. Call me cynical, but I'm not a big believer in unconditional love."

"In other words, we'll never be anything other than what we are now." Men, beasts, alone.

"Maybe that's all we deserve to be." Fin sounded as if he was thinking about that time before.

"Aren't you afraid I'll tell everyone?" How did Kelly feel about him? Did it matter? Even if she loved him, he wouldn't put her through what Fin had described.

"Hey, tell away. I don't care. It won't change a thing. We still have to work together so humanity can survive, and I still won't tell you what you want to know."

"A lot of the guys would hate you for this."

Fin's laugh was harsh. "I've been hated by experts. I don't react to the emotion of others. It can't touch me, Ty. Nothing can touch me."

"Then I feel sorry for you." Ty rose and left Fin still staring out across a darkened Houston.

When he walked into the suite, the lights were on, but Kelly was in bed. She was asleep. Exhaustion had taken its toll. He turned off the lights, then stood staring at her. Moonlight bathed the room in pale light. He'd always remember her this way.

Finally tearing his gaze away from her, he went into the bathroom, peeled off his bloody clothes, and stepped into the shower. Hot water washed away the gore and eased some of the tension from his muscles.

But it would take more than a hot shower to do the same for his mind. Would he tell the others? Probably not. Maybe after they got rid of Nine. He didn't know, wasn't sure. Did he want to be the one who tore the Eleven apart?

Once out of the shower, he dried off and walked back into the bedroom. He slipped under the covers beside Kelly. Ty smiled. She wore another nightshirt. He wore nothing. Habits were hard to break.

He loved her. Fin was right. Ty closed his eyes and thought about Kelly. Did she love him? Didn't matter. The whole love thing was a lose-lose proposition. Even if she did love him, he'd never let her take the chance of trying to claim his soul. And if she didn't love him? Well, either way he ended up miserable.

As Ty drifted off to sleep, he hoped Fin did lots of dreaming about the past he'd denied the rest of the Eleven.

Chapter Sixteen

Kelly lay with eyes closed, savoring that drowsy moment right after waking when her mind was completely empty, her body relaxed, and everything was right with her world.

Too bad it only lasted for a few seconds. Then reality started trickling back into her consciousness. The good stuff? If she opened her eyes and turned her head, she'd find Ty sleeping next to her. The other stuff? Nine was still out there, and she was sick of werewolves. A good night would be one when she didn't see a werewolf, didn't talk to a werewolf, and wasn't an entree on some werewolf's menu.

She opened her eyes and turned her head. Kelly smiled at the gorgeous guy watching her with serious intensity. "What's wrong? You don't look happy. I'm sure happy waking up next to you."

His sensual lips tipped up in a smile. "Just thinking."

"Care to share?" She rolled to her side to face him.

He'd only pulled the covers up to his hips, leaving everything else bare. The wide expanse of golden skin over hard muscle was enough to make her light-headed. She had an almost uncontrollable urge to kiss every inch of his spectacular chest and ridged stomach before slipping the covers down a few more inches.

Ty folded his hands behind his head. "How powerful is human love, Kelly?"

She blinked. That wasn't what she'd expected him to say. "Be a little more specific."

"Say a man loves a woman. How far does he have a right to ask her to go for him before it becomes selfishness on his part? We're talking hypothetically, of course."

"Of course." Kelly glanced away. His question came uncomfortably close to emotions of her own she hadn't sorted through yet. "I've never been in love." *Getting really close, though.* "But I don't think there's any do-not-proceed-beyond-this-line sign posted when two people love each other." She gave the question more thought. "If I loved a man, I'd lay everything out and let *him* decide. It wouldn't be my call to make."

"Maybe." He didn't sound convinced.

She met his gaze. "Is there a point to this?"

"Just trying to get a handle on human emotions. They're all new to me." His smile looked a little strained. "I was thinking about Neva and Macario. She's giving up the life she knew to live in his world. It won't be easy for her."

"Love usually isn't." Kelly smiled. "But the perks are great."

Speaking of perks, the perks of sharing a bed with Ty should include the right to touch. Sounded fair to her. Before her brain could marshal a string of reasons why she should keep her hands to herself, Kelly reached out and slid her fingers over his chest. Smooth, warm, male. Tactile heaven.

Drawing in a deep breath, he rolled to his side and then kissed her. It was long and deep, and the force of it pushed her onto her back. She wrapped her arms around him and pulled him down with her. The sensation of his body—hot, naked, and definitely ready to play—promised that her day would start on a high note.

And then it was over. He broke the kiss, and as he rolled onto his back again, she glimpsed regret and something else in his eyes.

He turned his head to smile at her, but his gaze was shuttered. "I'd explore possibilities right now, but Fin is expecting us downstairs in—" he glanced at the bedside clock—"about fifteen minutes."

Reluctantly, she moved away from him and swung her feet to the floor. She tried to push aside the thought that if he really felt motivated, fifteen minutes would've been more than enough time. Sighing, she shuffled into the bathroom.

And exactly fifteen minutes later she was seated at the dining room table with Ty and Fin, eating breakfast at 2:30 in the afternoon. Someone had collected their clothes while they slept, washed and dried them, then returned them to their room. Wearing clean clothes and drinking her first cup of coffee made Kelly feel almost normal. No, make that *dissatisfied* and almost normal. Sexual frustration was a terrible thing.

Fin tapped his fingers on the table as he thought. "It's interesting that Nine is keeping a sorcerer with him. I'd bet black magic is a big part of this guy's repertoire. Nine needs as much dark energy as he can get."

"If Nine is so powerful, why would he need a sorcerer?" Kelly slid her glance to Ty. He was being strangely quiet around Fin.

"Power of any kind can run down if you overuse it. Nine wants to keep his battery strong, so he's hired a sorcerer to do the small stuff." Fin stopped tapping his fingers and met her gaze. "And Ty is quiet because he's angry at me. I told him some things last night he didn't want to hear."

"Fin." Ty's voice held a warning.

Fin ignored him. "Since a lot of what I said involves you, I'd get him to fill you in sometime soon if I were you."

Uh-oh. Ty was starting to broadcast. Fin just grinned at him.

Ty pushed his plate away. "What should we do tonight?"

"I spoke with Jude, and he was able to give me a good description of the sorcerer. Vampires seem less impulsive than werewolves. They think before they kill. One of Jude's crew took the time to get some information out of one of the nonhumans before he tore his head off. The sorcerer's name is Thadeus, and I'll have Shen e-mail you a full description."

Shen. Kelly felt guilty for not asking about him sooner. "Is Shen okay?"

Fin looked distracted. "Shen is resilient. It would take a lot to kill him."

Kelly subsided. She'd be willing to pay good money to be in the audience if Fin ever displayed any real emotion about anyone or anything.

Fin turned his attention back to Ty. "Take Q with you and see if you can find any places in the city with connections to the occult or magic. Check out stores or clubs where someone might know our Thadeus."

Ty nodded, then rose from the table.

"Why don't you play your music before you go, Kelly?" Fin remained seated.

She took that as a royal command. Luckily, she'd brought her flute down with her just in case they had to leave right after they ate. She quickly assembled it, then played her brain music for Fin. It really was an amazing little tune, and the acoustics of the huge room gave the melody's Celtic flavor an ethereal feel. Or maybe she just thought it was amazing because it was a part of her.

"If we're lucky, that'll be the last thing Nine hears before you banish him from Earth for another sixty-five million years." There was almost a fanatical gleam in Fin's eyes.

Kelly looked away, pretending to concentrate on taking her flute apart and putting it back in its case.

Ty locked gazes with her. "We'll find another way." He ignored Fin.

Turning away, Ty strode toward the door. She ran to catch up. No way would she try to question him while he was in this mood, but sometime soon she'd find out what Fin had said. If it concerned her, she had a right to know.

He didn't speak all the way down to the parking garage, but she didn't mind. It just gave her more time to think. Absently, she noticed it was overcast outside. Maybe they'd get some rain.

Silence reigned during the drive to their apartment building. Finally, on the way upstairs, Mr. Somber and Silent spoke. "Kelly, how would you feel about being a driver for one of the other guys?"

"What?" She felt as though he'd gut-punched her.

"You've seen a lot more violence than any of the other drivers. Maybe you need a break."

He was lying. She sensed it in a part of her that was intimately connected to him. And wasn't that scary. Violence had nothing to do with this. Maybe *he* was the one who needed a break. Add depressing to scary.

What to do? If her feelings weren't all tangled up with him, she'd simply say okay. Let him do what he wanted to do. But walking away from Ty now would be like slashing an emotional artery. She'd bleed out fast. So she took the let-me-think-about-it path. "I need time. Let's talk again later about this."

He nodded before disappearing into his apartment. She

stared at his door for a long time. Ty still wanted her. Kelly was woman enough to recognize the signs. But he'd been pushing her away since last night, *since he'd talked to Fin.* The next time she got Ty alone, she'd worm what Fin had said out of him.

As Kelly let herself into her apartment, she lined up the things she wanted to get done before they left for the night. She definitely had to call Mom and Jenna. Then . . .

Closing the door behind her, Kelly looked around. Something was different. A scan of the room showed nothing out of place. But suddenly it hit her. The drapes were closed. They'd been open when she'd left.

Before she had a chance to react to the discovery, a cowled figure emerged from her bedroom. Its hood was pulled so far over its face that she couldn't see any features clearly in the darkened room.

"Who the hell are you?" She fumbled, trying to unzip her purse so she could reach her gun.

"Don't panic. It's just me. Jude sent me over to pass on some info he found that could help you." The figure glided forward. "I have to dress this way so I can go out during the daylight."

Kelly relaxed. She'd gotten a good look at the person's face. "God, you scared me. Why didn't Jude call instead of making you play messenger?"

The figure leaned close. "Because it's very important information."

Kelly's sudden realization came too late. She felt the prick of a needle even as she blurted, "Wait, how'd you get past Fin's security?"

While weakness made Kelly stagger and darkness pushed at her consciousness, the vampire laughed. "No security keeps Mr. Wyatt out."

The vampire's laughter followed her into the blackness. Kelly felt her flute case slip from her grasp as she fell.

Ty propped his feet up on his coffee table as he let Q run out of rant.

"Fin sent a freaking fish along with you instead of me."

"Lio isn't a fish. He's a swimming reptile. You saw the stuff Fin put on that CD."

"Same thing. I can't believe it. I could've done the job. Who helped you take out the red wolves? This whole thing sucks." Q continued pacing, flinging his arms around to emphasize his outrage. "Fin screwed me, that's what."

"Hey, we're partners. Fin just thought it'd be a little easier for Lio to handle anyone who went into the water. It was dark, and you might've had trouble spotting them from overhead. You should've relaxed and enjoyed the night off."

Q didn't look appeased. "So it wouldn't have pissed you if Fin decided to leave *you* home last night?"

"Okay, point made. Look, it's over and we'll be hunting together tonight." He'd bring Q up to date, and then they'd go over to pick up Kelly.

No matter how much he tried to deny it, the thought of being with her again excited him. At least a dozen times this afternoon he'd almost given in and walked across the hall to her. It was tough trying to do the right thing.

Ten minutes later he'd told Q everything and shown him the description of Thadeus. On their way out, Ty knocked at Kelly's door and waited. He knocked again. Nothing. Frowning, he tried the door. Unease touched him when he found it was unlocked.

After calling her name and getting no response, Ty walked into her apartment. Q followed him inside. Without speaking, the two men searched the place.

"No signs of a struggle." Q swung in a circle, taking in every inch of the living room.

"She wouldn't go out and leave her purse on the counter, her flute on the floor, and her door unlocked." Unease slid quickly into fear. Along with guilt. If only he'd come over earlier. And where the hell had his famous sense for wrongness been? When it counted the most, his talent had failed him.

"Better let Fin know." Q raked his fingers through his hair. "Crap. First Neva and now Kelly."

"We don't know that for sure." But he did. Ty tried to control his rising fury. If anyone hurt Kelly, neither heaven nor hell could save the bastard.

Q's expression softened. "Contact Fin, man."

Ty nodded. Forgetting his earlier anger at Fin, he opened their mental link. He didn't wait for Fin to acknowledge him. *"Someone took Kelly out of her apartment this afternoon."*

Fin's response was immediate. *"Get the disks from the security cameras. I'll send someone to pick you up. I'm calling in the rest of the Eleven."*

That was it. Fin never wasted time soothing fears or pandering to emotions. This time, Ty was glad of Fin's ability to coldly and unemotionally focus on a problem.

An hour later, the Eleven sat around the long dining room table in the condo. Fin scanned the group with hard eyes. "We've looked at the security tapes. A figure wearing a cowl carried Kelly out the door. I'm assuming he or she had a car pulled up right outside. We couldn't see a face, but the cowl might serve as more than just a disguise. The figure wore gloves. I'm thinking we're probably dealing with a vampire. A vampire would have had the strength to carry her out of the building, and a vampire would have to protect all exposed skin from daylight. I've already spoken to Jude. Only a few of his people are old enough to rise before sunset. He'll see what he can find out."

Ty listened to Fin with barely controlled anger. "How do we find Kelly?"

Fin hesitated. "I don't know yet."

"That's not what I want to hear." Ty's words were forced through clenched teeth.

Fin met his gaze. "I think Nine ordered Kelly taken. He's the only supernatural entity in Houston strong enough to bypass my security. I think she's still alive, and my best guess is that Nine intends to use her as bait."

"If he's smart, he'll know we won't fall for that." Lio's expensive suit gave no hint of the soul that had torn apart werewolves and vampires alike last night.

"I don't care why he took her. I just want to know where she is so I can go get her." Ty could feel his T. rex shaking the bars of its cage.

Fin looked away from Ty. "Emotion sometimes makes people choose an unwise path." He pushed his chair away from the table. "I want all of you to begin searching for Kelly. Let me know immediately if you turn up anything." His attention returned to Ty. "If you think you've found her, call *me* before attempting a rescue. Got that, Ty?"

"Yeah, I've got it." Ty couldn't stay here one more minute. He rose and stalked to the door; Q was right behind him.

"We need to wait for someone to drive us home, Ty." Q glanced back to where Fin was watching them.

"Like hell we do." He was tired of being carted around like a helpless baby.

He yanked open the door, reached the elevator in a few angry strides, and stepped into the waiting car. Within seconds Q and he were walking toward the desk where the two doormen were stationed. "Call a taxi for me."

Without waiting to hear their response, he strode out into the darkness. Ty drew a deep breath of night air. Sure, it wasn't the unpolluted air his primitive soul longed for, but it was the air he was stuck with for the present. And when the taxi came, he let Q take care of talking to the driver. He had other things to think about.

Once they reached the apartment, Q tried to reason with him. "Don't do anything stupid. You know Fin is on this. As soon as he comes up with something, he'll call us. If anyone can find her, it's Fin."

Ty knew his answer was an inarticulate snarl, but he couldn't help it. He was filled with so much rage and terror that he almost couldn't hold his emotions in. He had to control them, though. A T. rex tearing up Houston wouldn't help Kelly.

Once inside his apartment, he couldn't settle down. Pacing back and forth, he tried to think rationally. But it didn't work. Ty kept imagining what she was going through. He remembered the horror of finding Neva last night. Only Neva's werewolf strength and ferocity had kept her alive. Kelly didn't have that advantage.

But she's strong inside. God, let that inner strength keep her alive, because he was going to find her. Damn it to hell, he was coming for her. Flinging himself across the room, he almost ran from his apartment. Kelly's door was still unlocked. He'd been too upset when he'd left to think about locking it. After all, the most important thing inside was already gone.

Relieved, he discovered her purse still sitting on the counter. Rummaging through it, he found the keys to the SUV. For only a moment, he paused. Was he really going to do this? Stupid question because his choice was already made. He'd drive into hell itself if he had to.

He grabbed her keys, raced out of the building, and climbed into the car. Ty had watched how Kelly drove. He could do it. He started the SUV and steered it out of the parking lot.

Lucky for Ty, he had lightning-quick reflexes and a good memory. Both served him well tonight. A few drivers never knew how close they came to death as he tried to concentrate on his driving and search for his destination at the same time.

When he finally pulled into the parking lot at Hermann Park, Ty shut off the engine, then took a minute just to breathe. His adrenaline was shooting through the top of his head.

He was way too early, so he sat in the car thinking about Kelly. And sometime during the lonely hours before midnight, Ty made his decision. When he found Kelly, he was going to ask her to share a part of his soul, because he never wanted to be without her again. He was too damn weak to walk away from her.

Finally he climbed from the SUV and walked to the circle with the big statue of Sam Houston in the center island.

Ty waited, afraid his one chance to find Kelly wouldn't show and knowing exactly what he would have to give up for that chance. He was staring into the darkness when someone spoke behind him.

"I suppose we all eventually find something worth losing our souls over." Seir sounded dead serious.

Ty turned to face the demon. "The immortal we call Nine has taken Kelly. She's—"

"I remember her." Seir smiled. "And I think if you have

to loan out your soul for a night, she's definitely worth the sacrifice." His smile widened. "Although you might find being in the passenger seat when I take the wheel more of a rush than you expected."

"Yeah, I can't wait. So let's make the deal. My soul for a night in exchange for Nine's location." Ty tensed, knowing that if Seir backed out now, he'd be hard pressed not to tear into the demon. Losing control wouldn't help Kelly, but it'd feel damn good.

Seir nodded. "My choice of time and place to move in."

"Done." Ty knew making that concession could come back to bite him, but he was desperate. He didn't have time to negotiate.

"No backing out, no matter what?"

"No backing out. Now give me the damn information." T. rexes weren't known for their patience.

Seemingly satisfied, Seir got down to business. "I don't know where he is now, but Nine sent out a call for all his Houston recruits to meet at midnight tomorrow in the Astrodome. He'll have Kelly with him."

"Thanks." Ty started to turn away.

"Don't you want to hear the rest?" There was definite laughter in his voice.

Seir's tone had a "gotcha" quality to it. This wasn't going to be good. "Tell me."

"By showing up tonight you saved me the trouble of hunting you down tomorrow. I've done a few little jobs for this guy. My latest one was to pass on my Astrodome info to you. I not only did that, but I got your soul in the bargain. Nice night's work. And by the way, he calls himself Mr. Wyatt."

Ty gathered himself, death in his soul. Seir had played him, and demon or not, he'd pay for that.

"Don't go all silent-and-deadly killer on me. Hear me out."

"Talk fast." *Calm.* He clamped his will around his fury.

"This is what Wyatt wanted to happen." The bastard was enjoying himself. "I was supposed to talk to you tomorrow night when you were out with your partner. I'd say I knew where Kelly was, but you had to follow me right then because Wyatt was getting ready to kill her. I'd make it clear that you didn't have time to call for help. I'd claim to know a way to sneak into the Astrodome without alerting the guards. Then once you and your partner were inside, Wyatt would capture you."

Ty frowned. "What made him think I'd fall for that?"

"Wyatt keeps track of everything. You've met Balan. Well, he's been sneaking around on big cat feet spying on you and then reporting back to the boss. Wyatt suspects how you feel about Kelly. He's counting on emotion to overcome your common sense."

Taking a deep breath, Ty relaxed a little and tried to think. "Okay, assuming I'd fall for your story, what does he have planned for Q and me? We'd be damn tough to kill."

Seir stopped smiling. "He's one of the most powerful entities I've ever seen. He could take all of you except your leader. And he wants to stage the ultimate fight for his followers before he leaves Houston. You and whoever you bring with you. I'd vote for that Spin guy from the other night. If he can make it happen, Wyatt will impress the hell out of his recruits and leave everyone with a can-do attitude."

"And he doesn't think Fin will find out?" Ty decided not to say anything about his mental link with Fin, although Seir would probably suspect anyway.

The demon shrugged. "He's counting on Fin being too late or *his* head guy keeping *your* head guy distracted."

One more question. "Why are you telling me all this?"

Seir glanced away from Ty. "I get a kick out of making people think I'm something that I'm not. And this Wyatt guy is an arrogant bastard. Besides, I can't possess your soul if you're dead."

That made sense on some demonic level. "Do you know where Eternal Pleasure is?"

"Montrose? Vampire club?"

Ty nodded. "Meet me there tomorrow at eleven."

Seir looked at him. No smiles this time. "Don't underestimate this guy." And then he was gone.

Back in the SUV, Ty opened his link to Fin. It took only a few minutes to fill Fin in. Then he started the car and began the drive back to Fin's condo.

Chapter Seventeen

Kelly fought her way up through the fog, feeling as if she'd been doing the same thing over and over for a very long while. But this time was different. This time she'd break the surface.

When her mind finally cleared enough for her to think, she knew she'd made it. She kept her eyes closed, trying to remember. Gradually it all came back. Walking into her apartment, finding the vampire, the needle, and then oblivion.

Waves of nausea rolled over her. Oh, God, she didn't want to throw up. Stoically she forced back the urge to heave until her stomach settled a little.

She had to know where she was, so reluctantly Kelly opened her eyes . . . and met the bright stare of the vampire who'd taken her.

Kelly's first impulse was to throw out a few damns and hells as she leaped off the couch or whatever she was lying on. After a few exploratory movements, though, she changed her plan. Her wrists and ankles were bound to a . . . She took a good look. It was some kind of padded table, not a couch. Since she was at a disadvantage here, she probably should hold the curses.

"You cut it close. I was afraid you wouldn't wake up in time." The woman grinned at her. "Oh, and I'm Lee. Jude never introduced us."

Lee was still pretty, with big green eyes and curly red

hair. Unfortunately, Kelly had seriously underestimated Jude's bodyguard. She was definitely not too cute to hurt anybody.

"Where am I, and why'd you bring me here?" Kelly craned her neck to scan her surroundings. Looked like some kind of locker room. Not in great condition, either.

"You're in the Astrodome." Lee pulled up a folding chair and sat down near her. She glanced at her watch. "I guess I have time to fill you in. It's the least I can do after all you've done for me." Lee crossed her legs and looked smug. "I got the idea of snatching you after Jude told us how Yvette had taken Neva out of the club right under everyone's noses. Sounded easy. Mr. Wyatt loved the idea. Gave me my own hunting territory. No more running around keeping Jude's ass safe."

"Mr. Wyatt?"

"You call him Nine."

Oh, shit. As her mind cleared, Kelly started to get a really bad feeling. "Since I'm still alive, I suppose your Mr. Wyatt needs me."

"Of course. You're the bait that's going to lure the Gods of the Night into a trap." She frowned. "Or at least the one who's gone all emotional over you." Her frown cleared. "I still don't get the corny Gods-of-the-Night name. Nothing godlike about any of them that I can see so far. Yeah, they can turn into dinosaurs, big deal. But they can't take down Mr. Wyatt."

"How?" All emotional over her? Omigod, Ty. They were going to use her to capture him.

Lee shrugged. "I don't know. Mr. Wyatt didn't tell me all the details. I only know that a demon who works for him is supposed to leak your location. When your guy comes here looking for you, Mr. Wyatt will be waiting."

The whole plan was transparent. Ty would have to know it was a trap. He wouldn't walk into it for her, would he? Her mind raced in circles. How could she escape? "Demon? Does it have a name?"

"Seir."

Silly, but Kelly felt a moment of betrayal. But that was what demons did, wasn't it?

"You're probably thinking about escaping, but forget it. Even if you got past me, someone else would stop you."

"How long have I been out?" Did she still have time to figure out a plan?

"More than twenty-four hours. Now it's time for you to meet Mr. Wyatt." Lee left the room for a minute, only to return with two hulking helpers. "I wouldn't fight this. The guys here like to hurt people. Don't give them something to smile about."

Kelly didn't take direction well. She fought and screamed while the vampires transferred her to a rolling office chair and then tied her to it. Finally they wheeled her out of the locker room and down to the floor of the Astrodome. Oil-lit tiki torches were stuck into the ground at regular intervals around the arena. The flickering glow from the flames cast shifting shadows across the arena's dirt floor, giving the whole scene a menacing feel.

The man waiting for her looked disappointingly ordinary. Middle aged, medium height, suit and tie, brown hair. *Ordinary.* Until you met his gaze. What she saw in Nine's eyes scared her to death.

Lee parked Kelly's chair beside where Nine stood. His smile was almost fatherly. "It's so nice of you to join me, my dear. I'll admit to having warm fuzzy feelings for you. Without you, this couldn't happen." He swept his hand to indicate the inside of the Astrodome. "I apologize for the primitive lighting, but we didn't want to draw attention from outside."

Kelly followed his gesture. The Astrodome had been the first domed stadium, the Eighth Wonder of the World in its time. Now it just seemed old and worn. But not quite empty. What looked like a few thousand people sat in a circle around the floor of the stadium. *Waiting.*

Nine beamed at her. "Thanks to your charming self, Ty and one of his friends will rush in to rescue you from my evil clutches—" he glanced at his watch—"in I'd say about ten minutes. When that happens, I'll be here to greet them. Don't worry, you'll see Ty again. After all, he and his friend will be our guests of honor."

"Won't they be a little tough for you to handle?" After looking into Nine's eyes, she didn't really believe her words, but she wanted to keep him talking while she tried to figure things out.

"Look at me, my dear." He tilted her head up, forcing her to meet his gaze.

Kelly couldn't help it; she shrank away from him, her heart pounding hard and fast. Billions of years of death and destruction shone in his ordinary brown eyes. She fought back her renewed nausea.

"Now you understand. I'll handle them just fine. Once I've shown them to the middle of the arena, Thadeus, my very capable sorcerer, will cast a circle to keep them inside. Then . . ." He seemed to pause so he could savor his next disclosure. "Then I'll take away their memories of everything except their previous lives. The souls of their beasts will consume them. They'll no longer be human, and they'll revert to the wonderful predators they once were."

She stared at him in horror. Wasn't it enough that Fin had stolen Ty's memory of another time? Now this creep would take away his memories of this time. *Of her.*

He seemed pleased by her reaction. "You have to agree, it's brilliant. Primitive instincts will take over, and they'll try to kill each other."

"But they're immortal." Kelly hung on to that truth.

"Ah, I see that Fin hasn't told you everything. When their dinosaur souls are dominant, they're invulnerable to most attacks. But . . ." He dragged out the suspense, rolling it around and playing with it. "They *can* kill each other."

Kelly stared back at him, forcing her expression into one of calm confidence, but inside her terror shrieked and babbled.

"And now you'll have the honor of sitting at my side as I address my Houston recruits."

He shifted his attention to the crowd, and Kelly exhaled the breath she hadn't known she'd been holding. Panic pulled at her, but descending into mindless hysteria wouldn't help Ty.

Her flute. She could picture it lying on the floor of her apartment and felt the despair of knowing that her only real weapon was beyond her reach.

Lee leaned down to whisper in her ear. "Mr. Wyatt gave you to me. You'll be my first live meal in a very long time. I just wanted you to know how special you are."

Kelly clenched her teeth, refusing to give Lee the reaction the vampire was hoping for. But as Nine picked up a microphone and started talking, she forgot about Lee.

"This night is for you, future rulers of Houston. From this night forward, you'll reclaim the darkness." The audience roared. "The humans will disappear, a few more each night. And by the time December twenty-first, 2012 arrives, the human population will be in a frenzy of fear. At that moment, you, guided by me and the ones who came with me, will rise up and destroy all of them."

Overdramatic but effective.

Nine paused to acknowledge the cheers.

"Tonight will be my last in Houston. I'm leaving to take my message to another city. But the organization will be left in capable hands. If needed, I can return instantly." His thinly veiled threat, aimed at anyone who subscribed to the when-the-cat's-away philosophy, had the desired effect.

Kelly could almost feel the fear radiating from the crowd. What could make a vicious mob of supernatural beings so afraid? Maybe she didn't want to know.

"As a going-away offering, I've planned something special for you. In a few minutes, you'll witness the ultimate fight, a spectacle no one on Earth has ever seen. Enjoy."

There was an excited buzz from the audience.

Fear clogged her throat, not for herself, but for the man she loved. Amazing how easy the thought of loving him was now that she couldn't tell him. Would she ever get the chance? Kelly drew in a deep breath and calmed herself. She'd find a way to help him. Somehow. She'd just have to center her concentration and think. Fin? He'd realize Ty was in trouble in time to do his god act, wouldn't he? She only hoped he was as powerful as Ty thought.

Ty sat in the SUV with Seir and Gig, waiting until everyone was in place. He knew his backup was out there, but he couldn't spot anyone. The parking lots were empty. Everyone had parked on side streets where cars wouldn't be noticed. Come to think of it, he wondered where Nine's people had parked. It sure wasn't here.

Q, Lio, and Al crouched behind small trees and buildings close to the Astrodome. Fin never sent all of the Eleven into battle at once if he could help it. No use in giving the enemy a chance to wipe them all out in one attack. Fin had said he'd be nearby, too, if they needed him.

The huge parking lots around the stadium didn't offer any cover, so Jude and his vampires were pressed flat atop the roof of Reliant Stadium next door to the Astrodome, ready to jump into battle. Macario and his wolves were skulking in the shadows. They must be doing a good job of it because he couldn't see them either.

"Ready to go in?" Seir glanced at both of them.

"I'm ready to kill." Gig's smile was a scary thing.

In fact, all of Gig was scary. Big, with those pale eyes and that wild mane of hair, he had a lust for violence. That was why Fin had chosen him. Gig's soul was a Giganotosaurus, a meat eater even bigger than the T. rex. Between the two of them, they'd tear up the Astrodome.

Ty nodded at Seir. "Let's do it."

Seir eased the SUV into a spot in front of one of the stadium's doors. "I don't know what'll happen once we get inside. You'll have to wing it. I do know that Wyatt had his pet sorcerer ward the entrances. Thadeus will be waiting for us so he can drop the ward. The cover story is that he's my friend on the inside."

"Right." Tension coiled in Ty's stomach. Kelly was alive. He could feel her as surely as he could feel the wrongness of this whole place.

Ty and the others silently approached the door. Then they waited. Suddenly the door swung open and a tall thin man scowled out at them.

"Get in fast." Thadeus's eyes were as black as the clothes he wore.

They stepped inside, then waited while the sorcerer replaced his ward. He waved at them. "This way." He led them down a dark tunnel. At the end, Ty could see a faint light. Somewhere along the way Seir disappeared.

"This doesn't feel right," Gig muttered behind him. "We should kill the sorcerer now and then do our own thing." Obviously, he liked the direct approach.

Ty didn't get a chance to reply because suddenly light flared in front of them. Within the light stood a man. An ordinary-looking man. But there was nothing ordinary about the power surrounding him, power strong enough to push Ty back.

The man glanced at the sorcerer. "You may go now, Thadeus. Make the preparations." Thadeus silently departed.

Ty trusted his instincts, and his instinct said to act now. He gathered himself, ready to rush the man. Ty sensed Gig doing the same.

The man didn't say anything, didn't do anything, but suddenly Ty felt as if his body were encased in cement. He couldn't move. What the hell? He strained against whatever held him. Nothing. Gig stood frozen beside him.

The man smiled and shook his head. "If I were you, I'd save my energy. You'll need it." The glow surrounding him wasn't from any light. The glow came from *him*. "I'm sure you've already guessed my identity. I can't believe Fin calls me Nine." He looked insulted. "Nine really doesn't speak to all my individual talents."

Ty cursed himself. He'd been arrogant enough to think he could just waltz in here, catch Nine off guard, find Kelly, and escape with her. Even with Fin and the others waiting outside, he was afraid they had underestimated Nine. And, yes, he'd undoubtedly let his fear for Kelly cloud his judgment. He wondered now whether Fin had realized he was probably sending two of the Eleven to their deaths.

"But enough of my chatter. We have a show to put on. Follow me."

Nine didn't even look at them when he said it, but Ty's feet started moving. He wasn't in control of his body anymore. Hell, this couldn't be happening.

They emerged from the tunnel into the arena to the roar of excited voices. Nine marched them to the middle of the field and stopped.

"If you'll look around . . . Oh, wait, you can't. Well, I'll tell you what you'd see if you *could* look around. All of my shiny new recruits are waiting for the show to begin. And your friend Kelly is sitting directly behind you. Since you can't say hello, I'll do it for you." The creep waved.

Evidently tired of his game, Nine finally got to the point. "Here's what's going to happen. You'll free your animal soul and fight each other. To the death. I promised my people a spectacle, and it can't get better than that."

Ty wasn't able to speak, but he hoped his eyes said that Nine couldn't make him fight. Besides, he and Gig were immortal. They could fight until they fell over without killing each other.

Nine smiled. "Oh, but I *can* make you. In just a few minutes I'll take away all your memories of this time. Nothing will remain but your animal soul and the memories that go with it. As I told Kelly, you *can* kill each other. Fin really should've explained that to you." He looked thoughtful. "Of course, there's always the possibility he didn't know, but I doubt it."

Ty wasn't surprised that Nine could read his thoughts. He made a concentrated effort not to think about anything Nine could use.

Thadeus came into Ty's line of vision. He was tracing a large circle that would take up most of the arena floor. "As you can see, my sorcerer is casting a circle. Once he closes it, neither of you will be able to escape."

Crap. Ty was now a believer. He had no doubt Nine could deliver on his boasts.

Nine watched Thadeus do his thing. Then he nodded. "I'll leave you now. And you have my sincere gratitude for making all this possible." He walked away.

Fin. Ty's last shot. Taking the chance that Nine wasn't in his head right now, he tried to open his mental link. Nothing. Nine had closed all doors, physical and mental. Ty was out of ideas. Now all he could do was survive. For Kelly.

In those last few minutes, with his memories intact, he thought of Kelly. Would the others get to her in time? He had to believe they'd both come out the other side of this alive.

Ty watched Nine step outside the circle. And as Thadeus closed it, Ty felt all that made him human slipping away. His last link with humanity had Kelly's name attached, and then it too was gone.

Kelly watched the scene unfold with numbing fear. She was a spectator at a tragedy she couldn't stop. As soon as Nine had come out of the tunnel with Ty and another member of the Eleven, she'd realized he had them under his control. What had he done to them?

Fury and a fierce protectiveness tightened her chest. She'd been known to help spiders out of tubs, but right now she'd kill Nine without one regret. Despair tugged at her. She didn't have the power to kill Nine. No one did. But she could have stopped him, if only she'd had her flute with her.

Who was the guy with Ty? She took a closer look. Gig. She remembered his name along with his pale, scary eyes, but not what soul form he'd take on. She'd find out soon enough.

The crowd roared as Thadeus closed the circle. She could see the flare of the energy barrier. Too bad the sorcerer wasn't on the inside of his little creation.

Suddenly, Nine released Ty and Gig from whatever hold he had on them. But before either man could move more than a few feet, their souls took command.

Kelly bit her lip, her heart pounding in tandem with her silent cries of *no, no, no.* She watched as the two massive dinosaurs took form in the middle of the Astrodome. Omigod. She'd thought nothing could be more intimidating than a T. rex. She'd been wrong. Gig looked a lot like Ty, only bigger and even more terrifying. Fear such as she'd never felt before left her cold and shaking. Ty couldn't die here. It wouldn't be fair. But fair didn't have a lot to do with life.

Both dinosaurs roared their challenges as they flung themselves at each other. The whole building shook with the savagery of their coming together. The shouts of the mob played counterpoint to the sounds of the death battle. Blood began to flow. *Real* blood.

The flickering flames of the torches threw shadows across the dimly lit arena and the massive animals in its center. Ty came in fast on the larger, but maybe a little slower, Gig. Opening immense jaws, he sank his teeth into Gig's neck, tearing and rending. Gig's enraged bellow drew screams of delight from the audience.

The scent of blood made Kelly gag. She wanted to look away, but she couldn't. God, Ty had to win. But at what cost? Nine wouldn't let the winner live anyway.

Gig threw all his weight at Ty, and they went down in a cloud of dust. The floor vibrated beneath her.

Ty lost his grip. As they lurched to their feet, Gig struck at Ty's side, tearing a long, bloody gash in his flesh. Blood poured from the wound onto the dirt, where it seeped into the earth. Gig raised his head, and his huge teeth dripped with Ty's blood.

The proof of Ty's vulnerability hardened something in Kelly. *Enough.* If her hands had been free, she would have swiped at the tears sliding down her face. She was done with tears. They wouldn't help Ty or Gig. Frantically, she looked around. There had to be someone who could help her.

As if on cue, a voice spoke softly behind her. "Don't turn your head. Don't talk. Just listen."

Seir? She opened her mouth to tell him what she thought of him, but something in his voice made her shut it again.

"Good. Wyatt looks like he isn't in any hurry to rejoin you. So while he's busy playing the asshole, I'm going to get you out of here. That's what Ty wanted."

She felt him working at her ankles and wrists as the thuds of huge bodies colliding and the shouts of the crowd battered at her. At last she was free. Taking a deep breath, she tried to think. Oh, God, she couldn't focus. But she had to come up with something before one of the combatants died.

Both Ty and Gig looked unsteady on their feet, but still they fought on. Even as she watched, Ty gouged flesh from Gig's flank right before Gig swung his lethal tail, hurling Ty to the ground. She held her breath until Ty got to his feet again. They left a trail of blood as they battled across the Astrodome.

"I don't know what you're planning," Seir whispered, "but forget it. Ty's friends plus Jude's and Macario's people are outside ready to storm this place as soon as you're safe."

Kelly still wasn't sure whose side Seir was on, but he'd freed her, so she'd give him the benefit of the doubt. "Do you really think anyone outside will be able to get in? You've seen what that immortal dirtbag can do. If Fin can protect his condo from attacks by Nine, then I bet Nine can do the same thing. I bet he'd added extra juice to the sorcerer's wards. Have you tried to reach anyone on your cell phone?"

"Yeah. Nothing."

They were both silent for a few seconds, the screams of the mob's bloodlust and the roars of the two crazed predators a Greek chorus for their thoughts. Kelly stared unblinkingly at the two animals trying to destroy each other. *At Ty slowly dying.* "I can't see his humanity."

"What?"

"Always before I could see Ty's human form at the heart of his beast. He's not there this time." Kelly felt tears slide down her face. "I won't leave, Seir. You try to get out and tell everyone we need them *now.*" Before it was too late for Ty and Gig.

Seir's deep exhalation had all his frustration with her stubbornness packed into it. "You can't help him."

If only she had her flute she could . . . Wait. Fin had said it was the *melody* that would send Nine back to where he came from. Sure, he'd seen her playing it on a flute in his vision, but it was the actual tune that had the power.

Okay, it was grasping-at-straws time. She didn't have the flute, but the melody was carved into her mind and soul. Every time she closed her eyes she heard it, every note perfect.

Fin had said he'd seen the future, but the future wasn't immutable. People had free will; they could change the future. So why did she have to play her brain music on the flute?

She took a deep breath. Inside the circle, Ty and Gig continued to circle and strike, searching for that moment of weakness when they could move in for the killing blow. Covered in blood and physically overmatched by his larger enemy, Ty refused to give up. He had huge gashes and bites over most of his body, but at least nothing seemed broken. Again and again Gig knocked him to the ground. Again and again he rose from the clouds of dust. Gig's growing exhaustion was the only thing saving Ty. But he wouldn't last much longer.

"I'm going to try something. Can you protect me for even a few minutes?" Kelly didn't have much hope that Seir could. Nine's power would probably trump everyone's except Fin's. Sure, Nine couldn't kill her directly, but he had a few thousand true believers ready and willing to do it for him.

Seir surprised her by not arguing. "What do you want?"

"Pick up the hand mike that Nine left on the floor. Make sure it's turned on and then hand it to me. After that, do whatever you can to protect me." She paused. "And if you can't, thanks for trying."

"You'll have all the time you need." He sounded sure of that.

She swallowed hard, trying to relax her throat muscles. Oh, what the hell. She gave up and nodded to Seir. Out of the corner of her eye she saw Ty go down again. She willed him to his feet. Struggling to rise, he finally righted himself, but soon he wouldn't get up again. Hurry, she had to *hurry*.

Seir grabbed the mike and passed it to her. Standing, Kelly blocked out the horror taking place inside the circle. Then she sang. As the first notes filled the stadium, the audience fell silent. All faces turned toward her even as Gig swung his massive tail once again, catching Ty a blow that staggered him.

At first, Nine just looked startled, and then dawning realization twisted his face into something grotesque. "You bitch!" His scream reached her across the space between them. "Kill her." Nine's order fell on deaf ears because his followers seemed frozen in place as they stared at her.

What the . . . Kelly shot Seir a quick glance. Was he powerful enough to control thousands of nonhumans? But she didn't have time to think about Seir now. She sang on, her voice perfectly pitched, the melody true and clear.

"No!" Nine started to shimmer as he thrust his arms out in front of him. A blast of power vibrated and pulsed before smashing into some of the speakers. The speakers vaporized.

Oh, shit. If he couldn't hear her voice, this wouldn't work.

"Don't worry, I have it covered." Seir's quiet confidence eased her panic.

Seir didn't move, but the next blast that Nine aimed at the remaining speakers hit whatever shield the demon had thrown up. Brilliant flashes of diffused energy sparkled and hissed against the invisible wall Seir had erected.

She sang on, her voice soaring as she neared the end. Kelly refused to look at what was happening to Ty and Gig. She couldn't take the chance that what she saw might stop her song. Only the melody mattered.

The shimmer around Nine grew as he flung blast after blast at the speakers and then at Seir. The walls of the Astrodome threatened to cave as each blast shook them. Seir stood strong. Whatever that shield was, he should patent it.

In final desperation, Nine clapped his hands over his ears. Too late, much too late.

And as she sang the last notes of her melody, her eyes

widened. The crowd sat paralyzed as they watched. Even Ty and Gig were silent. She was afraid to think what that might mean.

Nine began to disintegrate into glowing particles from his feet up.

"No! I was promised more time. I'm not ready to go back. I waited and waited and—" His screams were cut off as his head became just so many glowing bits. Then the bits coalesced into one whirling ball of light and winked out.

For a moment after her song ended, none of the thousands in the audience made a sound. Trying to hold panic at bay, Kelly turned to look at Ty. She was just in time to see both men's human forms return. Ty's hair was matted with sweat and blood, and it seemed that every inch of skin exposed by his torn clothes was cut. Wiping blood from his face, he staggered toward her. Gig didn't look much better. But both men were alive. *Alive.*

Almost sobbing with relief, Kelly started forward. Seir put his hand on her arm. "Wait." She watched him walk across to the sorcerer. She didn't have any trouble interpreting the expression on Thadeus's face. Terror. A moment later, he did something to the circle. Seir returned to her, dragging the sorcerer with him.

"Okay, Ty and Gig can get out of the circle now. I'd wait here for them to come to you." He glanced around at the audience as an angry buzz rose, growing louder with each second. "I think they're a little ticked at having their fun spoiled."

Frantic, Kelly searched the crowd. "Ty. Where is he?"

"Here." Ty was suddenly beside her. His voice sounded exhausted but relieved.

And inexplicably, she was furious at him. "Don't ever, ever scare me like that again." Then she wrapped her arms around him, drew his head down to hers, and kissed him.

Covered in blood and sweat, he was still the most beautiful man she'd ever seen. His kiss was hot, crazy, and primal. And it didn't matter at all that the mob was working itself into a killing rage.

Seir interrupted. "As touching as this reunion is, we'd better get out of here fast. In a few seconds, everyone's going to realize their great leader is gone for good, and then they'll be looking around for someone to eat."

Dragging a frightened Thadeus along with him, Seir led the charge toward the exit. Behind them, a howl of fury from the audience suggested they'd gotten out of Dodge just in time.

"Damn, that was incredible." A limping Gig was grinning as they finally reached the door.

"Get rid of the wards, sorcerer." Seir's voice held the promise of death.

His hands shaking, Thadeus did what he was asked. "Please, don't kill me. It wasn't my idea. He forced me. Don't kill me, don't kill me, don't—"

With a disgusted grunt, Seir shoved Thadeus back down the tunnel. The sorcerer recovered his footing and ran into the Astrodome again.

Kelly had her arms around Ty, trying to keep him upright as they reached the SUV. She glanced back to see Jude and some of his vampires standing near the entrance, waiting for whoever came out. That's when she realized Seir was gone. He'd just disappeared. But she didn't have time to worry about him.

She was ready to get into the driver's seat when she realized it was already occupied. Fin grinned at her. Gig got into the passenger side. Kelly and Ty scrambled into the rear seat. Q sat beside them, while Al and Lio crowded into the very back of the vehicle. Then Fin backed the SUV up.

Fin put lots of space between the car and the Astrodome before stopping. Kelly watched as his gaze grew distant. After a few seconds, Jude's vampires and Macario's wolves erupted from every side of the building as they raced from the stadium.

"You said something to them, didn't you?" See, she was learning. "What did you say?"

Fin's gaze remained fixed on the Astrodome. Suddenly, a giant crack opened under the building. As she watched, horrified, the crack widened and widened and widened until with a thunderous boom that shook the ground and rocked the SUV, the whole Astrodome imploded. Disbelieving, she watched as the remains of one of Houston's landmarks sank into the gigantic hole and disappeared. Then the hole closed.

It had happened too fast to be real. She listened for screams. None. She looked for escaping bad guys. Not one.

Fin met her gaze with his cold silver one. "I told them to run like hell." He glanced back at where the stadium had been. "Who knew there was a fault line under the Astrodome?"

Silence filled the SUV. As they watched, the vampires and wolves disappeared into the night. Shouts of alarm were rising from nearby neighborhoods, and in the distance Kelly could hear sirens.

Fin drove calmly away from the stadium. "And, no, even if they dig, they'll never find any bodies."

"Son of a bitch." Gig's contribution to the discussion.

What was Fin? He hadn't even been trying hard when he took down the Astrodome. "Why did you do it?" Kelly couldn't believe how calm she felt. Knowing Ty was safe did that to her.

"To send a message to Zero. 'Don't mess with me or my people.'" He stared at Kelly when he said "my people." Then he grinned. "Oh, and did I mention that I get a rush out of doing stuff like that?"

Ty put his arm around her waist and pulled her close. She stared at the back of Fin's head. "Do you have a license?"

"I'll produce one if I have to."

She glanced over at nearby Highway 610. Even at 1:00 A.M., cars had pulled over to gawk. "You know this'll make headlines across the country."

Fin shrugged. "I felt it when you expelled Nine from Earth. How'd you do it without your flute?"

"I sang."

"Congratulations. I didn't realize you were so inventive. Great job."

While Q and the others complained to Fin about not getting a chance to fight, Kelly looked up at Ty and grinned. She shouldn't care what Fin thought, but his praise felt good.

Then she forgot about him to concentrate on Ty. "Come over to my place and I'll get you cleaned up." She frowned as she touched a gash in his shoulder. "Do you need a doctor?"

"No. All I need is you." The emotion in his voice was everything she could hope for. Laying her head against his unwounded shoulder, she wondered how she'd convince him to take her with him when he left Houston.

Chapter Eighteen

Ty stepped out of the steam-filled shower and chose one of Kelly's big fluffy towels to dry himself. His torn and bloody clothes lay in a corner of her bathroom. He'd toss them in the trash later.

Too bad he couldn't toss his beast into the pile, too. It still roared inside him. His T. rex had tasted blood tonight, and it wanted more. The adrenaline rush of battle still drove him.

Fear was his constant companion at times like this. What if the beast rose while he made love to her? How could she even *want* to make love with him after seeing his brutal battle with Gig?

Sure, she'd kissed him, but her reaction had probably been driven by relief they were both alive. What woman would want to spend forever sleeping beside a man who could lose his humanity as quickly and completely as he had tonight? And what man would be stupid enough to ask for such an unlikely forever? Guess that would be him.

When they'd finally made it home, she'd forced him to relax on her couch while she ran over to his place to get his toothbrush and some clean clothes. By the time she'd returned, he was pacing her apartment. The beast wouldn't let him rest.

He stared into the steamed-up mirror as he brushed his teeth. Why bother looking when he could only see a faint image? It made him think. Was that the real him? A faint image? Would he ever be able to offer Kelly all of himself? From the little Fin had revealed, he might not be a winning package. *Kelly, please accept me, my animal, and whatever the hell I was before.* Right. She'd jump at the chance.

Finished in the bathroom, Ty paused with his hand on the doorknob. Whatever happened, he'd have to leave Houston behind. If she didn't want him, he could still carry her memory wherever he went. Not much of a substitute, but it was the one thing no one could take away. *Fin could.* And no matter how hard he tried to dismiss the thought, it festered.

He was about to turn the knob when Seir spoke in his head.

"Except for all those cuts and bruises, you look pretty good. Women love wounded warriors."

Ty tensed. No, not *now.*

"I wasn't going to bother you tonight, but I have places to go and things to do."

"Can't we take care of this some other time?" *Like in about ten years?*

"Sorry, can't do. But I'll give you a break. I won't stay the whole night, only long enough to give you some pointers on how to rev up a woman's interest." The silence hinted that Seir was thinking. *"Not that Kelly needs any revving up."*

"You're not getting into that bed with Kelly and me." Ty spoke through clenched teeth.

Seir's laughter was free of his usual mockery. *"Relax. I'll be long gone. I'm just going to give you some help with what comes before. Now look in that basket on top of the toilet tank and take out the tube of body lotion."*

Ty thought about trying to fight Seir, but he'd made a deal. "Can I trust you?" What a dumb question. Seir was a demon. Demons lied.

"I'm all about good intentions tonight." The laughter was still in his voice.

Warily, Ty rooted around in the basket until he came up with the tube. "Vanilla? Tell me this is for Kelly. I'm not a vanilla kind of guy."

Seir didn't offer any comfort.

"Now what?"

"Now you let me in." The demon's voice sounded casual, but Ty sensed tension thrumming beneath the surface.

This was one of the toughest things Ty would ever have to do. He'd be handing control of his mind over to Seir, and Ty's memories of how he'd felt when Nine took control of his body were still way too fresh. But a promise was a promise. He'd known it wouldn't be easy when he'd made the bargain in exchange for a chance to find Kelly.

"If you try to do something that'll hurt Kelly, I'll fight you." It had to be said.

"No trust? I'm disappointed." And somehow Seir sounded as if he meant it.

"What do I do?" Ty tried to relax, but every muscle in his body felt stiff with apprehension.

"Invite me in, Ty. Out loud. Just invite me in. And don't worry, you'll be there to see and hear everything I do in your name." The amusement was back in the demon's voice.

Ty huffed out a nervous curse and said the words. "I invite you in." Then he qualified it. "But if you do anything to mess things up between Kelly and me, I'll follow you back to hell and tear you apart."

The demon's laughter echoed in his mind.

He opened the door and walked into the bedroom. Ty wasn't sure which "he" was doing the walking. Even though Ty's feet were the ones actually moving, it was Seir's mind doing the motivating. In this case, he and the demon were on the same page. His feet were taking him where he wanted to go.

Kelly was sitting on the edge of the bed. She looked a little uncertain. Ty thought she was the most beautiful thing he'd ever seen. Her short nightshirt bared the long sleek length of her thighs and legs, and her eyes were soft with emotion. She spoke to both the animal and human in him.

His body evidently didn't care who was in the driver's seat, because it reacted the same way it always reacted to her. He tightened and grew hard. And when her gaze slid over him and paused at his cock, he almost groaned.

"Are you hurting?" Her eyes, filled with concern, lifted to his.

Not in the way you think.

"A little. That's why I borrowed this." He held up the lotion.

A lie. Ty felt fine. He healed fast. Seir was evidently going for the sympathy vote. Not the way Ty would've handled it.

Kelly's eyes clouded. "Let me put it on."

Yes, yes, yes! Maybe Seir knew what he was doing after all.

"No, that's okay. I can take care of it myself." He pulled up one of the kitchen chairs and sat down facing Kelly.

What kind of dumb answer was that? Frustration beat at him. He wanted to yank Seir from his head and kick his demonic butt out the door.

Ty spread his legs, showcasing his obvious interest in her. Then he took the top from the tube and squirted a little on his arms. Slowly, he rubbed it in, using broad slow strokes. "I never understood the pleasure and power of touch until you."

Was that something he'd normally say? Ty thought about it. Probably not. He was more a doer than a sayer.

Her gaze followed every stroke of his fingers. She licked her lips, leaving them moist and shining.

Ty was at that tipping point where hard became hurt. Guess that's what they meant when they talked about pleasure-pain.

And when he squirted more lotion on his chest and rubbed it into his pecs and stomach with the same slow strokes, her eyes grew heavy with desire. "I bet there're places you can't reach."

"I bet there are." Ty wasn't sure he liked the husky tone of his voice. Uh, Seir's voice.

This was the perfect lead-in to the perfect line. *Hey, why don't I let* you *put the rest on?* Seir let the moment pass him by. Instead, he stood and turned his back to her. Spreading his legs, he bent forward and reached behind him to apply lotion to the backs of his thighs and legs. Then he rubbed up and down, up and down. His hair swung back and forth in front of his eyes in rhythm with the rubbing.

Okay, this wasn't him. Ty knew exactly what she could see with his legs spread. Seir must've worked as a male stripper, because no ordinary guy would do this. Would he? What did Ty know about ordinary guys? Fin hadn't filled them in on this kind of stuff.

Ty sensed the moment she slipped off the bed and padded on bare feet over to him. His hands stilled, and he held his breath as she stood behind him.

Then she smoothed cool fingers across his back and buttocks. "I'm *sure* there're some spots you can't reach." She leaned over him so she could speak close to his ear, her body pressing against his. "And lots of spots I *want* to reach."

He froze. Her nightshirt was the only thing separating them from skin-to-skin contact. That thin piece of cloth was his fire wall, the one thing saving him from a flash fire.

"I want you out. Now." Ty didn't do threesomes.

"That was fun, but I'm out of here as soon as I phone home." Seir sounded as if his attention wasn't on Kelly.

She was *touching* him, for God's sake. How could Seir not be paying attention? *"Phone home? What do you mean?"*

"You have a mental link to someone I want to talk to." Seir sounded dead serious now. *"He won't pick up for me. He will for you."*

Who? Just for a second, Ty tried to concentrate. It was tough to do with Kelly's hands on him. Mental link? *Fin? "You can't do that."*

"Sure I can. Just relax. It'll only take a few seconds."

In horror, Ty listened to himself call out to Fin. And Fin answered.

"What's up, Ty?"

"Not Ty." Seir didn't sound amused or mocking anymore. Anger and something else turned his voice thick with emotion. *"This is your loving brother. Just wanted to let you know I'm back."*

Then Seir was gone from his mind. Ty was so shocked, he spoke out loud. "Fin? He's gone. What the hell was that about?"

Behind him, Kelly made an impatient sound. "Tell Fin this is a bad time."

Fin was silent for a few beats too long. *"That was someone from a long, long time ago."* And then Fin cut the connection.

Under ordinary circumstances, Ty would have spent more time thinking about what had just happened, but these weren't ordinary circumstances.

He straightened and turned to face Kelly. "You're right, I have lots of places I can't reach but *you* can." *My heart, my soul.* He stretched out a hand for her.

She backed away, her lips curved in a sexy smile and her

eyes alight with playfulness. "Whoa. You know how to dish it out, but do you know how to take it?"

Ty let his gaze glide the length of her body. "Sure I know how to take it." He reached for the hem of her shirt and slipped it over her head.

Stretching her arms out in front of her to hold him off, she laughed as she shook her head. "Okay, let's try again. What you just did with the lotion was incredibly sexy." Her voice lowered to a sensual purr. "You excited me, and now that I'm excited, I want to play with the lotion. Can you take what I want to give?"

She was kidding, right? "Just tell me what to do."

Kelly didn't waste words. "Lie on your stomach on the bed."

Ty didn't follow orders well, but there were orders and then there were *orders*. Nodding, he stretched out. Resting his head on his folded arms, he waited.

Straddling his hips, Kelly squeezed a blob of cold lotion onto his back, then rubbed it in. Every stroke of her magic fingers left a trail of sizzling sensation behind. He shifted his hips to accommodate his increased excitement.

But with excitement came the return of his beast. It had hidden behind Seir until the demon was gone. Ty clenched his teeth, willing it away. Tonight it wanted to stay.

Kelly scooted back and squeezed a drop of lotion onto each buttock. "I love these. Firm." She dug her fingers into his flesh and massaged. "Sensual." Lowering herself until her breasts just touched his cheeks, she moved back and forth, dragging her nipples across his flesh. "Delicious." She bit his right cheek.

He swallowed a growl. His beast wanted to bite back. Anything that involved teeth turned the T. rex on. Ty grew harder, if that was possible.

Kelly murmured close to his ear. "That was for taking a call from Fin right in the middle of our foreplay."

Foreplay? That had been foreplay? Suddenly he felt more human. T. rexes didn't do foreplay. His beast backed off a little.

"Lie on your back." Kelly was moving right along.

He flipped over and looked up at her. God, she was gorgeous. Her hair was tousled, her cheeks were pink, and her eyes were filled with heat and emotion and so many things he couldn't ID. He hoped they were all good for him.

She looked mesmerized as she lightly traced the shape of his mouth. He didn't move as he held her gaze. Could she see his beast waiting behind his eyes? Did she even suspect the danger she was in?

Leaning close, she nibbled a path from the corner of his mouth and down the side of his jaw. "Your courage touched and excited me tonight. No matter how many times Gig knocked you down, you got up again."

Some of his fear eased. His primal side hadn't disgusted her.

She moved from his jaw back to his mouth. Her lips were soft, demanding. He opened his mouth and welcomed her in. And as her tongue tangled with his, his beast roared its need.

Just in time, she broke the kiss. His breath rasped in and out, laboring even more than when he'd fought Gig. With her breath warm on his skin, he felt her hunger as she kissed a path to his nipples. She flicked each one with the tip of her tongue until they felt so sensitive, he wanted to cry out and draw her down to him.

It was getting harder and harder to deny his T. rex. The beast flung itself at the bars in his mind, but for now they held.

Ty forced his body to still as Kelly smoothed her fingers over his chest and stomach. The scent of vanilla would always bring him back to these moments.

She paused to meet his gaze. "Do we have time for me to twirl my tongue inside your cute belly button?"

He must have looked horrified because she laughed. "Okay, your manly navel."

Ty struggled to hear himself above the now constant screams of his beast. "No. No time. Can't wait."

Kelly grew serious as her gaze came to rest between his spread thighs. "Here's where I want to spend some quality time."

Slowly and with maddening deliberation, she smoothed the lotion over the insides of his thighs. Every stroke was a slide of sensual torture.

"I was sure this was one place you couldn't reach. Aren't you glad I'm here to help?"

He couldn't stop the moan forced from the depths of his need for her, his *hunger* for her.

She didn't say anything else as she lowered her head and slid her tongue across his balls.

Warm, so warm. And wet. Sensation piled on sensation until the whole pile threatened to tip over. And still his beast cried for its release.

"Can't wait." He shook as he fought for control, his body's demands feeding on themselves. Ty needed to bury himself deep inside her right now, needed to tell her how much he loved her. Both urges were snowballing down a mountain built from all the emotions he'd felt since meeting her. But at the bottom of this particular mountain, a T. rex waited.

"I know." Her murmur was rough with desire.

And when she closed her lips over his cock, he almost came off the bed. Everything became a sexual blur as she swirled her tongue up, down, and around. The heat of her mouth drove him crazy. But when she nipped the head of his cock, she'd gone too far. His beast burst from its cage and roared its challenge.

No. He wouldn't let it control him. Ty held it at bay for the moment.

With an inarticulate cry, he pushed her onto her back and then rose over her. He knew his hair was tangled around his face and his body was sheened with sweat. He was almost afraid to think what she'd see in his eyes.

"Now." His breaths came in harsh rasps and his heart felt ready to explode from his chest.

"Now," she agreed.

Slipping his hands under her buttocks, he lifted her to meet his thrust. Biting his lip until it bled as he fought to keep from savaging her the way his animal craved, he eased his cock into her. *So wet, so hot, so ready.* Ty gritted his teeth as he tried to hold that position, his whole body shaking from the effort.

"I don't know what you're doing, but I want *all* of you inside me. Now."

Exhaling a huge breath of relief, Ty plunged into her. Kelly cried out her satisfaction as he drew almost completely out and then buried himself deep inside her again. She wrapped her legs around him and with every plunge, she rose to meet him.

As his orgasm became a rushing tide, pushing him closer and closer to that inevitable moment, and his beast's primitive soul fed off that most basic animal need, *it* happened again. What had happened that first time.

Ty felt like he was falling into Kelly, past the physical, into her yesterdays. He touched pieces of her humanity. Her fear when she first met him. Her joy when she played her first song. The excitement of her first date. The sadness when her first pet died. The love of her family. And then, beyond all that, he touched something bright and warm and wonderful. He touched her *soul*.

Just as he wrapped his arms around all that warmth and wonder, his orgasm exploded. He froze in that moment, time stopping while spasm after spasm rocked him. Dimly, he heard Kelly cry out as she joined him. Then the spasms rippled like pebbles tumbling over and over in the surf until the waves slid back to the sea, leaving the two of them still on the shore. Quiet and somehow peaceful.

And as he lay there with his breaths still coming in quick gasps and his heart pounding fast and hard, he felt as though he was more than he'd been before. He'd touched her soul and made a piece of it his. Ty closed his eyes. And he wasn't giving it back.

It took him a moment to realize something unbelievable. His beast was gone. She'd given him a piece of her humanity, and that humanity had driven the beast back to its cage.

"I love you." He lay on his back, staring up at the white ceiling.

"I know." Her voice sounded like it was clogged with tears.

He held his breath, the moment stretching into forever.

"I love you too." Only a whisper, but he heard it.

Her words repeated themselves over and over in his mind, echoing back to that long-ago time when he'd walked the earth as T. rex, and he knew that this was where he wanted to be. Forever. With her.

Ty tried to keep his voice calm, tried not to think he could lose her when he told her what loving him would cost. "I want you with me forever, but the price of loving me might be more than you're willing to pay. I'll understand if you choose not to go through with it."

She moved close and rested her hand on his chest. "I don't count the cost when I want something. Or someone. And I want you more than I'll ever want anyone in my life." Kelly looked as if she was wrestling with something. "I have to tell you something. I thought I could keep it to myself, but that's no way to start forever."

He nodded.

"Fin told me that you guys were something else before you were dinosaurs." Kelly's expression said she was waiting for him to explode.

"I know. He admitted it to me."

"When?"

"When he realized I love you. Fin thought I should know what you'd have to go through to claim me. Once I knew, he figured I wouldn't ask you." Ty glanced away. "But I'm a selfish bastard. Besides, I knew that if the shoe was on the other foot, I'd want to be given a choice."

Kelly looked outraged. "You bet I want a choice. Tell me what I have to do."

He told her—about his soul, her immortality, and the ceremony.

Her wedding day. Sort of. Oh, she'd have a traditional one with her family and friends, but this moment was for her and Ty alone. No white today. She'd chosen a short red dress. Red, a color that always made her feel brave and sexy, both things she wanted to be for him.

Fin stood beside her, radiating suppressed displeasure.

"Why don't you like me?" Kelly had to admit that even in a roaring bad mood, Fin was a beautiful man.

He looked surprised. "Why would you think that? I've always liked you. I just don't think marriage is a wise move for any of the Eleven."

"You don't think I'll still love him at the end, do you?" Foolish man.

"Some things should never be revealed and are best forgotten. I don't want Ty to be hurt." He paused. "Or you."

Shocked, she stared at him. He almost sounded human. "Don't worry. I love him too much to hurt him. Whatever I see, I'll survive."

Fin didn't try to change her mind. The time for that was past. Kelly looked around her. They were in the huge room on the top floor of Fin's condo. Someone had gone to a lot of trouble to decorate the place. But bright colors couldn't take away the knot in her stomach. *God, let me do this right.*

The rest of the Eleven, all dressed in tuxes, formed an aisle down the middle of the room. Ty stood alone at the far end. Waiting.

"It's time, Kelly." Fin's voice was soft as he took her arm.

She controlled a nervous giggle. Fin was giving her away. How . . . traditional. As they started walking slowly down the aisle, the men began chanting in a language she didn't recognize. It rose and fell, a joyful spill of words.

Startled, Kelly looked at Fin.

He smiled. "This ceremony is our tradition. For this one moment, I gave them back the memory of the wedding chant. When they're done, the memory will be gone."

"Will Ty have to say anything?"

"The words will be given to him."

Tears welled in her eyes. She didn't know why, but there was something wrenchingly sad about this small gift Fin was giving her and his men. "Thank you."

He nodded. "Are you sure you understand how this will change your life? When this is over, you'll be immortal like us. You won't age, so you'll watch those you love die.

You'll be facing some of the same dangers Ty faces until Zero and the other eight are gone."

"I understand. And I accept that my life will never be the same." She'd spent sleepless nights staring into the darkness, thinking about her family, her career, her *life*. Kelly was fiercely determined not to give up her family. Yes, she *would* tell them. And no matter how hard it was, they'd work it out because they loved one another. But she wouldn't trade Ty for a safe and comfortable future. She loved him that much.

And then she was facing Ty. He looked spectacular in his tux. *This wonderful man loves me.* The magic of it still boggled her mind.

Finally, the chant ended. Fin and his men moved to the far side of the room.

Ty looked into her eyes, his love filling her, completing her. "I love you, Kelly. Are you ready?"

"Yes." She bit her lip. She wanted to reach out to him, hold him, but she knew it wasn't allowed. Not yet. Nerves, not fear, made her stomach hop and skip, because as long as Ty was with her, she'd be safe. She'd always believe that.

So quickly that it made her gasp, Ty's beast towered above her. Within the dinosaur's massive form, she saw Ty the man waiting. Taking a deep breath, she began walking.

Kelly didn't slow down as she drew close to him. Ty would let her in. She would be his only mate, the only one who'd ever be allowed to walk into his beast.

Then she was through, Ty's form closing around her. Kelly didn't know what she'd expected, but it certainly wasn't this. Surrounding her was a world that had disap-peared sixty-five million years ago. Eyes wide, she watched the pattern of his days—the hunt, the kill, and the savage beauty of what he'd been. All the giants that had roamed that time filled her vision as far as she could see, alive once more.

But gradually the forests and plains faded to an earlier time, before the dinosaurs reigned. Nothing could have prepared her for this world. A kaleidoscope of darkness, death, and destruction spilled over into horror and evil that even the worst nightmare couldn't conceive. Kelly knew she was screaming, but no sounds came from her mouth. There was nowhere to run, no place to hide. Shadows she recognized as human drifted out of the blackness, but she couldn't tell whether Ty was one of them. She was too terrified to look very hard. Even though she knew it was useless, she ran. And ran and ran and ran.

And just when she felt that she'd collapse onto the hard earth and die, she found Ty. Tears streaming down her face, she reached for him.

He opened his arms, and she fell into them. The familiar feeling took her, the sensation of falling into him, becoming a part of him.

Ty spoke, his voice rumbling from beneath where her head pressed against his chest.

"You touch my soul, Kelly. You touch what I am, what I once was, and what I will be."

Kelly stared up at him. Words appeared in her mind. She spoke them. "I accept what you share with me today—your love, your soul. I give my love and my soul in return."

Dropping his arms from around her, Ty framed her face with both his hands. "Take what is mine, and let it join us forever."

Then he kissed her. It was a kiss for the ages, and Kelly lost herself in the magic of his mouth on hers. She hadn't expected to feel anything more than she'd felt before, but

this time was different. A sense of newness filled her, awareness that Ty was now a part of her essence, and her happi-
ness exploded at the unbelievable *completeness* of it.

When the kiss ended, Kelly realized his T. rex was gone.
She smiled through her tears. "I walked into the heart of
your beast, and I came out the other side still loving you.
Never underestimate the heart of a woman in love."

He held her close as he walked with her toward Fin and
the others waiting to congratulate them. "What did you
see?"

Kelly thought of the hell she'd glimpsed, thought of
what it would do to him if he knew. "I saw dinosaurs. Lots
of dinosaurs."

"Anything else?"

Some things should never be revealed and are best forgotten.
"Nothing."